Franchise

To

Kill

D.S.West

Local author, if you enjoy the book, please make a comment on my Face Book page. Don West. And pass on to someone else.

Other books by the author on Amazon
- Franchise To Kill
- Chasing Rains
- A Time For Change (syfy)
- A Time For Hope (syfy)

A former hitman, taken out of prison to help the government?
To quell the influx of drugs, killing city centres trying to stop the degradation of society.
Unknown to him, vengence is always in the background; he finds out his best friend is killed by a former drug king and seeks him out for retribution. The man who put him in prison strangely becomes an ally? A former military man, given the job to control him, and two drug lords hell-bent on revenge against people they feel, betrayed them, always in the distance and untouchable, or are they.

This novel is dedicated to one of my best friends, who sadly lost his battle against cancer Gary Bennett R.I.P.

Also, I would like to thank my family and close friends for their kind patience and support.

> Copyright D.S.West
> First Edition

This book is a work of fiction, and any resemblance to persons living or dead Is purely coincidental
The author asserts the moral right under the Copyrights, Design and Patents

> Act 1988 to be identified as the author.

All Rights Reserved. No part of this publication may be reproduced, stored in a retrieval system or transmitted, in any form or by means without the prior consent of the author, nor be otherwise circulated in any form of binding or cover other than that which it is published and without a similar condition being imposed on the subsequent purchaser.

Chapter 1

Paul Reed, formerly known as Paul Joesy, changed his name by Deed Poll after being caught by the police. Paul is a former special forces operative and police officer in (SCO19). He became a prolific hitman for hire, for the right price over sixteen years, had killed too many people to count, the police not knowing the true extent of his kill count. Three years into his incarceration, Paul sat down in his cell, a life sentence for his past deeds. Being ex-special forces his mindset to switch off from sounds and activities around him, pondering his life choices, strangely with no regrets, enjoying his life thoroughly before DCI Roger Leyland chased him down. His one regret, Julia, the love of his life and former wife and partner in crime, succumbed to severe depression and committed suicide when she heard of his life sentence, not being able to cope without him. While in prison, Paul is left alone due to his reputation keeping most prisoners away, only choosing to speak to Tony Stray and John Leech, both former serial killers, killing for fun rather than money in return. Conversations mainly were brief; on one occasion, they asked each other if they would do it all again. It unexpectedly all gave a resounding yes, such was the feeling and sensation it gave them, during and after the kill. John and Tony were caught quite early in their killing sprees, Tony within two years, John in three years, and both were inexperienced, leaving DNA on or near the kill. John was a killer of prostitutes; after one belittled him during their sexual activity, as he strangled her, he became more aroused and decided this was too good not to do again. In his three-year spree, Tony killed six women. He was a random killer, more on the spur of the moment type, all victims being in the wrong place at the wrong time, again DNA found, on a knife which he dropped, not realising when he was disturbed during his act of violence. Nobody in prison knows of Paul's skill set; even so, a wide berth would be taken by all, while in prison, he has still trained to his maximum fitness.

Paul has accepted he is in prison for life but, if an opportunity arises, he will take it however it comes to him and make a move to leave his rent-free accommodation. When he looks at the TV, he can see things are getting worse in the outside world; anarchy and drugs seem to be the leading causes. The judicial system is unable to cope. Poor sentencing and a lack of policing do not help, thinking in the back of his mind that somebody higher up must be picking up a financial remuneration to allow this to carry on.

Chapter 2

Sir Guy Long, former head of a government security think tank, has been summoned to a secret meeting. Only two other people are in the room, their names unknown, at this stage.

Sir Guy already knows to reach this level and the meeting taking place in a war room, and secrecy is the byword, all phones left in a different office one mile away, this is an important meeting indeed he thinks. Coffee and tea are placed on the table and a selection of sandwiches to reach all tastes, the secretary leaves the room, Sir Guy hears the operation of a switch and metal shutters seal the room, this is going to be interesting he thinks. The two men start the conversation, explaining that they are part of a government-backed organisation. Their main task is to eliminate all drug cartels in the UK radically by killing the leaders of each group and hopefully start to stop the build-up of drugs in the UK. They carry on explaining the country is being overrun with drugs, society, in general, is falling apart, and a sense of order must return before it all falls apart. They tell him that killing the leaders and if someone steps up to take their place, killing them too will start to deter them. We hope it will slow the intake of the drugs, so it becomes unprofitable and not worth the risks. Sir Guy tells them, 'We have our special forces, can they not be involved,' they reply, 'unfortunately not, higher up do not want the government seen to be involved.'

Sir Guy, 'how do you intend to achieve this then.'

The reply he got is not what he wanted to hear, 'that is your call.' Sir Guy, by the way, money no object to solve this problem.'

Sir Guy, 'by any means then, I assume.'

Man A, 'yes, as long as we know, so we can take the appropriate measures if required to help.'

Sir Guy, 'when do you need me to start.'
Man A. 'Asap, Sir Guy, it is that important that this situation is resolved.
Man B, 'by the way, there will be no electronic trail, we must keep these meetings by word only, no paperwork'.
Sir Guy, 'pretty sensitive situation, we have on our plates.'
Man A, 'as much plausible liability as we can, Sir Guy.'
Sir Guy, 'give me some thinking time; I will come back to you next week.'
Man B, 'we will meet in one week from now, at 10 am then.'

The shutters rattle as they lift; Sir Guy breathes a little bit better a sense of claustrophobia starting, for the first time in his life. Has he picked up his phone from its safe place? Guy has been given a coded phone number to arrange to see them when he needs to. Guy will check his phone when he gets back to his car, ever suspicious, a trait which has helped him on many occasions; he has never met these two gentlemen before; why stop now. While walking to his car, his mind thinking of options he can do to achieve his task, he opens the car door, sits down and opens the back of the phone, and Guy hopes there will be nothing there. Still, to his dismay and anger, he finds a device in it; he will wait until their next meeting before railroading them. Sir Guy has been careful about what he says while on the phone but has taken the precaution to buy a prepaid burner phone that he will leave in his car at their next meeting. The week passes quickly, and Sir Guy arrives for his meeting, the two men already seated waiting for him, general pleasantries are spoken, the coffee, teas and sandwiches are in place. Sir Guy explains that he needs one more day to put things in place due to unforeseen circumstances and would appreciate an external meeting tomorrow. Sir Guy writes down on his pad, passes it over to the two gentlemen, 'I will see you both there tomorrow at 10 am, do not tell anybody where we are meeting, it will be explained then,' and requests to leave the sealed room. Both men look at each other perplexed what has just happened but agree to his terms, the shutters raise, and Sir Guy goes. Twenty-four hours later, in a quiet country lane, the three men arrive in separate cars.

Sir Guy arrives in his second car, finding a device in his phone; he takes precautions that his main vehicle could have a tracker. It is 10.05 am; they are all settled in Sir Guy's second car; he starts the car and proceeds to drive away. Both men look at each other, 'just precautions, gentlemen.' Sir Guy had noticed a black Ford car not too far away and wanted to check if it would follow. To his disappointment, it did; he drives for approximately one mile and returns to their cars. Guy writes down on his pad, 'pass me your phones,' placing a finger over his lips to indicate silence. Both men pass over their phones, looking at each other. Why does he need the phones? On opening the rear of them, he finds the devices he hoped would not be there. If one were missing, he knew that would be the culprit. Instead, both had a device in them, which tells him these two men could be lower management or just naive. Both men stutter, 'what the hell is going on, seemly ignorant of the possibilities of someone listening to them, 'how long could they have been in their phones.'

Sir Guy informs them they are free to talk; he has a frequency scrambler in his car so that no one can hear. It is new to these men not realising what they have got themselves into. Sir Guy informs them, only to talk about the situation when asked and only to give minimal information until he can find out what or who has initiated this and purchase a prepaid burner phone each for future contact. He then asks them, did you tell anyone of our meeting, 'No,' was the reply. He then asks, 'who else is on the panel who asked them to speak to him and why?

They both look at each other, and they are not used to direct questions, which only confirms to Sir Guy how low these two people are in the chain. It makes him highly suspicious indeed. With no information coming forward, he decides to tell them he will not do anything further until they or their bosses are more forthcoming and more truthful. Sir Guy gives them twenty-four hours to come clean, or he will walk away, cards on the table if they want the job done.

Unknown to the two men, Guy's surveillance team have photos of the two men and the car, and the driver and his colleague are logged to find out who he is dealing with.

Twenty-four hours later, Guy has the names he was after and is happy to move forward, and he requests five million pounds to be placed into a dedicated account for incidentals, as he calls them. But, he further informs them, he will only contact them to update them or extreme emergencies; all people involved will be anonymous.

Guy has chosen a surprise element into the mix if he accepts his offer of redemption.

Chapter 3

Paul is in the canteen, enjoying the regular stew, which is standard for every Wednesday. Tony and John are next to him, and they complain it is the same meals daily, you can tell what day it is by the meal they receive they laugh. Suddenly Paul stands up, and if the seating had not been fixed, he would have kicked it several feet away. He has just overheard one of the inmates talking about his old friend Ethan Holton, and Paul goes over to him and whispers in his ear to get clarification. Twenty seconds later, Paul turns away from his discussion and leaves the canteen and goes to his cell, anger within starting to consume him. Paul had just learnt that his close friend Ethan had been killed in another prison two years ago. The other prisoner had confirmed that a former drug lord Jimmy Lees had initiated a hit on Ethan the day after he left the prison a free man, no proof, of course. Ethan, a former undercover police officer, brought Jimmy Lees empire down, he was undercover for three years, and many of Jimmy's associates were imprisoned.

There was a close bond between Ethan and Paul, and this has increased his desire to escape, enact his revenge on this individual, and give him great pleasure indeed. He would need some divine intervention to achieve his goal, unaware that intervention would be coming in a surprising form in forty-eight hours.

Guy has requested that Paul Reed be moved to a neutral room, with no cameras and no microphones all mobiles removed from the building. Guy has put in a high-level request to see Paul, also that he will most probably be coming with him.

Paul was surprised when told that a high-level government man wanted to see him, must be about the old special force days. He walked into the room, looking for any possibilities he might be able to escape. But, instead, Guy asks him to sit down, 'I will take your cuffs off, mutual respect I know your ability, and I hope you respect my offer.' Paul nods yes.

Guy carries on, 'I am here to offer you a form of redemption, if you accept, this will be your last day, in this prison.

Paul thinks there is divine intervention out there somewhere and replies, 'I am listening, by the way, who are you.'

Guy, 'just say, your saviour for now, till we get to know each other.'

Paul, 'go on then, tell me what you have on offer.'

'Freedom and for you to do, something you do best.'

'What would that be.'

'Kill people quietly.'

Paul smiles at this statement, life has a way of coming around, and his senses are pricked. He has just realised a chance to get Jimmy Lees, retribution for Ethan and a possible remuneration for a job well done.

Paul, 'tell me what it is that warrants me to leave this prison.'

Guy, 'I need a person of your skillset, to eliminate the leaders of drug gangs in the UK'.

'Sounds a bit desperate to me,'

'Being a former special forces operative, I need someone who can take orders, without remorse as to what that task is, a sort of franchise to kill if you will.'

'The remuneration for my loyalty.'

'Freedom and a new identity, a new life anywhere you want to be.'

'You forgot the money bit.'

Guy laughs to himself; it always comes down to money, 'one million pounds, in a bank of your choice.'

'I accept your kind offer.'

'There will be a few things we need to do to achieve this, one to change your identity.

'Experience tells me this could be painful.'

'Well, officially, you will die in a tragic accident so that you can become Mark Andrews.'
'Looking forward to it.'
'Before we go any further, we will need to remove your fingerprints; unfortunately, it will be painful.'
Paul, 'and next.' a smiling Guy, 'when we leave, you will be sedated and transported to a secure location; the reason for that will be self-explanatory.'
Paul, 'what if I try to escape.'
Guy, 'all along the route, I have trained snipers, all have the same ability as you, and instructed to kill on site.'
'As long as I am away from here, I will be happy.'
Paul and Guy leave the prison within the hour, heading for the secure location; on arrival, Paul is taken into a medical room and asked to sit at a table. On the table, there are two glass bowls, each having hydrochloric acid. Guy informs him this is the painful bit; we need to erase your fingerprints. Paul duly complies; most people would scream, but a slight wince on his face was the only indication of the pain he was feeling, the fingertips bandaged, and Paul sedated for the next part of Guy's plan. When the new man Mark Andrews wakes up, Guy informs him that Paul Reed sadly passed away within thirty minutes of leaving the prison. Paul was involved in a serious incident in which an articulated lorry wiped out the vehicle, and all three occupants were killed; two of the men were unrecognisable. The prison services were informed of the tragic circumstances, and all records were filed away to the depths of the bureaucratic system.
However, he tells Mark that technology has moved on. In the past few years, they have developed a new nano tracker, which has been installed in your bloodstream. It will work for two years; he will not be constantly monitored; it is purely a backup if you are in trouble.
Paul, 'how will you know I am in trouble.'

Guy, 'hopefully, your heart rate will increase, and we will see it.'

'What if I try to take it out.'

'Cannot be done; it is constantly on the move and virtually invisible.'

'All things considering, it is a small price to pay, to be free.'

'We will leave you alone to complete your task, minimum contact, only in extreme emergencies.

'When do we start.'

'We already have; good luck, Mark.'

Chapter 4

Two years earlier, the irony now is Jimmy Lees has set his operation up in Ethan's old town of Middlesbrough, far away from London, his old stomping ground. Jimmy felt he was known too well in London, arriving there on his first release day, noticing all his old haunts now gone to new houses and condos, even peachy little restaurants with outside tables, not his way of living, he must move from here quickly. Many of his old colleagues are now free, and Jimmy has arranged a meeting so that his old business can be resurrected, and the love of his life money will start to come to him again. While in the discussion, he receives a call from one of his old dealers in Middlesbrough, who informs him that Eric Lunn's (Ethan Holton) alias was working from here. Jimmy's warped sense of humour decided there, and then, this would be his new area of operation, lucky it is central to the country. A new base of operation was set up, and in two weeks, Jimmy and his family arrived in a posh neighbourhood, with the occasional ex-footballer present, surely a master drug lord would not live there.

In the following two years, Jimmy's empire grew quickly as he knew it would, addiction is an easy supplier of money, and everybody pays with his ruthless attitude.

The town now is overrun with drugs, the police are understaffed, with morale at its lowest point, every door opened is quickly slammed shut. It is the control of Jimmy Lees business empire, and he loved it. A recently qualified detective, who has risen from the ranks DS Simon James, a protégé of recently retired DCI Roger Leyland, bangs the table in frustration. Like the MET before him, he knows who the leader is but cannot prove it; it will take an outside influence to resolve this situation. Strangely enough, DS James's mind went straight to a former MET officer, who went undercover to beat Mr Lees previously, but then himself turned rogue and became the local drug Lord, which they brought down successfully. In the back of his mind, he knows they will get Mr Lees.

More staffing is essential to put pressure on them, but requests for more staff are falling on deaf ears in the government.

With Jimmy's astute business acumen, he has arranged different suppliers worldwide; he has purchased a large factory unit near the riverside. The main loading area located to the rear-facing the riverside, easy access to unload containers, small motor cruisers with false bottoms, all arrive at different times of the day to avoid a noticeable regular pattern to bring suspicion to his door. He is ironically using his old front as a wholesale flower trader. Under the name of Petals Flowers, a large car parking area with high-end security cameras fitted. Regular twenty-four hours of surveillance, he is determined he will be caught again. Very quickly, Jimmy's tentacles are spreading into the country, and it will not be long before he has total control of the most extensive drug networks in the UK. Such was the rapid speed in moving forward; he has decided to build a new house outside the town. He has decided that it will give him a more secure lifestyle away from prying eyes, but no one is invisible, and it can soon end for the right incentive.

Chapter 5

Mark has informed Guy things will not happen for at least two weeks; he needs to get accommodation and a vehicle.

Guy takes him outside, 'we have supplied a basic vehicle, with an upgraded engine, just in case you need to get out of somewhere fast.'

Mark appreciates his concern, but it is the victims that he should be worried. Even though his friend Ethan sold drugs, he hated the fact that the addiction destroys lives and families for the wrong reasons, one of the main reasons he declined his substantial financial offer. The only winners are the suppliers, and they do not care about the misery they cause to people and families if the money lines their pockets. Then Guy tells him he has arranged for him to be housed in a farmhouse on the outskirts of Glasgow; this has been chosen as his first kill zone, there is an area overrun with a drug problem, the intervention must be swift to send a message. Guy tells him that John Lane will meet him purely for geographical information purposes only. In the basement, there is a selection of armoury and tools to achieve his goals. Access is by a key card only, and this has been linked to the nano tracker so nobody can open it but him. It will be the same in other safe houses throughout the UK. Mark is impressed by Guy's efficient manner and feels he will get on well with him, but only if he achieves the right results. Then to Marks surprise, Guy pulls him to one side and tells him of his concerns regarding his meetings, which set this whole scenario in motion. During these talks, he tells Mark to be vigilant in everything he does; this is out of mutual respect for his service to our country. As far as he is concerned, we have a job to do, and we will complete it. Guy bids Mark farewell and wishes him luck, telling him that the police will most certainly try to find him after his first kill. However, with Marks ability, he is not deterred; he will be quick and efficient as Mark has always been; with his newfound freedom, he does not want to give it up again.

Mark walks outside and is shown around his basic car, a metallic grey Vauxhall Astra estate with a modified engine. He steps into the car, starts the engine and taps the destination into the sat-nav, only one-hundred and ninety miles to go; with a wry smile on his face, he drives off.

A few hours later Mark, turns left off the B road and enters a track into a field, thinking is this sat nav taking him the wrong way, two minutes down the driveway, he looks in the distance to see a car outside a farmhouse, he carries on up the track. On arrival, John Lane gets out of his car, and both men shake hands; John is unaware of Mark's task, he has been told to give him as much information he can on the drug problem in Glasgow, and the main area it has taken over. Mark and John enter the farmhouse, and both are surprised by how nice it is inside, very modern with a top-end kitchen and fittings. A giant TV and a superb white leather suite, on a raised seating area, basic foodstuff have been left to get him started with a choice of coffee and various teas from around the world. Mark offers John coffee; before they get started, John estimates around one hour to complete the introduction to the Glasgow scene. The discussions over, coffee drank John leaves and wished Mark good luck. Mark watches as John drives down the track out of sight; he makes his way to the basement area. It is close to the backdoor, and he makes his way down the old stairs, showing signs of wear over the years, the concrete steps having indentions where people have walked over them in the past two hundred years or so since it was built. Mark is thankful for the excellent lighting; the space is claustrophobic. As he reaches the bottom, a large steel door is in front of him; he places the key card over the reader. Mark is taken aback by the sound of compressed air as the door silently opens back into the room. In front of him, a vast array of weapons, Mark has just got excited he is back to where he wants to be, but the challenge is vast. He will have an early night; tomorrow, he will visit the area that has been designated to him; over the next few days, he will visit day and night to check how the dealers operate.

By day three, he has decided who will be the first unfortunate soul he will deal with. Mark has already chosen an old disused warehouse if required for his work to take place. Inside there are several old steel storage racks, and these will undoubtedly help for some interrogation purposes. He will need to buy chains and locks; the excitement is growing inside him, thinking to himself, 'it is good when you enjoy your job.'

Chapter 6

Having left Mark to achieve his task, Guy makes his way home, noticing the familiar Ford car following him in his rear-view mirror. He has not seen the car for a few days, constantly aware when it is following him, and he is now concerned that they may have seen Mark. A coded message to Mark is required for extra vigilance. Guy is busy making calls on his burner phone throughout the day, inside the safety of a specially built lockdown room installed twenty years ago. Commonly known as a panic room, Guy is not the type of man who panics easy, and everything is methodically analysed every avenue checked before he makes that decision that could cost someone their life. He has found out the four other men in the committee are well known and above reproach politicians, but he will look further. At least one is giving information out to a third party that Guy does not know about yet. Guy's network of contacts is vast and worldwide; he will have to pull out a few favours to get to the bottom of his problem. Locally, he has found out that the Ford number plate is false, so one of his specialist team will reverse the issue and follow it to this individual's abode; once there, an interrogation will occur. If the answers are what he expects, the individual will be staying at Her Majesty's pleasure a long way from here. Twenty-four hours later, Guy receives the information he is so desperate to have. To his surprise, the drug fraternity is aware of his task, and one of the four committeemen is involved, but the low-level individual did not know well above his pay grade. Guy now must focus his attention on who and why this individual is involved; he will look deeply into the past and present of all four men, no stone unturned. Unfortunately, three innocent men will have their lives torn apart to find the individual. Deep in the back of his mind Guy, knows it will be inevitable that large sums of money will be involved; it always is. So he sets in motion total surveillance of all four men, with all calls monitored. Covert tracking where they go and who they meet, he will find this person who values money over society.

Chapter 7

It is day four of Mark's freedom, and he is about to leave the safety of the farmhouse when he receives a text from Guy with three numbers which read 123, a coded message that he is in danger. Mark looks at the security screen, and it is the first time he has looked at it; that simple text has just saved his life. He can see an individual fifty metres to the left of the house. A smile comes on his face; this person does not know of Mark's skill set and is about to find out; Mark goes out the back door and circles behind his guest. Mark's adrenaline is pumping; he is within ten meters then quickly five meters, then he says a calm, 'hello,' as the man turns, Mark shoots him in the knee, he drops his rifle in pain, Mark hits the other knee, the man screams in pain he falls on his back. Mark stands over his prey and asks who sent him; the individual is not as skilled as Mark. It was only his second attempt to kill someone. His inexperience is now going to cost him his life, he begs Mark to let him go, and he will tell him what he knows; Mark nods his head. He proceeds to tell Mark he received a message from a drug cartel, the first person to kill him will get five-hundred thousand pounds; it was too much not to do it.
Mark, 'how did you know where I was.'
The reply shocked him, 'it was John Lane.'
'How much was he paid.'
'One-hundred thousand, on confirmation of your death.'
'How did you know what I looked like.'
'I didn't. I was just going to kill everyone in the house,'
'What do they want for verification.'
'A photo, to a website, it is in my pocket.'
Mark aims to shoot him in the head, the individual screams at him, 'you said you would let me go,' Mark informs him, 'in this game, there are no prisoners,' and

shoots him in the head. Then he takes a photo on his mobile, on the now dead man's phone, leaving the body for any other person to see as a warning.
Mark makes his way back to the house; he has already sent the photo to Guy to see if he can find out the identity of the unfortunate individual he had just killed. He is now aware that he is in constant danger; strangely, most people would be afraid.
Mark is different he loves this situation, more chance to kill, a bonus extra to his task. Mark rings Guy on the burner phone and explains what has just happened and his concerns regarding John Lane, also he is the only one who has seen his face, a short pause Guy surprised he has known John several years, only now realising this problem is a lot deeper than he thought. He must now reassess his procedures, and he is now forced to vet his personnel, which has become time-sensitive. Guy's methodical mind is running through the last few weeks, and in the back of his mind, why was he chosen? He must look to his past also to see if he can find answers.

Chapter 8

With his small task done, Mark heads towards Glasgow; the sun is setting he knows this is the best time for greedy dealers on the streets. It will give him plenty of chances to find his first victim; Mark parks up on the lower floor of the car park, near the area he needs to be, checks for cameras, silly the dealers have already destroyed them. Leaving the car park, Mark turns right towards what looks like slums, such as the degradation that drugs have brought to the area. Two hundred metres later, he turns into the street where he initially saw the dealer he had earmarked to be tested for information. As Mark does so, four young men are chasing the individual he wants to speak with. He slips on the floor two metres away; within seconds, the four men surround him, machetes in hand. One of them is just about to stab him, and Mark intervenes, 'guys, it is not fair, four against one.'

One of them turns seemingly to the leader, 'stay out of this old man, or you will be next,' pointing the blade within millimetres of Mark's chest. Mark instantly breaks his arm and snaps his neck, and the body falls; the three men suddenly realise what has happened. As they move forward forgetting, the man on the floor, Mark takes out his Glock, complete with silencer, and within seconds, three more dead people are on the floor. Instantly the man who Mark was going to torture has now become his new friend, and information will flow freely now. Mark leaves the bodies where they dropped, leaving a painted message on the floor, 'No knives, no drugs a change is coming,'

He asks his newfound friend to come with him to chat about his life choices, and he may be able to help change it for the better. A grateful Ewen Robertson looked about eighteen, and Mark could tell he had had a hard life, etched on his face. Still, there was a kindness in his manner; he accepted his liberator's offer and showed Mark into an empty house, furniture still in there, the original owners are long gone, due to the impact the drugs have had on the neighbourhood. Ewen explained that an Albanian gang took over the area two years ago, a familiar timeframe is emerging in Mark's head; this will be sorted in a couple of days, he thinks to himself.

Ewen carries on the leader is ruthless he is called Edon Kurti, the people who fail him, have his name burnt into their backs, he always has four enforcers around him for protection. If you do not deliver your quota of deals, he pulls your fingernails out; Ewen shows Mark his left hand with two nails missing, done recently. Telling him the four men who chased him would kill him because he was ten pounds short of what they expected. Also, he runs a people trafficking and prostitution ring; nobody is safe here; with your recent intervention, the streets will not be safe; they will put a price on your head. Mark smiles at this remark, thinking they will need to join the queue like everybody else; swift action is necessary to resolve the problem. Mark asks Ewen how he got involved with them; he tells him his parents fell into drug addiction and died, no one would take him in because they thought he might be like them, and three years ago I started dealing for John Mckay, he was a fair man, well as fair as a drug dealer could be and treated us ok. The Albanian's came in and killed John because he would not deal with them. His body was hanging off the local bridge, a warning this area was theirs now, Ewen continues, they rule by intense fear, everyone is scared.

Mark asks him if he wants to be free of the situation; if so, he can be if he can give him as much information he can on their movements, such as the way they do things, at regular times, if so were. Where do they stay, how many are they, what cars they drive, how many men are there, like the men who chased him. It is two hours since Mark's introduction into the Glasgow drug scene, suddenly the streets are full of men searching for him, Mark's humour thinking maybe I should have left the little message out, but his excitement is rising now. Then just as they are about to leave the house, Ewen can see two of Edon's enforcers coming down the street. Mark tells him to shout that he has knocked him out in the house and come quickly.

As Ewen does so, Mark positions himself on the stairs, three steps up in the shadows; there is no electricity in the house.

The men rush forward, pushing Ewen aside; they enter the doorway of the terraced house with no street lighting. There is little or no light in the hallway, trying to focus their eyes on the darkness. They hear a slight thud, and the first man falls; the second man feels and tastes the warm blood of his colleague on his face and in his mouth. As the second bullet hits him in the forehead, he falls to the floor. Ewen is in awe of his saviour; if only he could do the same to the rest of them. His prays would be answered and a way out of his nightmare. They drag the bodies into the dining room, Mark drifting back to his old days, poses them in a writing position, one of his old signature foibles. A happy Ewen thinks his new saviour is now extraordinary, but he has just saved his life; he can do what he wants. Mark continues to question Ewen on Edon's manpower and how many could be left. To his surprise, there are only four more men, and such is Edon's confidence that he has total control. Ewen carries on telling Mark they have taken over a small abandoned primary school. Using four classrooms has brothels, and the main hall is where he keeps the women to be transported back to Albania, all rooms chained and locked. Edon is located arrogantly in the headteacher's room, at the back of the building, two large containers, one for drugs, the other for the money, all the lock keys around his neck. Edon has had the four bodies killed earlier removed, and he does not want the police anywhere near them; he will resolve this matter in-house. He is unaware that his reign is nearly over, Mark assessing his next move, deciding it will be done tonight before he can muster up more men, and surprise is always the best form of attack; a diversion is needed. The school is located three streets away, so Mark casually walks with Ewen to tell him what he needs him to do. As they get closer to the school, Ewen runs in the direction of the other two enforcers, shouting. The man who killed Jamie and his friends are around the corner, and they run forward like blind fools, with no experience in warfare, only bullying.

Ten metres from the school entrance to the school, two quiet thuds, they land on the floor, one hitting a brand-new high-end SUV, the car alarm goes off music to Mark's ears. He finds it strange that people let their guard down, thinking their car is being stolen. True to form, Edon runs out, suddenly he stops when he sees the two bodies, then a searing pain in his knee, Edon screams as he hits the ground. Starting to crawl to the safety of the school, he feels a hand on his shoulder and screams obscenities in Albanian, Mark tells him to be quiet, and he will help him into the school for a bit of a chat. Mark hears Ewen callout as the last two men with machetes run towards him, Mark not wanting to do hand to hand fighting instantly, unloads two bullets into the two men, they drop to the floor also. Mark and Ewen drag Edon towards the school hall, ripping the keys from his neck. As usual, the last key is the one to open the hall door lock, and they walk in; the women scream and start crying tears of joy, realising what is happening. Ewen opens the other four doors used as brothels, asking them to follow him to the hall. Many of these women have never left their prison for months; one of them, Marie, had been there for fourteen months. Mark had tied up Edon on the wall bars, wrists and legs bound; he explains this man is pure evil for what he has done to you all. Mark carries on there are two containers outside, Edon still shouting obscenities, now realising he is losing everything, starting to beg for mercy, saying he will leave everything if they let him go.

Mark, 'as I was saying, in the two containers one has drugs, the other money, I will take some money with me, the rest is for all of you to share and start a new life.' There are tears of happiness as they realise from this day, they are all free. Mark also tells them that he will destroy the drugs so that they can tempt no one. They must leave their past behind them now; they all cheer. Mark, 'you can do what you want to him; hopefully, revenge will heal some of your scars.' Mark and Ewen head towards the two containers, complete with keys to open the locks.

Opening the first one, they find a vast amount of various drugs,
Mark asks Ewen to help him put the four bodies outside the school into the container; this job is now done. Mark sets the drugs alight along with the bodies, leaving the doors slightly ajar to fan the flames. Opening container, number two, a slight intake of breath from young Ewen having never seen this amount of money in his life. He is suddenly distracted; all he can hear are the screams of Edon in the hall behind him, all the women exacting their revenge, his body starting to become unrecognisable. Mark takes some money and tells Ewen to do the same, explaining it is to get him started in a new life and tell the women the same thing, or he will be back, to finish the job

properly. They return inside the school and go to Edon's room, Ewen surprised by Mark's next move, rummaging in the desk drawers, Mark finds two SUV keys. Mark then asks Ewen to bring the woman who has been held the longest; Ewen and Marie return; Mark gives them both the keys to the SUV's, telling them to change the number plates, they will most certainly be on the police radar and wishes them luck. Ewen thanks him and watches as he walks away towards the car park.

Chapter 9

Now Guy is very conscious that John Lane now knows what Mark looks like; he will need to check John's background thoroughly, now believing that he may well be a long-term undercover informant for a drug cartel. He then thinks it could be simply greed, or has he got gambling debts, and it could even be that someone is holding a gun to his head. Guy makes a quick call to his closest ally; Guy has known Harry Graham for over thirty years, who like him supposedly retired, working within the government, you never really retire, he thought to himself. If it is greed, he will be disappointed with John, but he is sure it will be something else in the back of his mind. Guy called Harry Mr Forensics, and he has an uncanny knack of tracking leads down, which other people would leave alone; to date, he has never been wrong. Guy explains using his burner phone; what has been happening. Harry is immediately on board for the challenge, and Guy gives him John Lanes details. Harry starts straight away, and he locks himself in his favourite room, three computers and a name just what he likes.

Guy has just been told that John is missing; this does not look good for John; Guy instigates a search on his car. It is a government car to track its GPS, to check where he has been in the last seventy-two hours. Guy follows the route from the farmhouse, nothing unusual it is heading towards his hometown of Newcastle, living on the outskirts in Ponteland, a nice affluent area close to Newcastle airport. The cars route is then spasmodic, stopping and starting in several regions as if he is looking for something, possibly someone, more questions than answers as usual Guy thinks. A phone call from Harry verifies that John had no debt, no need for the extra money there has got to be a different reason. Guy tells Harry to investigate John's wife Linda;

thirty minutes later, Harry calls back to confirm she is missing, and John's car has been in the airport car park.

Guy contacts the local police to check the car but treads with caution and uses the guise of a possible terrorism situation, bomb squad etc. The airport now cordoned off, several police cars and the bomb squad arrive, piercing sirens breaking over the sound of aircraft, traffic coming to a standstill. Bomb personnel approach the vehicle, do their checks and inform the police a bomb is underneath the car, and they can see two bodies inside the car. The situation is now escalating, and something Guy could do without he feels it is now like the old Mafia days, fighting for control, trying to bring back a normal society. If only all these people that the youth look up to did not do drugs, he feels it might not spiral out of control. The bomb squad have made the car bomb safe, and the police forensics are checking over the car; Guy has been informed that John and Linda were executed hitman style, with a single bullet to the back of the head. He must now tell the local police that the situation is above their pay grade and pass all information to Harry on a secured IT line. Several phone calls later, all of Guy's team have full disclosure of the battle they are getting involved in. The police have been requested to supply all security footage for the past three days, and Guy hopes to pinpoint a face near the crime scene. Finally, a call to Mark to update him about the situation, Mark telling Guy they are closing in on loose ends, but they do not know who I am yet.

Guy's obvious question, 'how can that be,' Mark's answer made him smile, 'I sent a photo of the man who tried to kill me, so they think at this moment in time I

am dead.' Guy now knows why he was so successful in his previous line of work and everything taken in his stride. Mark asks him to send a name and photo of the hitman if he can; he is on his way to the farmhouse to sleep. Guy issue's his customary, watch your back.'
'Always, by the way, what's your name,' a short pause, 'Guy,' nothing else said as they both put their phones down on each other, mutual respect. Guy contacts an old friend within Interpol, seeking crumbs that might help in tracking down the killer of John and Linda Lane,
his contact will ring back within forty-eight hours.

Chapter 10

Mark is happy with his very eventful evening, and that rush he missed so much is back; if only his wonderful wife Julia were with him, that rush would be complete. However, after discussing Guy, he is now totally aware he could be a target; as Mark turns off to the farmhouse, he notices three cars. These cars are placed four hundred metres away from the entrance, inexperience again from so-called assassins he thinks or is paranoia starting in his head. Luckily in his armoury in the farmhouse was a drone he had played with for a couple of days just to get the hang of its controls; after all, you never know when you might need a drone.

Mark takes the drone out of the back of his basic car, sets it in motion; it is ultra-quiet as it rises thirty metres into the air, with the cameras set to night vision. He can see three bodies crouched on the floor, noting their positions, and he moves in for the kill. As Mark moves forward, the drone is lined up directly above his first victim, a slightly muffled sound as he cuts the man's throat, only two to go. Then, moving to the right twenty-five metres, the drone slightly more forward he settles it above his prey, once again the familiar muffled sound, Mark wipes the blood off the knife on the man's jacket. He will now try and glean as much information from his final victim; his habitual shot to the knee always works for him. Confidence high, he casually walks up to his last victim; he thinks I have just shot a wimp; he has never heard anyone scream so much, luckily no neighbours; Mark drags him to the farmhouse. Mark tells him to stop screaming no one can hear him, and he sedates him to get some sleep; Mark will interrogate him in the morning, making sure he is handcuffed to the radiator. Mark has given his visitor enough sedation to keep him out for eight hours, bandaged his knee so he did not bleed to death; Mark needs some answers. It does not take long for Mark to go to sleep, he is used to short rest periods, so when his senses wake him early, he jumps out of bed.

Looking at the security screen, he can see two more men coming towards the house.
Mark rushes to the basement. It is rifle time. Has he gets to the basement, 'bollocks,' he has left the key card in the kitchen, racing up the steps, he gets the card and returns to the basement. He can see the men circling the farmhouse; one has a rifle, the other an AK47, Mark thinking they are bringing in outside help now. Rifle ready, he as the element of surprise, he lines the crosshairs on the man with the AK47, instantly one shot to the chest, the AK47 releases a volley of bullets into the air, he falls back into the bracken. Running to the back of the house, the camera has picked up the second man one hundred metres away. Mark goes upstairs, open the bedroom window just enough for the barrel of the rifle to go through. He thinks, 'head, neck, chest which one, damn it the neck it is.' Mark hits him in the jugular and leaves him to suffer, and he must now talk to his friend downstairs, who is oblivious of Marks morning escapades. Mark starts to smile, his warped sense of humour coming to the fore, thinking he is creating his little cemetery outside. Still, it will be good for the soil, and his visitor will soon be with them. His visitor, now coming around, wincing in pain, Mark uncuffs him and offers him his final coffee; unfortunately, he does not know it yet. Mark instigates the conversation, 'why did you come here.'
Visitor, 'bounty on your head.'
'It is not me; the man you are looking for is dead outside; a photo sent.'
'They know you are not dead.'

'How do they know.'
'The photo is the son of the man who wants you dead.'
'Who would that be.'
'None of us knows; it is all by e-mail or text.'
Mark, 'do you know why they are after me.'
'Only rumours.'
'Which is my friend.'
Visitor thinking with this statement he could be going home today, 'that you are trying to close the drug cartels down.'
Mark, 'ok' he then takes him outside, to the nearest victim and cuts his throat, leaving him to die next to his dearly departed friend, more fodder for the land. Mark now must become someone he never imagined, a police detective not second nature to Mark, but he realises that Guy has access to more information than he can get. He goes back to the kitchen and picks up some sealable plastic bags, and Mark is in luck indeed; then, he goes back outside and proceeds to photograph each assassin. Numbering each bag, the same as each photo sent to Guy, Mark uses each individual's blood to create a fingerprint on a small writing pad and places these into the plastic bags. A phone call to Guy explains the situation, and Guy gives him a PO Box number to send the blood samples to. Mark also tells Guy he will not tell him where he is going; next, there are too many leaks; Guy reminds him he is the only one who has access to the nano GPS, so he will be aware of where he is if required. Guy then tells him to take what firepower he feels he needs and not go to any safe houses; Mark agrees.
He gathers the tools of his trade, that he has made his own, loads up his basic car, gathers the envelope to send to Guy, surprised that there were stamps with the envelopes, Guy is very efficient; indeed, he is starting to like him a lot. He sets off down the track towards the B road, turning right heading towards his next

destination, adrenaline high in anticipation of what lies ahead. Mark enters a quaint village on his way to the motorway, a post box on the high street, envelope posted; he settles in his basic car and heads towards Newcastle.

Chapter 11

Now Guy is taking stock of what is happening, fully aware that there could be a large body count. That he did not envisage in the next few weeks or months, disappointed in himself with his years of experience showing a certain naivety over the situation. Now concerned Guy may have sent Mark Andrews to certain death, Guy has never known the number of assassins after one man, and after the killing of the drug lord's son, whoever that may be, things are only going to get worse before they get better. Another call to Harry to see if he has come up with any anomalies, with the four politicians and hopefully a culprit. Again, things are not as they seem all four politicians have issues in their pasts, supposedly well-hidden from any form of investigation, but for Harry's inquisitive mind. He makes a list of the problems for each politician for Guy to use in his talks with them, which might turn into an interrogation to get the answers he needs. Guy's realisation the vast amount of money being used to try and stop them, there must be help from an external source, he must talk to Mark and ask him about his past. Mark has gone dark to avoid detection, running everything through his head; Mark is coming to a similar conclusion as Guy. Looking through the documents that Harry has sent him, having already found out the names of the two people he first met that started this chapter in his life. Harry's information has eliminated these two as pawns, being pushed to the front as a diversion tactic, warning bells in Harry's head. Both of their backgrounds indicated, well too do families, well educated. There are no signs of any radical involvement, no police records, and no drug abuse indicators. The four main components of this committee all have minor issues. But they are not significant enough to raise any warning flags. He is abruptly aware in his years in the government. How easily a smoking gun can be hidden in bureaucracy. Guy requests a meeting with Samuel Hornsby, the first name on the list, and already put into the queue; he is unavailable for at least three days.

He does not take this statement lightly and is not the type of man to be messed around. Within one hour of his request, Guy storms into Samuel Hornsby office, slamming the door behind him. Mr Hornsby's secretary request's security, not realising who Guy is; by the time security get to the office, Guy has introduced himself, they are told to carry on with everyday duties. Hornsby is two metres tall, immaculately tailored, starting to lose a bit of his dark brown hair compensated by a well-manicured beard. He asks Guy to sit down in the well-worn black leather chair in front of him. Samuel asks Guy, 'why the dramatic entrance.'

Guy, 'you formed a committee to track and trace a drug network.'

'Nobody is supposed to know about that.'

'Why would that be.'

'It was classed above, my pay grade, told to keep quiet, need to know only.'

Guy, intrigued by the answer, replies, 'do you know who oversees getting that information.'

Samuel, 'actually, there are only two people who know; they needed four for the forum to get it passed; in fact, we never met, I do not know who they are.'

'Why did you agree to it.'

'A career move, up the ladder, seemed an easy move for the right reasons.'

Guy accepts his answer and apologises for his aggressive entrance and thanking him, and leaves. Harry was monitoring phone calls from his office phone already, any texts etc., from Samuel's mobile. Guy's back up, never really trusting people he has not met before, Harry will inform him if he feels anything is of use to him. Number two on the list is Terence Ward; the appointment booked a different department strangely. As Samuel, a lower league government employee informed Guy the same story, all attention is on the last two on the list, Charles Raven and John Hurst.

These two names were suspicious that Harry had checked; even to Harry, their backgrounds were too perfect; I had his senses tingling, a sure sign he was on the right track.

Eliminating Samuel Hornsby and Terence Ward, Guy asks Harry to increase covert surveillance on the other two; he may need extra help in this task and asks him to contact David Jackson for assistance. David was Guy's go-to man if the workload was too much, meticulous like Harry for sourcing information that was buried deep. But, having been brought up to speed, he also is intrigued by the knowledge he has been given, also sensing something is not right, which is music to Harry's ears, more confirmation they are on the right track.

Chapter 12

While Mark has been busy, things have escalated in his old free accommodation three days after leaving his only two friends. Tony Stray and John Leech were both killed. Both prisoners were poisoned by different prison guards, each one having weaknesses that an outside source could use to their advantage. Why dirty your hands when broken people can be manipulated easily, with the right incentive given. One prison guard Shaun Hart, a habitual betting man, constantly trying to find that winning fix to pay that last debt off, which only seems to be moving further away. Especially when your family's lives are at stake, he was approached just as he was about to walk into the local betting shop. The offer to place a truth serum in the water of their victim. To find out where Paul Reed now Mark Andrews would be, a simple task for all, his debts to be gone. The well-suited man would be outside the betting shop at the same time tomorrow to get the answer from Shaun Hart. At the same time as these connections were made, serial adultery prison guard John Willis is approached by a woman in his local bar. A few drinks later, he follows her to the nearest hotel, a room paid for the night, giggling they walk to the room, two hours later, John caught in the old hotel sting, flashing lights, photos taken to send to his wife, which he loves dearly, he tells himself. John went to the hotel room like a bull to slaughter, and it goes to show when your privates stand to attention, you will always go forward and not backwards out of the room. John is given the same offer as Tony, and he must get information from John Leech as to where Mark is, a meeting arranged to get the answers they require. The two prison guards, oblivious to each other's task, a simple job they both think, not realising this request, will be the last they do. Both men did not get the answers their requesters asked for; their fates sealed, and they would be dead in twenty-four hours. The serum given to Tony and John contained a new synthetic poison slow-acting, taking forty-eight hours to take effect, both men looking as though they died of natural causes. Nothing was unusual about their deaths until the two prison guards did not arrive at work to do their duties. Then, urgent phone calls from supervisors to each guard's home, for them to be informed they had died in their sleep, within one hour of each other. The people who asked the guards to get the information also gave them the serum to check if they were telling the truth, a guise just to provide them with the serum without hassle. Unknown to John Willis killers, being set up professionally, he had written two letters and given them to his solicitor to deliver if he died within seven days of him giving him the letters. One to his wife, baring his soul and apologising for past indiscretions, the other to the Prison Director, with instructions to pass it onto the man who took Paul Reed away.

Before Guy had left the prison with Paul Reed, he had left instructions with the Prison Director, if anything untoward happens to send him a letter through the PO Box number he had given, not to use any form of electronic mail or phone calls. The director duly sends on John's letter along with an update of his own. As to what has happened and his concerns about the matter at hand. Guy goes to his PO Box daily at different times, part of his past, never let them know when you may be there, sometimes using his staff to collect items. It is 7.00 am. Guy searches into the small amount people out and about at that time of day, looking for a stranger's face, a different car; happy that all is okay, he collects the items from the PO Box. He is surprised to see two letters, one he knew about from Mark, regarding fingerprints. He had collected at the safe house, the other with the prison franked on the back, of where Mark used to have his free accommodation; surprised by this, his curiosity is high indeed.

Chapter 13

With Mark's intervention, one of Jimmy Lee's revenue streams has ceased moving, a substantial amount of money has not reached him. Jimmy is unaware of the impact that Mark has dealt him, and he is desperately trying to contact Edon on their encrypted phones, not knowing that one tentacle of his operation has ceased trading. Trying to find why his money has not arrived yet, he contacts the Newcastle branch to send someone up to find out what and why his money has not come through yet. Within five hours, he receives news that he never expected they had found the mutilated body of Edon; the area is like a ghost town, with no one willing to speak. More interested in the money and drugs, Jimmy asks them if they found anything. Only to be informed that all drugs burnt down and four bodies inside were unrecognisable, and all the money had gone. They then tell him of the painted sign on the container (no knives, no drugs, a change is coming). The loss of drugs does not bother him either, but losing the money hurts him more than Mark realises; even Jimmy Lees must pay his suppliers. Even though he has lost one of his money streams, the small impact can be felt, but if two more were closed, he would be in significant financial trouble, such as the outlay to bring the drugs into the country. Jimmy decides to call his eldest son Ian, no response from his phone; Jimmy has not heard anything from him for a couple of days; he calls his youngest Glenn to see if he knows where he is. Glenn notifies him that his brother went to Scotland to do a job for someone on the internet, said he would be a couple of days, and he would be five-hundred-thousand pounds better off, for the holiday fund, a knot now forming in his stomach. It was himself who put that bounty up, and a friend had informed him that the government was trying to close him down. He was trying to find a hitman who had done work for him many years ago, who efficiently disposed of an informer, never to be seen again. He remembered him because he wanted Jimmy to pay for a holiday for two in Benidorm as part of the payment. Why the hell would he do that? Glenn tells him we have plenty of money; he just wanted to prove he can bring money into the business for you.

A bead of sweat forms on his head, that knot has just got tighter he starts screaming obscenities at people, at that point his phone pings a text has come through, he opens it to see the picture of his dead son, a note stating is this the hitman you are after.

Jimmy drops to his knees, and this man does not cry easily, tears falling, screaming he will be avenged at all costs, money no object. One hour later, Glenn and his mother Janet are at Jimmy's side, all crestfallen. But, more annoyed at his stupidity, there was no need; Jimmy's bond to Ian after sixteen years in prison had become close, always together, Jimmy teaching him all he knew about surviving the drugs game, now wasted. Nobody knows who killed Ian; Jimmy has vowed to find that silent hitman who could do the job properly; he will search the dark web. Hopefully, he still has the address at home, and the police did not find it eighteen years ago when he was arrested.

After another phone call to his Newcastle branch, he requests them to bring Ian's body back home. On arrival at the farmhouse, even seasoned drug dealers were shocked at the war zone they encountered around the house.

They searched amongst the bodies, and none had any identification, a sign of their professionalism; unfortunately, only Ian's body had ID, strangely something Mark forgot to do. Otherwise, he might be a little closer to who is after him, and it must have been the excitement of the day.

Chapter 14

As Mark enters the outskirts of Newcastle, his phone rings, pulling over into a nearby layby, the last thing he needs now is to be pulled over by the police for using a phone. Only one person knows the number; Guy informs him they have an ID for the hitman who killed John Lane and his wife Linda; he is well known to all levels of police organisations but seems to be untouchable. He carries on telling Mark his name is Rudy Stem, a former Dutch special forces operative working primarily for drug cartels around the world. Mark laughs, Guy surprised by this, asks if he knows him, 'no I don't,' came back the reply, 'if he killed John, we must assume he is coming for me then,' Guy concurs; what are you going to do then Mark, 'I do not like to assume, but if he is still in Newcastle, he must have the address of the safe house,'
Guy, 'what are you going to do next then, Mark.'
'Old school surveillance.'
'Leave you to it, and any issues, let me know.'
Mark makes his way, on the A696, towards the village of Belsay, just on the outskirts of Ponteland. Noticing bed and breakfast on the way, he stops and books in for a couple of nights. Mark settles into his room and then walks down to the local pub; after a couple of pints, Mark is relaxed and running various scenarios through his head. A wry smile on his face is the first time he is the hunted, but soon the hunted will become the hunter. Watch out, Rudy, and you may not see what hits you when the time is right for Mark. Walking back to his B & B, he has decided to walk towards the farmhouse. With the drone in his case, this item has become a vital tool to keep him alive. Unfortunately, the road is poorly lit heading towards the farmhouse, and he needs to be careful. He sees a five-bar gate to the right, lifting the handle, opening

the gate, and resting behind the fence. Five minutes later, the drone is airborne, scouring the fields; Mark has estimated a one-thousand-meter range if the hitman is as good as the indicators are.

Sure enough, he is lying in position, rifle in hand; Mark thinks he will return tomorrow; he will not sleep if Mark is old school, giving him a tactical advantage. So, drone back in the case, he casually walks back to the B and B, opens the bedroom door and gets ready for a good night's sleep, more than Rudy in the field, then he hears a loud thunderclap and thinks a very wet Rudy indeed.

During the day, Mark has purchased another phone; he asks for the local yellow pages and puts three takeaway places, pizza, Indian, and Italian, into the phone. Having had a substantial breakfast, the people who own the B and B are old school, all their clientele leave, with bellies full to last the day. Mark is used to waiting; patience has been one of his better virtues; as the time drifts away, 10 pm come around time to do what he does best. Mark pays his bill and thanks the owners for their kind hospitality, and he will recommend friends to come and stay. Mark gets into his basic car and drives up the road, a short distance, parks near the five-bar gate; within minutes, the drone is in the air; sure enough, Rudy is still there. Mark gets out phone number two and calls the local pizza shop asking how long it would be to deliver to Belsay farmhouse. One hour at least came, the reply, Mark puts the phone down, cursing under his breath. Next call the Indian takeaway, the same question they can deliver in thirty minutes, Mark orders a Chicken Masala a Garlic nan and mushroom rice, he tells them, when you drive up to the house the lights will come on when you get near to the house. Mark puts the phones on silent and heads towards Rudy; twenty minutes later, car headlights are coming down the farm track; Rudy shuffles into position, thinking his payday is about to happen. Mark guessed the lights would go on; you need to see who is coming to your door. Rudy is about to shoot the delivery driver, when he feels pain in his ankle, warm blood running into his sock, instinct comes to the fore, he turns gun in hand, to late more pain and blood running down his arm, two more shots, one to his right knee then the shoulder. Expletives in Dutch, Mark asks him to calm down while he makes a call.

Mark calls the Indian takeaway, telling them he is running late and to leave the meal at the front door, offering his apologies. Rudy is in excruciating pain, lying on the floor, screaming at Mark to get it over with. Mark asks who put the hit on him, Rudy replies he does not know directly other than a large cartel is after him, one bullet to the head all is quiet, Mark takes what is becoming a chore, the flash of the phone and he has his picture, stored ready to send in the morning. Mark directs the drone to the house; using his key card, he enters the house with the drone and his takeaway, pondering his night's work, enjoying his meal. Finishing his well-earned meal, Mark goes back to Rudy to see if he has anything on him. Just his phone he will send to Guy's PO Box number, then he walks towards the five-bar gate. He collects the drone case, gets into the basic car, and drives to the rear of the farmhouse. Back in the farmhouse, he goes to bed relaxed, one small problem eliminated. At the back of his mind, thinking, 'I must have pissed somebody off, but who the hell is it.'

Mark settles down for a good night's sleep, getting up nice and relaxed in the morning. Wanders into the kitchen, he turns on the coffee machine and takes in his surroundings. Noting how Guy has made sure all safe houses are the same in décor, even the kitchen is the same in every detail. Mark smiles on the raised floor, a white leather suite; he likes Guy even more. Picking up the key card, he heads towards the basement, more spacious than the last one. Key card over the reader, the familiar sound of compressed air, and even better selection of tools of the trade, taking stock of what he has, heading upstairs a call to Guy required. Within seconds Guy answers the phone; Mark proceeds to give him details of the past forty-eight hours, a photo will be sent in ten minutes, and the phone will be at your PO Box tomorrow. Mark informs Guy that the only thing he could get from Rudy is that a large cartel has put the hit on him. Guy asked if he thought it was UK based; Mark replied, 'I think it could be international.' Guy thanks him and he will make some enquiries, through Interpol.

Chapter 15

Ian Lee's body has arrived at Jimmy's house on the outskirts of Middlesbrough; unfortunately, they will need to bury him somewhere in the two acres of land they have. The body is placed on a table in one of the four garages, and Jimmy tells Janet and Glenn not to enter the garage. Naturally, they will not like what they see, and it was bad enough for him looking at the text he received.

With the house just recently been completed, there is still a small excavator on the grounds, and he arranges for a grave to be dug two-hundred-metres, opposite the main door entrance, so he can see the gravesite when he leaves daily.

They decide to pay extra to a local funeral director and pastor to do the service, no questions asked, especially when the body has a bullet in the head. Like everything in life, if you pay enough money, it all goes away. So they inform them, if they tell the police, they like their son will be out of business permanently. The bead of sweat on their heads was confirmation this incident would go no further. Ian's favourite music was playing while family and friends were at the house. Sandwiches and cakes are supplied, for them, while they give Janet and Glenn their condolences, Jimmy watches as the excavator is levelling the soil over Ian's grave, fists clenched a single tear running down his face. Although he is annoyed at Ian's senseless death, there was no need; he had nothing to prove to him. Within twenty-four hours, the guests leave and make their way back to various parts of the UK, many not knowing the true reason Ian had died. One hour after the last guest has gone, three large SUV's come up the drive, three individuals shown into Jimmy's lounge. Janet brings the coffee and biscuits and leaves; in all her years with Jimmy, she knows when not to say anything. Janet, another woman, was trapped in a marriage of no love when Jimmy was sent to prison, having had a couple of steamy affairs, and this released the real woman in her.

It seems every drug lord who dishes out money thinks it buys love and loyalty; in many ways, this could play into Mark's hands. Unknown to Jimmy, his wife has had some extra hidden cameras installed, which automatically download to a remote computer in a friend's house. Of course, she will deny any knowledge of these if found, 'you know I do not know anything that has wires on it,' hopefully, she will not need to use this excuse. The death of her eldest son has now spearheaded her desire to get out of this marriage. Realising her youngest is also on the wrong path, she has already lost him to greed like his father. The three men are shown into the dining room and sit down around the table opposite each other. All the men were in prison with Jimmy and were his get the job done people if inmates tried to complain about his extortion and racketeering scheme to generate his favourite commodity money. Their loyalty rewarded with substantial areas to supply drugs, in effect a drug franchise to each of them without paying a start-up fee. John King given Manchester, Mo Sam, was given Leeds and surrounding areas. Finally, Joe Hodge was given Newcastle and surrounding areas up to twenty miles of Middlesbrough to control and with significant effect. It was a sad time to meet, but Jimmy is a pragmatic businessman, money always on his mind facing the reality of the situation at hand. Jimmy asks the men if they have any idea who might be involved, have they heard if another cartel is trying to take over, the three men nonplus, void of answers. He tells them he has an old friend, in high office he will try to find some answers, or they could soon be out of business, that is something none of us wants. He tells them to pay for more men to secure their operations, and they all agree that we must nip this in the bud now. Four hours later, the three men leave, they shake his hand, giving their false condolences, driving down the road; John King texts the other two to meet in a pub car park two miles away.

Chapter 16

Mark contacts Guy in the afternoon, telling him it might be conducive to staying low for a few days after the past few days. And if it is okay with him to take a short break. Guy agrees that our enemies might think it was just a one-hit situation and step back their paranoia.
Mark, 'is my tracker still online.'
Guy, 'yes, any particular reason.'
'No, just going to Manchester to pay my respects.'
'Anyone I should know about.'
'My mother-in-law passed away six months ago.'
'Sorry, Mark.
'Thank you, and I think my sister-in-law was left my wife's house.'
'Will that be a problem.'
'No, never met her.'
'Should be interesting,'
Mark laughs, 'I suppose so.'
Guy, 'good luck, contact me when you are ready to carry on.'
At the back of the farmhouse, there is a two-story extension with a flat roof; Mark manoeuvres the drone onto it; he might well need this when he gets back. He second guesses himself and decides to take the other drone from the basement, and he has found them to be too helpful to leave behind. Mark gathers more tools of the trade and puts them in the false bottom in the boot, and the car is well modified to accept several tools, then make his way to the A1 heading south. Pondering what lies ahead, he makes his way to Julia's old house, wondering if he is making the right decision. It must be the three years in prison that has made his mind stale. Usually, all his decision making was instant, with no second thoughts, just clinical. Mark drops into a service station off the M62 to fuel up and get a bite to eat, avoiding cameras. There

seems to be more than usual; after all, it is three years since he was in these parts. After his meal, he calls into one of the shops to buy a larger brimmed cap to help hide his face, returning to his old mantra.
Steadily, just habit, he arrives in his old haunts, passing the house on Highfield Road, now a new house, after he blew it up in a time of need a few years ago.
Surprised the council have let them build a very modern house, so out of character, for some reason, he worries society is just getting worse. But, noticing half a mile away from the decay now starting, as housing estates are laid bare to drugs. He will not leave here till he has left his mark, he tells himself.
Then passing his old house, he can see the new owners are looking after it just as he and Julia did. Mark smiles as he passes the driveway; he will be outside Julia's old house in four minutes. He has not met Julia's sister or seen any photos; Julia kept her away due to their clandestine work, as hitman and hitwoman, worrying that she could be harmed or used as leverage against them.
A deep intake of breath as Mark walks up the drive, stopping should he carry on is he doing the right thing, suddenly Mark realises he is ringing the doorbell, no turning back now. A voice from behind the door, 'who is it at this hour.' Mark lost in time, forgot how late it was, he replies using his original name of, 'Paul Reed,' a gasp behind the door.
The door slowly opens, the hallway light shining in his face, he sees the slim figure of Julia's sister Lydia, he looks at her face she is the younger version of Julia, he breaks down on the step not believing his eyes. From Mark's response, she knew it could only be him; trying to come to terms with the situation, she puts her arms around him, even using the same perfume as Julia, Mark lost for words. Showing Mark into the living

room, she makes coffee and calms him down just as Julia would do. He closed his eyes; the tone and undulation of her voice she was the re-incarnation of Julia.

Lydia can see he is tired, explains they can talk tomorrow and guides him to the second bedroom, and Mark falls asleep instantly. In the morning, Mark is now woken by the smell of bacon and eggs, the smell of coffee. Making his way downstairs, he can see the house has not changed too much, Julia's influence everywhere.

Lydia looks stunning, cooking breakfast, just like Julia makeup on if someone comes to the door, especially late at night, he thinks to himself. So, breakfast on the table, before he starts, he offers his condolences over Sharon, asking, 'was it sudden.'

Lydia straight to the point, just like Julia, she thought it was a broken heart after losing you both, she struggled, the main part was your jobs, she could not believe how two people like you could do that type of work. Mark was just about to respond and looked up to see Lydia smiling; she said to him, 'but me, that is another matter. I loved the thought of what you both did.'

Mark, 'what do you mean.'

Lydia licking her lips, 'Julia told me all about it and even taught me things when you were out of the country.'

Mark was surprised, 'she never said anything.'

'Some secrets are best kept hidden for safety purposes, Julia told me.'

'That must have been the only one then.'

'Of course, she loved you too much to have any other.'

Mark now tucking into his breakfast, Lydia sits next to him, Mark with raised eyebrows, wonders what surprises she may have instore now. Resting her chin in cupped hands, she informed him; Julia even confided about your intense lovemaking in bed; after a kill, it turned her on, she said. Mark was extremely surprised by her remarks, more surprised when she took his hand and guided him to the bedroom. He is now glad he decided to come back, the next two hours brought back memories of Julia, and her sweet sister Lydia is just as intense. The nano tracker noticed that Mark hoping there would not be a knock on the door, remembering his heart rate would have increased. He excuses himself, telling Lydia he needs to check-in. A bemused Lydia nods in acceptance, a quick call to Guy referencing the tracker. Guy explains if it is not S & M, it only picks up on intense pain, strangely a sigh of relief from Mark. He could be doing the same thing again in a couple of hours, this time without a care in the world. While he is in the kitchen making coffee, Lydia glides down the stairs.

Then, in a mild state of euphoria, she looks at Mark, 'now I know what Julia meant,' a big smile on her face., a bigger smile on Mark's face, 'glad to have been of service, young lady.'

Mark asks her to sit down, Lydia's smile disappears. Could this be a one-night stand only, not after that performance; she is hooked on Mark as Julia was. Mark starts to explain his situation, laying all his cards on the table and telling her everything. Truth and trust between himself and Julia was the bond that kept their relationship together. He is expecting total rejection; on the contrary, she grabs his hand, laughing just like Julia and puts her arms around him, kissing him passionately. She takes him back upstairs throws him on the bed, no words spoken, just complete acceptance of each other.

Chapter 17

Two miles away from Jimmy Lee's house, John King, Mo Sam, and Joe Hodge meet in a pub car park to discuss their recent meeting with Jimmy. John opens the conversation that he has never seen Jimmy so spooked, and nothing has ever done that before. Jim points out that he has just lost his son; it is bound to affect him, he is grieving. John tells them both, I have known Jimmy for years; nothing affects him. He even beat up his father with his brother; they smashed his legs to a pulp, unable to walk ever again. John is ambitious; he wants to take over from Jimmy; recently, maybe the lever he needs to oust Jimmy. Ever manipulative, John is starting to plant the seed that Jimmy is losing control. Unfortunately, Jimmy did not tell his former protectors that everyone in Glasgow was killed, only singling out Edon's mutilation, wandering who could have done it. Jimmy only ever knew his leaders, not caring about the minions, regarding them as hangers-on. The only bad management choice he has made; without them, nothing works. The three men agree to meet in two weeks if things have not improved. They shake hands, get into their cars and make their way home along whichever road the satnav has chosen for them. Each man goes their separate ways, two unsure what to do, the other just looking for that little gap or mistake that he feels Jimmy will make soon, he will be ready, and he will be the new lord of the manor. The other two men are in turmoil; both realise that they would not have the trappings of their chosen profession without Jimmy's input, but with mixed loyalties between Jimmy or John, this will play hard on their minds. Both men carry on with normal day to day tasks, everything as usual, but a storm is brewing as to which side they choose; rightly or wrongly, there will be no winners in this game of power.

Unknown to Guy and Mark, their intervention in Glasgow has caused a ripple effect in a different direction, if only they knew they may have lit a fuse, where the infighting might do their work for them.

Chapter 18

Deciding to stroll down the lane towards the local village, a fresh crispness in the air, with early morning dew on the ground, Guy's eyes constantly searching for something unusual or out of place. After several good mornings to local villagers, he is well-liked, having been involved in local projects to keep the village sustainable, using contacts that have helped throughout the years. He steps into the small post office also the local food store for his morning paper and picks up items sent by Mark. In one hour, one of his colleagues will pick up these items, and hopefully, by the end of the day, he will have some information for Mark. Even with their years of experience, Harry and David are struggling to glean anything. From their searches into Charles Raven and John Hurst always suspicious when firewalls are put in their way. Somebody buries their past so efficiently; there must be reasons a great deal of money has been used to achieve this. It is sending warning signs to Harry and David. Details are coming through to Guy, not as fast as he would like, but he realises that this will minimise any mistakes. So Guy has asked all his colleagues to hand deliver all information, make only one copy and delete all other material. He will be the only one who has all the information. A knock on his office door, an A4 envelope hand-delivered, opening it two pieces of paper, one with blood results the other a name to the first photo sent by Mark. Even Guy is surprised by the ethnicities of the blood results, Rudy Stem the dutchman he knew about, the rest known through Interpol outlets worldwide. Thanks to various police forces worldwide, each an untouchable hitman from different parts of the world, one Mexican, one Columbian and one from Italy. With this type of firepower, some raw nerves have opened; Guy is worried now. They have been drawn into something far more significant than they thought; have they bitten off more than they can chew? Guy calls Mark.

Explaining everything to him, regarding the people he disposed of, then the surprise that Mark did not expect, his first kill had familial DNA to a known drug kingpin called Jimmy Lees.
Mark opens to Guy, telling him that it was Jimmy Lees who ordered the hit on his friend Ethan, a slight gasp from Guy, Mark carries on 'it looks like I may have killed his son, well that is one less to go after.'
Guy, 'any idea about the other contingents.'
Mark, 'the countries have just reminded me of something.'
'That would be,' with bated breath.
'Before I was so rudely interrupted by Cleveland police, I was employed to dispose of the heads of a cartel in Holland. Taking out a Mr Columbia and a Mr Italy, Somebody, else who hired me took out Mr Dutch, they were all done on the same day.'
Guy, 'good grief Mark, you do not do things by half, do you.'
Mark, 'a different time, for another reason, Guy.'
'My instinct is telling me, we have two separate issues, which have overlapped, just the timing is wrong.'
'Guy, one is my problem; I will deal with it on completion of our original task.'
Guy thanks him for his loyalty but tells him, 'We are in this together, do not feel you are out on a limb,'
'Can you give me another couple of days before I start up again?'
'Certainly, oh how did you get on with the sister-in-law.'
'A lot better than I had hoped.'
'Good, contact me when you are online, so to speak.'

'You will know by the news and media, believe me.'
Guy, 'goodbye, Mark.'

Chapter 19

Mark is now also besotted with Lydia, and their conversations are like an old married couple; Lydia has gone to the corner store for a few essentials. His relationship with Lydia is a bonus beyond belief; he will take it all as long as it lasts. Marks original reason to return to Julia's house, his old business burner phone, which is in a cavity above the rafters in the garage; Julia had hidden it when he was arrested. In the thirty minutes, Lydia was away; Mark had found the phone, now charging on the kitchen worktop. She looks at the telephone, wincing at how old it is. Mark explains what it was used for; her hair stands up on her arms, a sense of excitement just like Julia. Her cheeks start to flush, with that glow of anticipation of what lies ahead.

Lydia cannot contain herself. In two days, her world has been turned upside down, to her for the better, and she now understands why Julia loved their lifestyle. After two hours of gentle banter and the phone is charged. Marks' website was closed just before DCI Roger Leyland caught him. So to have any messages would be a shock. But a surprise indeed one message a few days old the message even more surprising to him. 'Hello, this is Jimmy Lees; you did a job for me several years ago, eliminating a snitch called Harry. He still has not been found, and I need your services urgently.' A phone number was left, Mark thinking should I contact him, curiosity killed the cat, they say, but this is life and death. It might be one way of finding out what is going on. He is so confident in two days of their relationship, and he tells Lydia the scenario that is building up. She is so excited, she purrs in his ear, 'you must call, or you will never know.' Unusually Mark crosses his fingers and makes that call, the phone rings four times, and the cockney tones of

Jimmy Lees answers the phone, 'Jimmy who is it,' quite sternly.
Mark, 'you left a message a few days ago.'
Jimmy, 'is that the guy who disposes of rubbish.'

Mark, 'that would be me.'
Jimmy, 'I need your help desperately.'
Mark with a sincere 'yes how can, I help you.'
Jimmy, 'the hitman, has killed my son.'
Mark interjects and offers his condolences; Jimmy accepts this and carries on, 'I realise it will be difficult, I do not have a photo or name yet; in fact, I do not know where he is.'
Mark, 'have you any idea why this hitman killed your son.'
Jimmy, 'my fault, Mark gasps for effect, Jimmy carries on, 'I put a hit on the hitman, my contact high up in the government informed me about his the task to shut us down, do they not realise how big I am.'
Mark, 'how did your son become involved.'
Jimmy, 'he was trying to prove himself to me.'
Mark, 'sorry about that. Do you think you can get any more information about this hitman?'
Jimmy, 'I will squeeze my contact.'
Mark, 'I will not do anything till you contact me again.'
As mark walks into the kitchen, Lydia is smiling; having listened to his conversation, her hormones rise. She grabs Marks's hand, and within minutes they are naked on the floor out of view from the neighbours. If the neighbours could hear, they would have thought the kitchen was getting replaced, such was the noise and intensity of the passion, both sweating they move to the shower room.
Another hour later, Mark is on the phone with Guy, and he is not surprised at the information of a government man being paid by Jimmy. There is a slight sound of laughter down the phone as Guy realises that Jimmy

has hired Mark to kill Mark; the irony does not slip past Mark's mind either.
Mark tells Guy that he will have to be careful as this hitman is quite good; they both laugh at the situation at hand. Guy then asks Mark when he will be available, 'give me two more days; I need to rattle a machete supplier first.'
Guy, 'call me when you finish, I will chase down our drug benefactor, I hope.'

Mark, 'bids him farewell,' then goes on the internet to find the machete supplier on the dark web.
Surprisingly, they have the audacity to put the address and phone number on the website, either naïve or they think they are untouchable.
Mark rings the number, a gruff voice at the other end asking what he wants. Mark continues that he has looked on the dark web and would like to purchase many items from them. Now the voice changes to a more business-like manner, my name is Phil, amazing how money changes things. Mark carries on saying, 'he would like to come down tomorrow at 6 pm to pay for a large consignment.'
Phil quite aggressively 'we close at 5.30 pm.'
'If you want a big order, it is 6 pm or nothing.'
'How much are we talking about.'
'At least half your stock.'
'6 pm it is then.'
The phone call finished, Mark makes his way to the Manchester safe house, on entering he smiles, everything the same as the other two. Key card over the reader, walking into the armoury, picks up some extra items that he will most certainly use. Next, a visit to the small industrial estate just to see what he is up against. The unit is at the head of a short road, and if you are in the unit, you can see everything around you. Mark was hoping access could have been a little bit

better, but the surprise element wins all the time. Phil is not expecting anything, only thinking about money. Mark notices the two cameras on each corner and the fancy sportscar outside, trappings of his trade. Mark will arrive a little different than he usually looks. The next day Lydia, just watching how Mark is preparing for his task in hand, everything Julia had told her how meticulous Mark was, a cold-hearted killer who enjoyed every aspect of his work. Two hours before he is due to leave, he goes upstairs. Telling Lydia to stay downstairs; thirty minutes later, he comes downstairs a different person. Mark had put on a brown wig slightly greying, a brown beard again with grey steaks and wearing a pair of spectacles, Lydia speechless at the transformation.

Lydia's mouth is still open, and Mark kisses her on the cheek, saying, 'just nipping to work should not be too long.'

As he walks out of the front door, she rushes to the front window to wave goodbye, inside hoping and wishing he would return soon.

Mark is on the motorway, running various scenarios in his head, always ready if something might change. His only unknown is how many people are in the building. He parks up around the corner taking his briefcase from the car. Starts to walk towards the unit; the owner, Phil Steel, had installed signage above the front door, proudly telling everybody (supplier of quality steel). Mark thought he would not know what a 4 x 2 steel channel was; as usual, Marks' heart rate had slowed down. A technique he had developed during his time with special forces. Opening the door, he enters the unit, conscious of where the cameras are, not too worried that they will be gone when he finishes. Two men stand behind the counter; Mark asks to speak to Phil, he has an appointment with him, one

of the men moves forward to frisk him, Mark asks, 'why.'
The other introduces himself as Phil, 'precautions I do not know who you are.'
Mark replies, 'that's the same for me; I do not know who you are either.'
Phil, now getting annoyed, 'just do it, or my friend may have to break your arm.'
'Strange way to do business, especially the amount of money I am talking about.'
'Well, that's where it got suspicious, that amount of money and why.'
'It is an obvious reason, really.'
'And that is, my friend.'
'Firstly, I am not your friend, and I just wanted to get them off the streets.'
Phil laughed, 'you are more of a fool than I thought; you might be.'

'Maybe, but can I ask who your supplier is.'
'I don't mind telling you; you will not be leaving here tonight, Hoffman Steel in Holland.'
'Thank you, that was easy.'
'What do you mean.'
Mark, 'after tonight, you will not have a business; you will be dead.'
The other man never got a chance to frisk Mark; he cut his throat with lightning speed, blood pouring from his throat. Mark ironically points out the danger of selling knives. Phil's demeanour changes instantly, begging for his life; Marks's favourite move the shot to the knee, Phil screaming in agony.
Mark tells him to sit down, 'your knee must be hurting,' Phil sits down grasping his knee, 'what are you going to do now, you bastard.'
Mark, 'why did you get into this business.'

Phil, 'an old friend suggested it would be a good money-making venture.'

'You did not care what you were supplying to the youths of today.'

'Why they are idiots, it was an easy way to make money.'

'Who was your friend.'

'Jimmy Lees said he had the ok from a guy high up in the government.'

Mark thanks him, then proceeds to cut him with different knives and machetes, explaining, this is the pain you are selling on the street; it ends now and shoots him in the head.

Mark then finds the main office, disconnects the computer with surveillance cameras, and places it in his briefcase.

He proceeds to place charges around the building, slams the front door shut and walks to his car. He arrives at Lydia's front door, putting the key into the door. She greets him as would Julia, coffee on he says to Lydia, 5,4,3,2,1 and cups his ear, an explosion in the distance, a childish squeal from Lydia, they both laugh together in each other's arms.

Chapter 20

Within minutes there was the sound of police and fire service siren's racing to the scene. The building was standing alone at the head of the road. Utility services have been cut off to minimise issues that may affect other facilities, and burglar alarms start piercing the air as power supplies are turned off. Police are talking to fire officers to decide if they should let it burn to the ground as the flames are intense; constantly aware safety of life is paramount. Fire hoses reeled out, and they proceeded to douse the building with water, one seasoned fire officer speaking to a police officer, pointing out this is not an ordinary fire.
He asks, 'what do you mean.'
Fire officer, 'the heat is too intense; I have never seen metal melt like that before.'
It takes several hours to bring the flames under control; the problem of having a steel cladding exterior has all melted into a mass of molten metal.
Two hours later, the police are knocking on Phil Steel's door, and Jane Steel answers the door, startled to see two officers, one male, one female. They ask, 'is Mr Steel in,' she replies, 'he has not come in from work yet,' the female officer steps back and mumbles into her comms with an update that he is not at home.
The male officer carries on, 'what time do you expect him to come back,' Jane replies, 'he normally rings me, as he is leaving the office.'
'What type of car does he drive,' at this request, Jane starts to shake, 'has he had an accident? Please don't tell me he has had an accident.'
'We cannot say, Mrs Steel, there has been an incident at your husband's business.'
Jane starts to cry, 'please tell me what has happened.'
'We do not have the full facts yet. For example, does your husband have any work colleagues?'

Jane, 'only one Jake Howard.' 'Where does he live.'
Jane, 'Three roads down,14 Wier Close, why.'
'We will send someone to Jake's house.'
Jane 'but why what is going on.'
Having just received some information, the female officer asks Jane if it is possible to come inside, to talk rather than on the doorstep; still shaking, she agrees. As they enter the lounge, Dawn, her daughter, is sitting on the settee, already having heard most of the conversation, showing signs of stress herself. She rises from the sofa to turn the TV off, just as a news flash comes up about an explosion, both police officers annoyed at how quick the media brings it to air. Dawn turns to her mother, 'mum, it's dad's place, oh my god, what has happened? He only sold knives,' both women burst into tears. The officers can only wait till the tears subside, the usual a nice cup of calming tea, and the kettle switched on. Ten minutes later, tea made, both officers trying to calm them down, saying, 'that it is early days in the investigation and all avenues will be checked.' Again, both women calm down, not wanting to believe what has just happened. Finally, one officer asks, 'if you would like one of our liaison officers to attend,' a polite nod a call for Susan North to attend, she arrives one hour later. It releases the two officers to assist in any investigations.

On the other side of the coin, Mark and Lydia have just seen the news footage, with a different reaction, Mark has noticed Lydia's cheeks start to flush up, thinking, 'I am going to need Viagra if this carries on,' they rush upstairs, nothing more to say. Twenty-four's later, and the building is still steaming, the heat so intense, it is one mass of steel, it will be another couple of days before any investigation can occur. One fire officer has indicated a professional hit; the police ask why surprised by this comment. The fire officer tells him he

was an explosives expert in Afghanistan up to three years ago, and to create that amount of heat, it could only have been thermite charges.
At this stage, no bodies were found, but the police are already setting up a murder investigation.

The police thought that Phil Steels business was a steel supplier, but the steel was another word for knives and machetes, so inquiries have started into his business. The following morning, Jane and Dawn have accepted that Phil was in the explosion, no replies to their phone calls, he never fails to answer, added to the fact that Jake Howard is missing. Jane has asked the police to leave now; she has things to do. Unknown to the police, Jane and Dawn are the business brains behind the knife operation. She is callous and driven by money, and she does not care about the lives she ruins. However, if she gets her bling and expensive holidays, her daughter is a chip off the old block and highly driven, just like her mother. So instead of arranging a possible funeral, she contacted her suppliers to hold the last order. Her next call is to arrange a viewing on another unit near Wythenshawe, not far from the airport. It is now a bittersweet enquiry; on the surface, some police are glad the knives are off the streets, but they would rather Phil Steel was in prison. They do not believe in vigilantes on the streets offering out punishment at will. Others are over the moon that someone has taken over the cause and does something they cannot do. It could be a long-drawn-out investigation indeed for some officers, who do not have the heart to solve it. There are now individuals around Manchester within the drug fraternity. Wondering what is going on, strong rumours of the demolition of their Glasgow colleagues is filtering down the chain. Creating fear has always been their mantra, but now they are afraid, and for a good reason, they do not know who or what is coming their way.

Chapter 21

John King is gathering his men in Manchester with the recent explosion at Phil Steels property. He is asking for vigilance from all of them; anything unusual they must come to him straight away. However, he is presumptuous as his future antagonist plans to return to Newcastle, loaded with information on Jim Hodge, Marks next victim.

Lydia has packed sandwiches for the trip, asking if she could go with him, but accepted Marks' reasoning. He did not want her to get hurt till he had time to test her abilities. She agrees, uttering her disappointment, telling him to come back soon. She shouts out the door, 'looks like it is therapeutic shopping for me then.'

Mark waves goodbye and smiles and gets into that basic car and points the car North. Lydia will go shopping, straight away she has decided to buy some special lingerie for his return, he will melt into her arms when he comes home. Guy is now informed that he is on his way to Newcastle. Guy knew, of course, what is a tracker for. The journey will be around three hours if you do not use it, depending on toilet breaks. Mark drifts left onto the M1 from the M62 heading North, and as usual, the heavens open, torrential rain for the next forty minutes and then the sun breaks through the clouds, not long now, he will be at the farmhouse. Ever cautious, Mark pulls up to the five-bar gate, gets out of the car, goes to the rear, and gets out the drone controller; he will do a thousand-meter scan of the surrounding area. As dusk is falling, the drone he had left parked on the two-story extension lifts silently. Within minutes it is scouring the area, five hundred meters from the house at opposite sides, two individuals are poised with rifles. Mark thought this was starting to get a bit intense now, 'still, I better move out to one thousand meters, just in case,' nobody else there, time to deal with these two individuals. Mark makes his move to the nearest one, drone overhead, he picks up a rock, one of the oldest ruses to trick someone, throws it to one side.

His victim moves to the right trying to focus on the dark, then grasping his neck, trying to stop the blood flowing, dead in seconds. Mark is searching the body for clues, no wallet, no phone, only car keys. Mark circles round to the other side, drone above his prey again. Staying still, Mark sends the drone back to its parking space on the extension. One-shot in the shoulder an utterance in English, he drags him to the farmhouse, the man trying to get away, thinking, 'why must, I have to shoot them in the knee, a quiet thud,' he screams, Mark pushes him to the farmhouse.
Mark, 'good grief, now I know why I kill them, it is less hassle,' but he needs essential information, so he puts up with his annoying guest. Mark informs him that depending on what he has to say, he will determine if he leaves here dead or alive. The man considering his options asks Mark what he wants to know.
Mark, 'just one simple question, who sent you.'
His victim, 'I cannot tell you.'
Mark, 'why not.'
Victim, 'we do not know, it is on the dark web, we accept the job, send a photo of the kill, then the money is sent to our bank account.'
Mark, 'how do they know if you have the right person.'
Victim, 'we have to send a photo of ourselves to confirm our kill, please let me go.'
Mark, 'too late, my friend, an eye for an eye, you were quite prepared to kill me for money.' Mark grabs his face with a sudden movement, the victims neck broken, and silence descends on the farmhouse. He takes the dead body outside and lays it next to the other victim,

and he thinks there will be loads of flowers here next year, time for sleep. As Mark gets ready for bed, pondering his options for tomorrow. Gathering up the file on Joe Hodge from the white leather three-piece suite and reading about his history of violence towards society in general, this man is nasty; indeed, it will be a pleasure to get rid of him from this world, he thinks.

Chapter 22

While sitting at his desk at home, Guy does not want any form of information found in government offices, and things are getting quite sensitive. Once you indicate, there may be a problem within the government, and the doors start to close in. Any requests fall on deaf ears. Scanning the daily papers, he can see what remains of a building, which he is almost certain is the handy work of Mark. The media have found out that it supplied knives and machetes, giving it a high-profile front-page coverage, with headlines about a vigilante whose son was killed by thugs with knives. He smiles, yet again the media are overthinking for the sake of extra sales of their newspaper; if they only reported on the truth and not half-truths, the public would respect them more. Then as he is turning the pages, he suddenly realises that the newspapers may help their cause and create even more paranoia, hopefully keeping their enemies at bay, thinking of other things. A couple of anonymous phone calls later, the media have been told that drug kingpins used the building via his burner phone. Initially, they disbelieve the caller, but the seed has been planted; Guy is sure that some more stories will emerge by the end of the week. A call to Harry and David can they come to his house for an update, and he will inform them of the current situation, and please watch your back for anybody following. He is starting to think who is winning this game now, his paranoia coming to the fore, he will need to stay grounded. Four hours later, a coded knock on the door of Guy's home, the door opens by itself, Guy operating it from his panic room. Harry and David have been before and making their way to Guy's little haven in the house. As they settle down for discussions, a single tap on the door, opening the smell of coffee, floats into the panic room;

Guy's wife, Mary, always up to speed, walks in and that knowing nod between a long term married couple always knowing what they think. Harry and David thank her, biscuits have gone before the tray touches the table.

Shaking his head, nothing left for him, Mary, 'I will be back, with your biscuits Guy,' she laughs as she leaves the room. As Mary walks back to the living room, she reflects on their lives together, childhood sweethearts from fifteen years old meeting at the mixed comprehensive school. Married in their early twenties, two children in their late twenties, blissfully happy with very few crossed words in their marriage. Children in good jobs with their own lives ahead of them, up until the last couple of weeks she was happy, she has noticed a change in Guy this new job is worrying him, her sixth sense is on edge. He started his career in the army, his abilities were noticed quickly, and he was sent to the Royal Military Academy Sandhurst. Fast-tracked, he soon climbed the ladder within the military, becoming the youngest Brigadier in the military. Approached by government agencies, MI5 then moved to MI6; whilst in these positions, he was privy to the most sensitive information, for your eyes-only status. While he was in the military, she loved travelling and, best of all, the Captain's Ball, mixing with people who loved what they did. Wearing beautiful clothes, bringing out the jewellery, the ones for that special occasion, just what every woman wants, watching her husband mingle with possible future politicians. She would smile when Guy would ask her to dance, and he is looking handsome, in his bright red braided tunic, the pencil crease in the black trousers, shoes polished so you could see your face in them. He always pointed out that he did so to see if she was wearing any knickers, then laughed to herself as she never wore any, and they think to days, youth are promiscuous. Oh, if only her children knew what they were like, stories for another day, you never know they might make them blush with embarrassment. Guy had learnt the art of social climbing with ease, but not in a bad way, possibly because it worked so well. He was well respected by all who met him. Guy had been sent to many places that no one needed to know. The art of being a politician at times pulled him out of many situations.

As the years progressed, counter-terrorism became the main subject of Guy's work, Mary still not knowing what he did.
Mary tapped on the panic room door, opened the door, walking in with a cafeteria of fresh coffee and biscuits just for Guy; Harry and David smiled at each other; he was the boss after all.
In all his years, sadly, Guy had only lost two of his team ten years ago, working undercover in Afghanistan tracking the money trail for a drug cartel supplying arms and drugs to the Taliban. John Rains and Carl Naim undercover for two years, passing information back to Guy's group; the information became spasmodic in their last six months. Guy hoped they had not been captured, using all his best resources to find them; all that kept coming back was that they had been caught and executed; Guy carried on for a further two years, constantly looking, but to no avail. In the end, he put it to the back of his mind with great difficulty, never wanting to lose anyone, part of the job, they knew what they were getting into, he would tell himself never really accepting it. Finally, Harry and David put on the table the little information they had. Both are surprised by how deep the firewalls are; nobody in their opinion is this squeaky clean, which

adds to their deep suspicions of both Raven and Hurst. Harry points out that this level of deceit is high indeed; a phenomenal amount of money has been spent to create this illusion. If only the people had not closed the net so tight around Charles Raven and John Hurst, they might not be looking so hard into their pasts. Harry points out that these two individuals were two small businessmen ten years ago, one with a building business and a small-time property manager. Then suddenly, nine years ago, they were in higher office, no questions asked; this is hard to believe. They must have something very incriminating on some politicians to get into such high office. Guy suggests they contact their Interpol colleagues to see if they can shake a few trees and see what may fall. Then, strangely two hours later, a call from Paul Wayne, an old Interpol colleague. Guy had worked several operations with him, so pleasantries passed.

But, he tells Guy, a possible breakthrough, intense chatter, is coming through of a rising drug cartel called Ramina, location unknown but a lot of money involved with the name. Guy tells everyone to prioritise tracing this organisation if only to remove them from their enquiries. Guy tells Harry and David that something is happening if Paul has picked this up, be incredibly careful indeed. As the two men leave the house, Mary catches Guy's eye after several years of marriage; he knows that she wants to talk and now looks like he is in trouble, which is rare indeed. Walking tentatively towards the main sitting room, Mary asks him to sit down, Guy thinking, 'oh no, not a pep talk, which is normally a dressing down situation.' Guy sits next to Mary, 'okay, what have I done wrong,' she smiles, 'nothing, just noticed you have changed a bit with this latest job. Is there anything I should know?'
'Mary, you know I cannot tell you anything.'

'I am your wife; if I can see something is wrong, so can others.'
'Why are you so good at this, Mary.'
'Just tell me you will be careful, Guy.'
'I will, Mary, just keep telling me if you notice anything out of the ordinary.'
'You know I will.'
'Thank you, Mary,' then kisses her and goes back to his haven to think. Constantly amazed at Mary's insightfulness, one of those things when you have known each other since their teens. He is surprised at a homeland situation, which is now gradually becoming an international one, and who the hell is the Ramina cartel. A call to update Mark on how the situation is escalating, Mark is unsurprised that drugs are involved, telling Guy, 'Looks like our little job has just got a bit bigger.'
Amazed at how calm Mark is, does he have any nerves at all, looking at the tracker marks heartbeat never faltering, wishing deep down he had more men like him, unofficially of course. Then a call from Harry, he has just found out that Raven-Hurst Holdings has bought up a large area of property and land in Glasgow at a low price.

Harry carries on, it is the area that Mark had cleaned out a couple of weeks ago, yet again more questions than answers, Guy thinks.

Chapter 23

Mark has thoroughly digested the information on Joe Hodge and is currently driving around his designated area to inflict some pain. Once again, the area showing signs of decay and degradation is an area of high unemployment strangely; this seems to fuel the fire of drugs. Everyone fighting to survive; hence the easy way to make money is to become a dealer, running the streets picking up easy prey, and the addiction starts, and that cycle of money rolls in too easy, no need to work, no tax to pay. Mark is annoyed the police seem to allow this to go on, making him think there are payoffs somewhere down the line. Something Guy might not have, thought of before; he can tell his moral compass is high and would not like to consider a servant of society would stoop so low. After two days, Mark has located his first prey, and he looks about twenty years old, currently just supplying an individual; he constantly has a friend with him. Mark pulls up just next to him and gets out; the first thing he notices is the young man's friend, who steps in front of him, then he sees the tip of a blade in his right hand.

Mark, 'what's the idea with the knife? I only want some of your product at the right price, of course.'

Friend, 'we do not know who you are; you could be the police.'

Mark, 'If I were the police, it would not go down well with them, you bloody idiot.'

Friend, 'nobody calls me an idiot.'

Mark, 'well, look at it this way, I could be carrying a knife as well.'

Friend, 'what's an old fart like you.'

Mark, 'well, that is where, you are wrong, a sudden movement from Mark and the friend is on his knees gasping for breath, blood coming from his throat. The twenty-year-old drops all his

packages and tries to jump over his friend; Mark grabs him and tells him he will be ok; information is all I am after.
The individual is called Aaron, gradually calming down, hoping that he will survive this day.
Mark casually asks him why you need someone with a knife with him; he replies, something happened in Glasgow, now all dealers have someone with them. Mark asks him how many dealers are on the streets; Aaron replies about fifteen now; it can be up to twenty depending on demand. Mark asks Aaron to come on a journey of discovery with him, which if he takes the right road will enlighten his life for the better, and possibly he would live a lot longer. Aaron is now thinking he's with a mad born-again Christian and hoping he will let him go in due time. Having already noticed a disused factory unit and no cameras insight an ideal bolt hole to question his new colleague. Mark picks the lock on entry; just a couple of storage racks left in the building, Mark cuffs Aaron to the rack, via both feet and one hand, and proceeds to question him.
'How long have you been a dealer.'
'Two years, most of us have been doing it for two years.'
Yet again, this two-year thing, just when Jimmy Lees was released. So, mark, 'are you, independent dealers.'
Aaron, 'no, we work for Joe Hodge.'
Mark, 'who is he.'
'He works for Jimmy Lees; most of the money goes to him.'
'Where does Joe live.'
'I can't tell you he will kill me.'
'Well, you have a difficult choice then.'
'What do you mean.'
'It's either him or you who dies tonight, your choice.'
'Oh my god, I am just small time I don't get involved with him.'

'What do you mean.'
'We work for two supervisors, and if we do not deliver, we are beaten up in front of everyone.'
'Well, it is a simple choice, a life away from this, which will shorten your life or complete freedom, which is what I am offering you.'.
You have got five minutes to sort your life out.'
Deathly silence then Mark asks, 'which is it then, young man.'
Aaron, 'even if I tell you, the supervisors will find out, and I am dead.'
Mark, 'I guarantee you will be free by tomorrow if you give me their names and address.'
Aaron, 'would you do that,'
'Yes, and when I let you go, you tell the others to walk away.'
'What do you mean.'
'No more drugs, you all walk away, or I will be back, and your lives will be no more.'
Aaron agrees and gives Mark two addresses; Mark has left one hand free and leaves water and sandwiches for young Aaron.
Mark leaves, and the door closes; it echoes through the empty building, Aaron has never prayed before, but he is now reaching out if he changes his ways. The two supervisors are brothers and blood cousins to Joe Hodge, which looks like a family affair for Mark to sort out. Luck is on Marks side; they both live next door to each other, recently buying some land with their ill-gotten gains, taking the two largest plots and leaving the four other plots to be sold soon. One of the houses owned by the two cousins, not the marrying kind, life is too good to involve any women on the scene; they would spoil the holidays to exotic places. Of course, the large extravagant house next door on the largest plot is Joe's, three new cars on the drive, both parties just moving in two days ago, boxes everywhere. Both

have extensive block paved drives, with lighting guiding Mark up to the cousin's house. He notices the garage door open; these people are overconfident no one dare come to their houses. Mark casually strolls into the garage, then knocks on the internal door to the house. Within seconds one cousin opens the door, a thud, and the bullet goes under the chin and through his head. Falling backwards, he hits a kitchen stool into the large brand-new kitchen.

On hearing this, brother number two runs into the kitchen shouting, 'what the hell,' not even completing the sentence, he falls to his knees, a bullet to the head. Mark then turned the gas taps on; luckily, these were old school and had an open fire blazing away. It should not take too long before the fireworks start.

Mark positioned himself behind a large oak tree, waiting for phase two to start.

He was getting impatient, and usually, the fireworks would have started by now, then remembering it was a large room to fill with gas.

Loading the magazine into his favourite Glock, just as he snaps it back in, the explosion, 'oh joy,' a smile across his face. Joe and his two sons run out, followed by his wife, and Mark takes her out first, then the two sons, as his family lay on the floor, he turns to see Mark coming towards him. Obscenities flow at Mark, falling on deaf ears, then the obligatory, 'why my family.'

Mark, 'simple you and your kind are selling death and addiction, killing society, so elimination is the only answer' then silence as Joe Hodges breaths his last breath over the bodies of his family, two shots to the chest. Mark goes into the house, turns the gas on and leaves; one of his special timers on the kitchen worktop gets into the basic car and drives away. Six minutes later, a call from a public phone box nearby to the fire services that two explosions had been heard at the address given. Mark can hear sirens in the distance, fire services arrive first and see the bodies on the floor, a call to the police as they attempt to control the fires. Two police cars turn into the road; they already know whose houses they are. They request the fire services to pull back, as there is no danger to life, the bodies located at the end of the driveways away from flames. Instantly they can see that a professional hit has taken place, no witnesses. It will be a lengthy investigation, currently assuming it is drug wars as information regarding Glasgow is just filtering through the system. Police chatter on comms about the victims, known drug kingpins they could not get evidence on. A confident DS Scott is now starting to sweat as he was there inside man, planted several years ago, his cash flow has just stopped. Mark returns to the unit; Aaron is at a crossroads; will he survive the night? As Mark approaches, he tenses to learn his fate.

Mark removes the cuffs, 'you are free to go,' Aaron thanks him, half expecting a bullet in the back, shaking as he walks towards the door. Mark, 'just before you go.'

Aaron a sense of panic coming to the fore 'yes.'

'Just thought about something, the money and drugs, where are they.'

'They kept it secret none of us knew.'

'Tell your colleagues to destroy the knives, or I will be back to kill them all; that is not a threat, it is a fact.'

'One last question, do you know if they have a snitch in the local police.'

'Only rumours.'

'Well, I suggest you find the money and leave the area, for your safety, also if you can destroy the drugs, before the police raid the area, which they will do now your, bosses are dead, or you will finish up in prison.'

Aaron is just about to leave the building when Mark booms out, 'you are lying, 'beads of sweat start to fall down Aaron's face.

'You all must meet at a commonplace to pick up the drugs and give them the money.'

'Oh erm sorry, I forgot about that.'

'Well, sorry, may cost you your life.'

'I did not mean to; I am so afraid to tell you.'

'Get it through your thick head, and this is a way to freedom and a better life, one last chance.'

'I will take you there.'

'Not too hard, was it.'

They leave the unit and make their way to the street where Mark picked up Aaron; as they drive down the road, Mark can see how the drugs are starting to affect the area. Aaron asks him to stop outside a large Victorian house; Mark asks if there are any guards about it, Aaron informs him there are always two on the bottom floor. 'Come with me, young man; I need you just to get inside, do not worry; nothing will happen to you.' They enter the house; on doing so, one man puts his hand on Mark's shoulder, a sudden twist of his arm a muffled scream as his throat is cut, he falls to the floor. Mark asks Aaron to shout the other man's name, a loud, 'John,' was heard.

He runs into the room, one bullet to the head, the house is now silent, and nobody else is around.

They both search the premises, each floor at a time. On reaching the top floor, there are three large rooms, two full of drugs and stacks of knives, supplied by Steels of Manchester. The last one with a substantial amount of money in it, Mark tells Aaron to bag as much money as he can take and leave immediately; this house will be in flames shortly. True to his word, the house starts to burn; Mark leaves, seeing Aaron in the distance. He goes the opposite way, heading to Manchester happy with his days' work; a new chapter in his life is starting.

On the way, he informs Guy of his suspicions regarding a bent police officer. Guy takes stock of his reasoning and will get Harry and David to investigate.

Unknown to Mark and Guy, DS Scott is making his way to the area where Mark had just left ten minutes ago to find the house, where he picked up his extra pay packet, now in flames. Distraught at the sight, knowing all the money and drugs gone, how will he now survive. He was recruited many years ago, unfortunate fate, himself and another potential officer with a gambling problem, both officers going into the same betting shop at the same time, he was the last one out. However, he was approached with a simple solution to his problem, one favour. He should have known there is always more favours required, incriminating evidence; he was on Jimmy's hook forever. He is now dragged into the underbelly of the drug scene, money coming easier; his habit continues, no turning back now. The favours becoming more desperate to hide information, threats on his family made sure he would toe the line. He thought his life was free when Jimmy went to prison, not so he became the guardian of Jimmy's slush fund to start up again, threats to his family always controlling him. Jimmy requested he join him in the Northeast, more demanding than asking, no way to turn he put in a transfer to Newcastle.

Four weeks later, he's Jimmy's lapdog again, his world spiralling out of control.

His wife always thought he was just a well-paid officer because the job could be dangerous.

But, enjoying their lifestyle in a leafy London suburb, close to amenities, excellent restaurants, regular nights out, she loved her husband's job.

Then the bombshell, 'we are moving to the Northeast,' Amy his wife's reply shocked him, 'without me.'

John Scott, 'we have to. I have an assignment up there.'

Amy has never been out of London, 'but it is dirty and industrial, no way.'
John, 'but it is Newcastle, a city which is vibrant just like here.'
Amy, 'I do not care, you are going without me,' she walks away crying, John cannot console her. His life starts to fall apart, and he must move without her; four weeks later, he had moved by himself. As soon as John moved to the Northeast, Amy was having an affair she craved for; with him gone, life is blissful. Six months later, John receives the half-expected letter, Amy requesting a divorce, accepting this easier than Amy expected. The settlement was straightforward, and he had settled in the Northeast, surprised at what it had to offer. But, now, with his lifestyle of deceit, he will struggle to survive on his miserly police wages; what can he do, who can he turn to.

Chapter 24

While things are happening elsewhere in the country, Jane Steel has just purchased a new unit in Wythenshawe to carry on her business supplying knives and machetes to the wrong type of people. Jane and her daughter Dawn have only one agenda: easy money and the markup on their products exceeds 200%, and with the existing drug trade, there are plenty of buyers. They have estimated that they should be up and running within seven days, with no thought about her husband, whose life was sacrificed for her love of money and holidays. The insurance company agrees that her husband died in an unfortunate accident; she has become a wealthy woman, no need for the new business; once again, greed comes easy. Police and fire services still sifting through the carnage of the explosion. As parts of the building are removed, the heat so intense the steel melted together, a large crane has been brought in to lift onto trailers. Whilst this operation was happening, lifting one section of melted steel a call from one of the salvage crew, he has noticed the remains of a finger, everything is stopped. Within one hour, a forensic crew arrive, the blue and white police tape placed around the no go area, people on their knees meticulously searching for clues; this job will take days. Mark is halfway to Manchester. When Jimmy receives a call from DS Scott, putting the phone down, anger consumes him. He starts destroying his office furniture, his colleagues taken aback; they knew he had a temper but nothing like this. Non-stop obscenities fill the air, the window getting smashed, people vanish quickly until it subsides, ten minutes later silence they return to find Jimmy on his knees, he tells them all to go home, come back tomorrow. Another revenue stream stopped; Jimmy thinks it is personal; what the hell is going on?

Who is doing this to him? A call to John King and Mo Sam, do they know anything about what is happening, obvious answer, they don't know anything about it, both shocked at the news. Coming off the phone, Mo thinks that John King could be involved after their last discussion.

Chapter 25

The call from Mark has Guy on edge. This problem is now getting more extensive than he had anticipated, yet another call to Harry and David they must investigate the personal files of the police force in Newcastle. To have people embedded in the police, they must have been caught early in their career, look for new people joining recently at any level, check all finances for any extravagant spending. Three hours later, Harry contacts Guy, and they have a name of a possible culprit, a DS Scott, a call to the police commissioner. After a lot of flustering and disbelief from the commissioner, he agrees to arrest DS Scott and send him to a local army barracks. He will be picked up and interrogated under the terrorism act, just a ruse from Guy to get him away from his kind. He is delivered to Catterick Army Camp, Guy, using his old status as Brigadier. A favour is needed for reasons he cannot tell the commander. However, he was still held in high regard within the Armed forces fraternity, and his request would never be refused. John Scott is now incarcerated within the camp; only two people know the situation's sensitivity. John is blindfolded while travelling, and he has no idea where he is, receiving two meals and water, through a bottom hatch in the door, even lying on the floor, he cannot see anything. DS Scott will not be informed of the reason or nature of his arrest; Guy hopes the silence will pray on his mind and will hopefully slip up. After two days, a knock on the door, he is told to put his back to the door and step one metre forward, he complies, then told, 'put your hands behind your back,' the cuffs are put on, a spit bag over his face.

A loud voice instructs him to come quietly; without hesitation, he follows the instruction, a door opens, he can feel the breeze outside, the sudden crunch of pebbles under his feet, where can he be. Then, a prod in his back, someone puts a hand on his head, 'you are being transported elsewhere bend forward to get into the vehicle.' John Scott, in all his years in the police force, has never known anything like this.

He now fears the worst that Jimmy Lees is involved; John knows he has tentacles all over, so why not another police force? If so, his days are certainly numbered. The journey is only two hours, but to John, it is a lifetime, not knowing the outcome of what is to follow. With no airflow in the vehicle, he is sweating profusely and the tension of not being told anything. He wants to scream but dare not, and he wants to cry; what has he got himself into. Finally, the vehicle stops, a request to get out, stepping out no pebble sound, no concrete feel but the soft texture of grass, his first thought, 'oh my god, it is an execution. Then the sound of a metal door opening, a slight sigh of relief, then two men, one either side of him guide him down some step he counts twenty, panic sets in he is going underground, two hundred metres straight ahead and he is guided into a room. Placed on a chair, then cuffs are put around his ankles to the chair, somebody from behind removes the spit hood, a bright light shining in his face, he can see no one. Then, out of the shadows, a quiet voice calm and collective, 'hello John Scott, we require information from you regarding Jimmy Lees empire.'

John's whole body relaxes, now realising they want Jimmy; he tries to barter his corner, 'firstly you cannot talk to me without council, I want a solicitor.'

Voice, 'sadly, DS John Scott, you died in an accident two days ago, your ex-wife has been told of your sad passing.'

'No, it can't be; what are you doing to me.'

'Well, after a visit to your house, via court order, we have found information that you are involved in a possible terrorist plot,'
'No, what are you doing to me? I would never do that.'
'Your computer gives a different story.'
'You are setting me up, you bastards.'
'Unfortunately, John, the courts will see it differently, especially with your involvement with a drug lord.'
'What is it you want.'
'We know you have been Jimmy Lees lapdog for years.'
'How do you know all this? Even the police do not know.'

'Well, we are not the police.'
'Who the hell are you.'
'We are asking the questions, John.'
John's voice starts to shake, 'what will happen to me if I tell you.'
'If you tell the truth, a softer sentence in a softer prison, your identity changed; if not, it is possible, you will never walk the streets again.'
John descends into silence, running things through his mind; he has no option really but to tell them everything, 'right what do you want to know.'
'How did it all start.'
John begins to tell them how Jimmy snared him, and he could not get out of it, only making sure investigations never went anywhere near him.
'What about John Lane.'
'Never heard of him.'
Guy now knows John Lane's death was a revenge killing, but for what? Harry and David must use every resource to find out.
'Tell me more about Jimmy's empire, how far does it stretch.'
'I was never told about other branches of his network; the less I knew, the better for me, I did not enquire.'

'Do you know who his supplier is?'
'The only name that kept popping up was the Ramina cartel.'
'Where are they based.'
'Don't know.'
'Why not.'
'They are a shadow cartel, and they contact you; nobody knows where they are.'
'Right John as I said, for your help, you will only be arrested for aiding and abetting Jimmy Lees in the facilitation of his drug empire.
'I suppose sorry will not help me.'
'Gambling was your downfall, these types of people pray on it, my colleagues will take you away now, spit hood back over his head, cuffs removed, John is moved to a new location.

Chapter 26

After the deaths of his Glasgow and Newcastle counterparts, Mo Sam is lying in bed, contemplating his next move. Could he be next? Should he tell Jimmy of the discussions they had in that pub car park. He will automatically ask, why is he only telling him now, what answer can he give, then he thinks better the devil you know, he will tell him he thought it was just bravado, but now Joe Hodge is dead came back to him. A sleepless night ahead, getting up for breakfast, coffee in hand still debating with himself should he make that call to Jimmy, palms sweaty he now wishes he never got into the drugs game. Strolling through his six-bedroom mansion, with a cinema room, large swimming pool and four-car garage, Mo Sam knows precisely why he chose the drug game. Walking past the swimming pool, shimmering in the sun, he carries on and into the vast garden. It is continually trimmed by a robotic lawnmower, going back and forth, mesmerised by how it does it and parks back into its charging unit for the next day. By the time he reaches the bottom of the garden, his hands even more sweaty, he auto dials Jimmy on his encrypted phone. It rings for some time, making this call even more complicated, finally Jimmy answers.
'Jimmy, we need to meet immediately.'
'Why, what is wrong with you.'
'It is regarding our current predicament.'
'Why can you not tell me over the phone.'
'Your ears only, it would be better face to face.'
'I will meet you at Wetherby services in two hours.'
'I will see you then, Jimmy.'
Mo Sam makes his way immediately, wanting to calm himself before Jimmy arrives; Mo pulls up to the service station and parks up in a very public area just in case anything happens. He has known Jimmy for

many years; he has a violent temper and witnessed many a person being beaten for petty things; that is why he is worried.

As he sits there waiting in his black SUV, this seems to be the norm for drugs people, and another black SUV pulls up next to him. This the moment of truth, he gets out of his vehicle and opens the door of Jimmy's SUV, sitting down in the fabulous leather, the seats having aircon; this is a high-end SUV indeed. Mo Sam begins to tell Jimmy his thoughts; unusually, Jimmy is calm, thinking that a solution to his problem has come out of the blue. He asks Mo if he thinks John can organise such treachery; Mo explains money changes people; Jimmy thanks Mo he will take over from here. A sigh and sense of relief from Mo as he gets into his car. The load now lightened and removed from his shoulders. Strangely Mo does not feel sorry for John, and he is prepared to stab Jimmy in the back; it could have been him next. Instead, he drives home feeling a lot better, and he has done the right thing, turning into the long driveway, fifty metres further on the automatic gates open. He parks up on the blocked paved drive, his wife and two daughters greet him, now not a care in the world, funny how your mood can change. With a sense of joy, Jimmy makes his way home, a quick call to his son Glenn to meet him at his office with an overnight bag, and bring Ricky and Paul saying, 'we have some retribution to deal out.' One hour later, Jimmy pulls up to his office, and three men step into his vehicle, complete with overnight bags and some extra baggage. John King was on his way home; he had just cashed up and had transferred the money to Jimmy's account, giving out the drug quota for his dealers. Everybody busy, he lets his enforcers go home, having one other work nightshift to solve problems if anything

arises untoward. The dealers are dropped off in various city areas to maximise all possibilities of making money, a well-run business machine John devised. John was one of Jimmy's original enforcers when the drug trade exploded, and the money was coming from all places.
They shared the highs and lows, avoiding the police skilfully for several years.

That was until an undercover police officer Eric Stot blew their operation apart, and they spent several years in different prisons. His loyalty to Jimmy was unbending, but as the years passed and he could see how Jimmy was putting other people before him, this was eating away at his soul.
When they got out of prison, his loyal people got areas to look after, but in John's mind, he felt it was an afterthought, not realising it was his freedom to earn more money. It was this reasoning that he wanted to take over Jimmy's empire and become super-rich. He is halfway home when he receives the call from Jimmy, and he wants a face-to-face meeting urgently about Newcastle; John is non-plus about the deaths in Newcastle. Not caring, it is a different area, nothing to do with him. John is even more surprised; he is only half an hour away; he rushes back to the office, trying to ring Joe Hodge to find out what had caused Jimmy to come his way. The phone was constantly ringing, no answer, he left several messages to contact him as soon as possible. On the way to Manchester, calm and collected, Jimmy tells his three colleagues of their predicament. The deaths of their friends in Newcastle and the reason for their visit. When he tells them of the conversation John had with Joe and Mo, their agitation having increased, basically wanting to rip John's head off, sufficiently wound up, they enter the road where John's office is. John was one of Jimmy's original

enforcers, capable of the same brutality as Jimmy in his hay days. Hence, he has brought his son along with Paul and Ricky. Ever cautious, John has installed security cameras above the entrance door; Jimmy knows this and told his men to hang back till the door opens. Unknown to John, he will not survive the onslaught that is about to come down upon him. He has reached the dark side of this industry. Jimmy presses the button to be let into John's office, the buzzer sounds, the magnetic catch opens, the door slightly ajar.

John, only noticing Jimmy gets up to greet him, not looking at the security screen; the other three men rush past Jimmy. Then, handing a baseball bat to him, they start raining blows onto John, the first to his knee. They continue to hit him as he falls, dead before his head touches the floor. Stupidly in Jimmy's anger, no questions asked, no information they have just killed an innocent man, blood-spattered all over they do not care revenge has been served. Wiping the blood off the baseball bats and placing the rags into a bag along with the blood-spattered coveralls they were wearing, they then make their way to the nearest hotel, book in, and order drinks as though it was another day at work. As blood slowly oozes from John's body onto his office floor, his mobile phone constantly ringing, his wife distraught knowing Jimmy was coming to see him. She also knew of his violent temper, she is thinking the worst of the situation, but because of their involvement in the drugs trade, Martha cannot call the police. What can Martha do? Who can she turn to? A call to the single enforcer doing the nightshift, he answers the phone, taken aback by what John's wife has to say, he tells her he will go back to the office to check on John. It is another agonising forty-five minutes before John's wife receives the news, she already knew, the scream down the phone piercing in the enforcer's ear. A few minutes pass and the enforcer gets a call from John's wife, her two sons, and her uncle will come for the body; nobody must know what has happened. They arrive with a bag to put the body in, seeing John's body so badly beaten; the three agree it is an all-out war against Jimmy Lees, the body carefully placed in the back of the large estate car. John's men informed of the betrayal, but the local press will have a column in a couple of days, telling of the sad passing of John King, dying in his sleep a shock to everyone he was only in his fifties. Little does Jimmy know his act of anger will cause repercussions throughout his network, saving Mark and Guy a lot of work. Another day at the office as Jimmy settles into the hotel room with his Glenn. Neither looking at each other, get into bed both asleep instantly, totally oblivious of their actions and what they have done. Then, as the morning sun shines on their faces, they get up and go for breakfast while they mumble to each other over the table, coffee poured, a large breakfast in front of them.

Jimmy suddenly realises the stark reality of what they have done. He has given John's team cart Blanche to retaliate, and he must try and control the narrative before he loses control.

What was he thinking of? There was no need for John to kill the Glasgow and Newcastle crews; it was revenue he would have if he took over? What the hell has he done, the death of his eldest son? Jimmy is not thinking straight, and he must get his head back into a semblance of order. With his mind in turmoil, he instantly thinks it could be Mo Sam creating infighting to takeover. He turns to the other three, 'finish up, we must get back quickly to John's office, or there will be retaliation,' the three men obey and leave immediately, collecting their bags from their rooms they meet at Jimmy's car. Driving back to John's office, he explains to the other three, we must take control of this area, telling his crew that John was trying to take over from us, we have given him everything, and he wanted to betray us. Jimmy knows the daytime enforcers and calls them to meet at the office to sort out the situation that John had caused them, pushing the blame onto him. All attend the impromptu meeting, and Jimmy puts his cards on the table, telling them of the treachery John was about to inflict. He then surprises them, telling all that if he must come here to run the show, their lives will be hell. He gives them time to digest the situation and surprises them by saying, 'right then, I propose that your senior enforcer Vince Small take over running this little enterprise.' Vince tries to say 'no', but to no avail, he is now the head of Jimmy's Manchester branch. After killing a man, Jimmy has pulled back a volatile situation to his advantage, showing who is the actual boss. Jimmy will stay a few days so that Vince knows his role in his organisation precisely, he sends Ricky and his son home to look after the Middlesbrough branch, leaving Paul and himself to control things. One hour later, Jimmy calls Glenn to double up on security, and all people are paired up and prepared for anything unusual. Surprisingly, Jimmy organises flowers for Martha King; he has known her for several years.

He writes a personal letter explaining the situation to her and telling her it is only business, and a fund will be set aside to carry on their lives.

Martha is a pragmatic woman and, deep down, secretly knew this day would come and accepts the situation for what it is. She books a family holiday for one month in Florida to mourn John's death.

Chapter 27

Mark left destruction in his wake, leaving Newcastle. He can see the signage for the A1 South, drifts casually onto the motorway and tunes into a radio station, playing music from the nineties. Even Mark is surprised how many he could remember, bringing back memories of a fonder time. Before he met Julia, the time passed quickly, he called into a perfumery, it was Julia's favourite shop and collected some perfume for Lydia, which he had pre-ordered. Thirty minutes from home, he calls Lydia, asking if she wants something bringing in for dinner, a gleeful reply, dinner is all ready for you with a special dessert, it is something I am sure you will want a repeat course again and again. Mark laughs; she has the same sense of humour and quirkiness that drew him and Julia together, but he must remember not to forget she is a different woman and not draw comparisons. He pulls up on the drive, wondering what Lydia has up her sleeve; as he reaches the door, again, the backdrop of the hall light casts an aura around her, making her look quite angelic. As Mark steps into the hall, she puts her arms around him, kissing him passionately on the lips; after being away for a few days, his arousal is instant. She pulls away and takes his hand, guiding him into the dining room. Even he was amazed at the presentation of the meal, knowing that his favourite meal was Hungarian goulash, garlic mushrooms, sauté potatoes, Julia had confided in her, and it had stuck in her head for some reason. Lydia poured out the red wine, and they started to discuss what he had done in Newcastle; Lydia wanted to know every detail of his kills; Mark saw the tell-tale signs as Lydia's cheeks began to flush; she was getting turned on just like Julia. She then gets up, 'I will get dessert now, I am sure it will be the best you have ever had,' and leaves the room.

Ten minutes passed, Lydia told Mark to stay in the room, as this dessert takes. Another five minutes pass, Mark is getting impatient as he stands to go into the kitchen.

Lydia appears at the door. Mark's jaw drops a vision of pure sex, yet again instant arousal, the whole attire in red lingerie, stockings and high heels, along with a bowl of strawberries.
She struts over to him, her hips moving in unison; with her glossy red lipstick, she plants a kiss on his cheek, leaving the mark of her lips. She giggles softly, whispering in his ear, 'oh my god,' Mark realises Julia has taught her. He softly lifts her in his arms and slowly takes her to the bedroom, both kissing gently, placing her on the bed covered in red petals on the silk sheets, this will be a night of passion for both, and they will remember for quite some time to come. Lydia gets up early in the morning, telling Mark it is breakfast in bed for you today. After that performance last night, Mark Laughs thinking, 'still got it, even after three years in prison.' Mark decides to shower and return to bed, and he did not want to disappoint Lydia as she is making breakfast, a call from downstairs, 'are you ready for breakfast,'
'Famished whenever you are ready.'
He can hear Lydia coming upstairs, next thing a hand with a plate at the door and one boiled egg. Mark is just about to say something when Lydia walks in wearing black lingerie and heels. Mark has now realised he is with a sex addict and shouts out, 'yippee.' He asks Lydia why the egg, she responds, you need your strength. They both laugh in unison, a perfect couple, it seems.

Mark contacts Guy to update him and tell him he will be off the radar till he needs his services as to where the next city is.

Chapter 28

Guy, Harry and David are involved in an intense meeting; the revelation that Jimmy Lees had a police officer undercover is nerving to Guy. They must deep dive into other forces nationwide, hoping that there will be no more; this will be time-consuming, which is getting shorter by the minute, they must go back at least twenty years, a monumental task. He does not want Harry and David tied up in this task, but it must be done. They must clear out the trash before they can move forward. Within three hours, the gods must be on their side, with four more names highlighted for investigation, all of them DS status, possibly a rare mistake to keep all of them at that level, as this was one of the main parameters the computer searched. They are based in North London, Birmingham, Liverpool and Middlesbrough. A request for local police chiefs to stay silent is put in place investigations into the name given at their branch. All suddenly started to have a high second income, some twenty years ago, a more recent one in Middlesbrough two years ago. The three men are in despair that people who are supposed to protect the people they serve are quickly taken in by money. Guy then says, 'we do not know the circumstances that may have dragged them into the wrong path.'

They carry on and discuss this mysterious Ravenhurst Holdings, a bargain price for land and buildings in Glasgow. It is too coincidental for their liking. Could that be why the drugs needed to be off the streets, their senses raised, there is something wrong, lives lost for a land grab, does not sit well with them? The price they paid is only twenty-five per cent of its actual value, surely not pure greed; there has to be an ulterior motive, where's the money coming from, more investigations needed. Regarding the homeland drug problem, it seems to be coming through the pipeline. Some infighting has taken place as to whether Jimmy Lees is losing his grip. Rumours of cash flow problems have exasperated his control, people questioning whether he still has the mentality to carry on. Unfortunately, Guy is more concerned about this shadow Ramina cartel; most law enforcement groups would know something, but little or no information on them worries Guy. There is usually a trail to their front door, and they rely on fear to control the narrative, but these are different, having new ways of working. He must find that little lever to open the door of information, how big are they, who are the leaders, how many people work for them, do they have politicians on their payroll. While they are discussing these issues, that annoying thought pops into his head again. Why was he chosen? Again and again, he runs through the scenarios. Finally, he decides he will contact two people for a secret meeting, hoping this will disperse these feelings, he has always stuck with his gut feelings, and this is something he must sort out, sooner rather than later. Guy excuses himself; he must make a call urgently. Harry and David know by his demeanour he has something he must sort out now; they have known him too long and are used to his decision making. Ten minutes later, he comes back, 'right, I hope by this time tomorrow, we will be a bit further forward in our quest to sort this out.'

They carry on sifting through the minefield of information, and then Guy remembers a long-time friend he met in his days working out of Ukraine, a well-embedded individual called Ron Walton. If anyone knows about this Ramina cartel, it will be him. He leaves the room again and returns ten minutes later, telling Harry and David that avenue is closed for two weeks. Ron is on a special assignment.

Chapter 29

All the names given to local police superintendents were completely surprised; many had been with the force for many years. With exemplary records of achievement, especially in Middlesbrough where DC Philpott had risen to DS Philpott, after his excellent work catching a long-time local drug leader and former MET officer Ethan Holton, now deceased. But having seen the amount of money that the deceased had accrued turned his thoughts towards greed, yet again money turning a good man sour. With Ethan gone, the money played on Philpott's mind; why him, not me? Everyone deserves to have a little more in their lives, and it became a mental obsession with him; how can he get this easy money. Time passed, and twelve months was gone in an instant, subtle changes to his personality that only his wife could notice, more arguments than usual, a bit distant, lost in his thoughts. Then the rumour mill started about Jimmy Lees, an opportunity he could not miss, the possible start of extra income and a lifestyle more becoming of his stature in society. Jimmy had only moved into the town two days previously, but Philpott took the bull by the horns and stated in his case the benefits he could offer such a fine businessman, such as he. If the money were conducive to both parties, they would shake hands on an agreed payment plan. Jimmy not used to such a direct approach liked that in him, and a new alliance was formed. Jimmy was never approached by any law enforcement, all activities under the radar. Until DS James started to enquire about Jimmy a year later but was blocked most of the time, taught by DSI Roger Leyland, his curiosity to keep on probing away for the truth, a trait Roger liked about him. So, when he was called to the police superintendent's office, told to close the door. 'This discussion is between you and me-only; usually, internal affairs would handle this situation, but I want it in-house, so no waves are created,' and nobody else spooked.

The police superintendent tells James of his concerns and would he take an outside perspective on the situation.
Initial surprise from James as to who the suspect was, he was held in high regard by all colleagues, not wanting to believe what he had just heard. Before he leaves the room, he asks the police superintendent, 'if he could call on the services of a former DSI if he comes, of course,' the chief laughed. 'That can only be former DSI Leyland.' After some deliberation, a resounding, 'yes,' James thanks him, and he leaves the room with the biggest grin on his face. Leyland had left his private number with his protégé if he ever needed advice, but always said, 'that he was always capable of doing the right thing,' and if he did call, he would know it was a serious issue. James, with slight hesitance, dials the number, four rings a woman answers the phone, taken back he says, 'hello this is DCI James, is Roger Leyland still at that number,' a giggle down the phone.
'Hello Simon, it's Holly Holton,' the ex-wife of Ethan Holton
A slight stutter, 'Oh hello Holly, it must be three years since we last spoke.'
'That's correct, how are you.'
'I am great, surprised to hear your voice.'
'Good to speak to you, oh here's Roger.'
'Hello Simon, must be urgent for you to ring, after two years, not that I am counting.'
Simon, still taken aback after hearing Holly's voice, stutters a 'yes'.
'What is it, young man.'

'Can I come over to see you? It is a bit sensitive?'
'See you in an hour is that ok, do not worry Holly will not bite you,' Leyland starts to laugh, DCI James in all the years he had known him, he never laughed, the job always came first, a trait Sir Guy would be impressed by. One hour later, DCI James is knocking on Leyland's door; Holly answers and invites him in, the smell of fresh-brewed coffee, drifts in from the kitchen.

Leyland invites him to sit down. Before doing so, James goes to sit down and Holly out of sight. A silent gesture with his hands to say what the hell is going on with Holly.

Leyland continues, 'sit down, and all will be revealed; Holly enters looking more radiant than he could remember.

It looks like this relationship is doing them both good, coffee on the table, Holly holds Leyland's hand, and they both look at James smiling, then they laugh. They explain that when Ethan got killed in prison a few weeks later, Holly invited Leyland over to the villa for a break, as he had now retired and as a way of thanking him for his support through the trauma of Ethan's crimes. Whilst there, they both found they had a lot more in common than previously thought, and a relationship out of the blue started, both not looking for commitment. It has since moved on in the last month, and we have got engaged in Portugal, with some local friends and Holly's sister Ivy in attendance; they now come back to the UK for occasional breaks to see relatives. 'You are lucky we are home, young James, '

'I do not know if I should carry on then, sir, as you will return shortly.'

'That depends on what your problem is; I assume it is serious, or you would not be here.'

'Yes, sir, but unfortunately, it is for your ears only; that is how delicate the matter is.'

Holly realising how sensitive it may be, gets up, saying she will make some sandwiches; James thanks her and apologises at the same time. James tells Leyland what has happened, and he cannot believe that Philpott could be dirty. His first question is where the information came from, is it one hundred per cent correct, have they verified it all. Leyland already knows he taught young James, and in many cases, he was more thorough than him, which only made him more eager to teach him all he knew. Leyland asks him if he can get the name and number of the person who forwarded the information,

James will come back tomorrow, cheekily asking Holly if she could put more cheese in his sandwich tomorrow, running to the door, Holly smiles she always liked young James. The next day at 11 am, James is knocking on Leyland's door.

Again the smell of coffee a cup on the dining table along with a sandwich with extra cheese; Holly smiles, he nods in mutual admiration.

James passes over a name and number on a piece of paper to Leyland; he looks at the name, 'are you sure this is the man,' James is unsure how to take Leyland's reaction.

'Yes, sir.'

'If this is the man, I can guarantee Philpott is dirty.

'What do you mean.'

'I worked for him for ten years ago, in a past life.'

'How do you mean, sir.'

'Cannot say official secrets act.'

'You old dog, you were a spy.'

'I cannot divulge anything.'

'Fair enough, sir, where do we go from here.'

'If this man is involved, this is bigger than it seems.'

'Should I get excited sir,' James, out of respect, still calls Leyland, sir.

'I will make this call in private and come back to you, do not, and I mean you do not speak to anyone about this, give me till tomorrow.'
'Yes, sir.'
'Can you come back tomorrow at the same time?'
James thanks Holly for the coffee and extra cheese sandwich; he is more intrigued by the situation, as this could escalate to other things, now excited by the prospect of some intelligence work hopefully. James heads home by the end of the workday, things running through his head, trying to sleep, but his mind is wandering to spy novels. So what is he getting involved in?
But, unfortunately, the reality is not the same as spy novels, and he drifts to sleep.
Leyland calls the phone number on the paper, 'Guy Long, please speak.'
'You have not changed, sir, Roger Leyland speaking.'
'My goodness, that is a name from the past; how are you.'
'Excellent sir, retired but with some concerns.'
'That would be.'
Leyland tells him what is happening, and Guy brings him up to speed with what they know so far,
explaining that it is now a major international situation and to trust no one.
Knowing Guy is the epitome of trust and loyalty, Leyland is deeply concerned things are not correct, he will abide by his request, they must get to the bottom of this conspiracy. The following day James alarm is getting louder; he is in a deep sleep. The next-door neighbour bangs on the wall, 'are you bloody deaf,' he jumps out of bed, still half asleep, stops the alarm. He has never done that before, hoping it is not a sign of what is to come, his mind all over the place thinking about Leyland's request not to talk to anyone.

Just as Leyland comes off the phone, the familiar knock on the front door, 'must get a bell; it must be softer than the banging,' Holly laughing at his statement. So in comes their regular visitor, Holly thinking the neighbours will start talking for sure, coffee, sandwiches extra ham just in case, he can take it off if he wants to, choosey little sod she thinks to herself. Leyland explains the situation, always take extreme caution, to monitor Philpott for now till a formal request from Guy and all the dirty police officers will be arrested at the same time. James finishes his coffee and extra ham sandwich, Holly thinking at least the plate is clean. James resumes his duties till further notice. Leyland has told him not to update the Police superintendent just as a precaution; they do not know how deep the corruption goes.

Chapter 30

Glenn and Paul are heading towards Middlesbrough in their hired car. Unusually, not a word was spoken, still shaken, as to what they have been complicit in, neither having killed anyone before.

Paul drops off Glenn in silence; before he enters the house, he looks over at Ian's grave, now realising the path he is taking is possibly the wrong one and most definitely a shorter life cycle to come. Entering the house, Janet, his mother, starts shouting at him, 'where have you been, where is your father.'

'He is still in Manchester.'

'What, why did no one tell me.'

'I thought dad would do that.'

'Like hell, he has, nothing from both of you; I was worried about you both.'

'I am sorry, mum,' then he breaks down the pressure of what they have done, finally breaking him, he explains what they have done. Janet puts her arms around him. To comfort, now the only son, losing Ian in tragic circumstances only weeks ago, she must act quickly to save him.

'Where is your father now.'

'Still, in Manchester, he will be there a couple of days at least.'

'Right, just go to your room and rest for a while; I have a few things to do first, then we will discuss our options.'

Not contacting Janet about where they are, Jimmy has inadvertently added more fuel to the fire and given Janet the perfect reason to leave him. Janet will not ring him as this gives her more time to disappear with her son, to a new life they both deserve, in the back of her mind. Unknown to Jimmy, she had filtered quite a substantial sum of money into a foreign bank account under her maiden name. The vast sums that Jimmy was dealing with before he went to prison meant no time to audit or count. Also, she took advantage of his time in prison to purchase a house in Strafford-on-Avon.

She would rent out as a holiday let, paying a local cleaner to keep it clean, all monies going into her foreign account until she needed it herself. So now she has the accommodation, transport not too easy, Jimmy will check all modes, trains, hire car, airports and buses. Janet opens Jimmy's safe, he trusted her one hundred per cent, but time in prison changes all parties, a large sum of money just sitting there, she decides to take only twenty-five thousand pounds, putting it into her bag. Next, she will call around to her friend who has the recordings she so desperately needs. These are her safety net, and these will stay with a solicitor. If anything happens to her, they are to be released to the police. After making all the arrangements to get into her own house, Janet and Glenn go to bed, and she has explained to him what they are going to do. She will not lose another son, and he agrees to go with her; if she had done it sooner, Ian would still be alive. It will pray on her mind for several years to come. A long agonising sleepless night for Janet, they must leave by ten, just before ten, two cars pull up, both men get out of the vehicles, one of the men hands over the keys, for a two-year-old Ford Mondeo, then they leave. Janet was telling Glenn, 'Your father cannot know what car we are driving.' Glenn succumbs to her reasoning, and bags packed, they leave the house. The door left wide open; phone smashed on the hall floor, a goodbye letter on the bed, begging him not to come looking for them. Once out of the drive and half a mile down the road, Janet stops and informs Glenn there are new number plates in the boot.

Can you change them over? Glenn is amazed at his mother's ingenuity and proud that she has taken the bull by the horns to give them a normal life. Ten minutes later, they are on the motorway to freedom, both starting to change. An hour into the journey, Janet hears Glenn laugh for the first time in two years; this is her old son coming back to her. Such is the pressure of having a father like Jimmy Lees, always trying to impress him.

Hence the reason her eldest son died. She starts to reflect on why she married him and quietly confess to herself.

Blinded by baubles and money, 'oh why, twenty-four years of her life wasted.' The two wild affairs she had when he was in prison, that sense of freedom and abandonment, why did she just not divorce him? At this point, a tear falls, the realisation of wasted years in her life. After a couple of tea breaks, they carry on, and in three hours, they turn into a road flanked by trees on either side. The sun glistering on the dew after a recent rain shower, Janet turns into a long driveway that starts to steam with the sun's heat. She turns to Glenn, 'welcome to your new home, son,' a contented sigh from him, surprised that his mother owned such a beautiful looking house. The drive opened across the front of the house, which looked late Georgian from the style of windows and doors. Janet opened the door with an old-style large key. Glenn smiled; he liked the quirkiness of the key, and they stepped into the hallway, the solid oak floors shining in the sunlight. She gives him a tour around the house all oldie world, till you reach the modern kitchen is an enormous extension yet did not look out of place. Glenn turns to his mother, I think we will be happy here,' Janet, ecstatic at his response, finally breaks down in tears, years of pent-up emotion finally released. Glenn puts his arms around her to comfort his mother; just that simple act that her son cared, was enough to know things will be ok. It will be another two days before Jimmy will be home, already getting annoyed that there is no response from the house phone or mobiles. Jimmy's time with Vince has shown him that he can run the Manchester branch with some extra incentives to keep him more loyal. Jimmy and Ricky head home; as they get onto the M62, Ricky reminds Jimmy to ease off the accelerator. We do not want to be stopped now; strangely, Jimmy thanks him and puts the vehicle into cruise control.

Ricky knows something is wrong; in all the years they have known each other, he has never said thank you to anyone. Although Ricky does not know that Jimmy cannot contact Janet or Glenn, surprisingly, Jimmy takes Ricky home, only ever being there once before; this has confirmed something is wrong with Jimmy. Ten minutes later, Ricky is left on the pavement watching Jimmy speed down the road, thinking, 'I would not like to be Janet or Glenn at this moment in time.'

As Jimmy enters his driveway, he can see the front door open; he speeds up more and slides to a halt, jumping out, leaving the door open and the engine running.

Shouting their names, seeing the smashed phones on the hall floor, thinking the worst that the thorn in his side, the hitman has killed his family. Running through the house, screaming their names at the top of his voice, hoping he does not find any bodies, seeing wardrobes open, thinking a robbery has now taken place. Finally, the sweat now running down his face, he reaches the main bedroom as he enters the room, he can see the envelope on the bed, a sudden realisation of what the content could be. Opening the envelope,

reading the content deep down, he could see why Janet took the decision, and he did not notice he had fallen to his knees; such was his adrenaline rush. He wants to shout and scream obscenities, but nothing will come out; his world is slowly falling apart; who the hell is behind it. Then the sound of his SUV speeding down the drive, an opportunist seeing the door open, has taken full advantage of Jimmy's circumstances, could anything else happen to him.
He feels his soul has been torn apart, and he must quickly take control of the situation.

Chapter 31

Mark has made enquiries into Hoffman Steel through Guy and his team; the information coming through has made him angry. They are about to dispatch a large number of knives to a new unit in Manchester, called Steels of Manchester. The revelation they are starting up again, the message has not got through, and who has sanctioned it. Further digging into their background, they have found the directors are Jane and Dawn Steel. It astounds Mark, after just losing her husband, what type of women are they. A phone call to Mrs Steel, explaining he is the English sales representative for Hoffman Steel. After their recent large order, could they discuss the possibility of renegotiating their terms for a better discount? Jane, who values money more than life, was over the moon and would like to discuss this as soon as possible, in fact, 'please come to our house,' an address is given and a time of 10 am was arranged the next day. Then just before she was about to put the phone down, Mark explained he had a female trainee, would it be ok to bring her, a resounding. 'yes', came back. As Mark put the phone down, Lydia, listening, ecstatic, grabs him and passionately kisses him, so excited Lydia is finally getting her chance to prove that Julia has taught her well. The next day they rise at 6 am; things to do, Lydia must show Mark how professional she can be. Mark prepares his disguise putting on the brown greying wig and beard; Lydia now becomes a redhead with the wig left behind by Julia and a dress to show off her curves, just like Julia showed hers, everything for distraction. The address given is in an affluent area of Manchester, two expensive cars on the drive, the houses are well spaced at least thirty metres apart, just to give that sense of privacy. Arriving outside the house at 10 am, Mark takes out a large briefcase from the car, and Lydia swings around from the other side of the vehicle, poetry in motion just like Julia.

Lydia rings the doorbell; the door opens both Jane and Dawn answer the door, inviting them into what many would call a foyer, a large crystal chandelier hanging from the ceiling.

Both dressed the same, trying to give an air of businesswomen, with a certain aloofness but wearing enough bling to weigh any ordinary people down in what Lydia thought was just tacky, and women can be pretty bitchy it seems. Mark notices the large garden, looking onto woods, the three-bar fence trying to keep stray animals out; he already knows how to use this facility in the back of his mind. Both women talk simultaneously, inviting them into the dining room; Mark offers his condolences for their recent loss before they start. Jane, with her non-plus reaction, showed him already what type of woman she was. Mark introduces his associate Maria, and they shake hands, Jane telling them both to sit down. Dawn asks if they want coffee and proceeds to go to the kitchen; Mark squeezes Lydia's knee, a sign to deal with Dawn. Lydia excuses herself, 'I will help Dawn if that is ok, Jane.' She nods her acceptance. Lydia walks into the kitchen, 'just come to give you a hand, part of the Hoffman service.' Dawn laughs, then she feels a needle in her neck, a cup falls to the floor. It signals to Mark to take his Glock out of his briefcase and point it at Jane, whose face instantly turns ashen. Unable to talk, worried that her daughter is hurt, Mark ties her to the chair, then walks into the kitchen to bring Dawn back. Now both tied up, Mark proceeds to ask Jane questions, 'Why have you started up again.'

Jane replies, 'why do you think it is the money with a certain arrogance.'

'But your husband has just died.'

'So, what.'

'Quite callous, Jane.'
'Money pays the bills, not dead people.'
'How did it all start.'
'A call from Jimmy Lees, he knew my husband.'
'But why would he need you to supply knives.'
'It wasn't for him.'
'What do you mean.'
'It was his suppliers, and they wanted their assets protected.'
'Do you know who they are?'
'Yes, but you must let us go.'
'Ok, I agree.'
Lydia is surprised, but Mark turns and winks at her; her excitement rises, he carries on, 'how do you contact Hoffman.'
'Internet the dark web, we have a special, numbered code.'
'Can you tell me what that reference number is?'
'Why, what is the point.'
'The point, Jane is whether you are alive when we leave, 'Number please.'
Mark grabs the computer, turns it on and waits, Jane now feeling sick and wanting to vomit, she asks for a plastic bag from the kitchen. Lydia walks back into the room; Mark cannot believe how calm she is. The computer automatically opens the page for Hoffman's, inserting the number Jane has given him. He types in an e-mail, cancelling all orders and informs them they are going out of business. He does not realise that this simple act has triggered a warning to the Ramina cartel. They know how much money was going to them, no reason to close the business; this is how they control everything money and send someone to investigate.
Jane thinks their ordeal is over and tells Mark that Jimmy's suppliers are the Ramina cartel, that bloody name again. Dawn is just waking up; she starts

swearing at Lydia, notices that she and her mother are tied up, and starts swearing again. Finally, Jane tells her daughter they will let us go; Mark interjects, 'erm, I will let you go, but my associate might have other ideas.' A look of terror from them both as Lydia explains that selling knives to kill people for profit does not fit well with decent people. Then Lydia explains that she will show them the pain their products inflict; she picks various knives from Mark's briefcase. Lydia rips the sleeves of the expensive blouses, and she turns to Dawn, her eyes begging her not to do anything, the first cut from shoulder to the elbow, just enough to cause pain breaking the skin. Dawn screams as the blood runs slowly down her arm. Jane is now in tears watching her daughter suffer, 'we will stop everything if you would only stop and let us go.'

Lydia responds, 'no mercy for the victims that your knives killed; why does money change your perspective.'

Lydia turns to Jane and does the same thing, once again a scream, now wishing the gap between the houses was not so big, a cut in the same place on the other arm of Jane and Dawn. The blood is starting to soak into the plush deep pile carpet. Mark is starting to wipe down any signs of them being there. He nods to Lydia; she cuts their wrists, the blood flow increases, the women beginning to lose consciousness, the glow on Lydia's cheeks, Mark knows the signs it will be a long night of bliss. Before they leave, Mark opens the rear doors to allow nature to enter the house for a free meal. Mark suddenly realises the security cameras may have recorded their visit, puts the computer in his case and removes the hard drive from the security device. If people had noticed the car, the false plates are removed a mile down the road, and these will be destroyed, both getting into the basic car, Lydia the same as Julia on that first kill, non-stop talking all the way home, he is in for a long night. Four days later, a stranger knocking on the door, an early morning call before he goes into the office its five am. With no response, he walks around to the back, seeing the doors open he walks in shouting for Jane, then he sees the bodies, within those four days foxes and other animals had made quite a meal of things, paw prints in the carpet stained in blood. The stranger being DSI Alan Mead, one of the men under investigation, not knowing the net is closing in, and one of the few who does not work for Jimmy Lees. The cartel caught him stealing their product on a drug bust, twenty kilos missing from a haul of one-hundred and twenty kilos, a bit naïve even from a police officer's point of view. Within twenty-four hours, two men called to his house, with pictures of his family, the children going to school, then the offer he could not refuse snared into the murky world of drugs. A call overseas, rather than his colleagues, he must keep this under wraps, so no investigation takes place. The cartel is now aware that they have a war on their hands, starting a power struggle between good and evil.

So, to minimise his involvement, knowing they are already dead, he starts a fire at the rear of the house. He goes out the back door closing it behind him, gets into his car and leaves. Unknown to DSI Mead, a nosey neighbour over the road has just come home from holiday and suffering from jet lag. Unable to sleep, the sun rose from the rear of the house. She was casually gazing out of the window, noticing the shadow of her home on the lawn. When she saw a man coming from the side of the house over the road, she moved behind the curtain to hide her modesty. Thinking who can that be at this hour, the man looks back at the house this made her look to the house as well, she can see the smoke, a call to the fire service, she also writes down the registration number of the car.

Within ten minutes, the fire services arrive, but the house is well alight no chance to save it. They douse the flames down; twenty-four hours later, they find the two bodies. While the fire services have people on site, police have arrived, and an entire forensics team have taped off the area with blue and white tape. The fire has burnt any evidence of the bodies being tied onto the chairs, having nearly completely burnt away. It offers no reason why the women did not leave, other than overcome by smoke. Two officers appear on the roadside, an audible 'yahoo' from behind them. It is Mrs Benn from over the road. She proceeds to tell them about the man and car she had seen the previous morning, giving them the car's registration number and a copy of the security video. A phone call to head office, the reply they got is not something they wanted to hear, the police surprised to find it is one of their own. If DSI Meads had just walked away and left things alone, his involvement would not have been noticed, and the bodies could have been there for weeks; no one would ever have known. After discussions with the superintendent, they decide to keep it quiet for a couple of days to investigate their colleague more formally. Four days have past and Meads is still unaware he is under investigation. He arrives for work as usual; on entering, he is approached and arrested. After discussions with Guy, the police superintendent immediately transfers him to Middlesbrough police station. Guy informs him he has an old colleague who will interview him on his behalf. He had requested that Leyland come out of retirement; he needs competent men like him. He was told of his rights and informed of the reason for his arrest. He pleads with innocence as most people do and is placed into a cell until his transfer is organised. Two hours later, he is on his way to Middlesbrough, a copy of the video is forwarded on, so Leyland and James can make an assessment, all the while Meads is screaming for his union rep. It is 3 pm when Meads arrives at Middlebrough and is formally charged again by DC Simon James. Unfortunately, Leyland cannot make it till the next day; one hour later, Meads is brought into the interview room. As they are about to question him, a loud knock on the door, James opens the door to a man in a dapper pin-stripe suit, too expensive for a policeman's salary, over two metres in height, dark beard and wearing expensive glasses. Who explains he would like to talk to his client. James asks who he is, and the man arrogantly shoves his card into James's hand. My name is Bennett, of Bennett and Bennett, 'I would like to speak to my client, please,' more aggressively. James steps aside and informs him he has ten minutes, 'that is all I will need, thank you.' James and his colleague leave the room and watch via the security camera; James is ever-suspicious, just like his old mentor and makes a call to the number on the card. The phone rings a slight delay as though it is getting transferred; James makes a note, then an eloquent ladies voice answers, 'Hello Bennett and Bennett, how can I help you,' James explains who he is and asks, 'who rang for Mr Bennett to attend the police station for Mr Meads.' The woman explains that she cannot divulge any information unless it is a court order, client confidentiality,' Bennett receives a ping on his smartwatch; this is to warn him about the enquiry by James he looks towards James. After the call, James senses something is wrong but cannot put his finger on it.

He turns to the screen to see the two men talking; Mr Bennett takes a packet of sweets from his pocket. All in strawberry wrappers except one he offers Meads a sweet he accepts, offering him the one with an orange wrapper. Bennett places the wrappers in his pocket. Both are eating the sweets nothing wrong with that, James thinks. Mr Bennett waves them in, explaining he has told his client not to say anything. He will be back tomorrow to carry on this conversation at one pm, and all will be clarified. Meads is placed back in his cell. Twelve hours later, they find him dead in his cell, and it looks like a heart attack. James informed he was making his way to the office, running things through his head. Arriving at his desk, he sees the card for Bennett and Bennett, making another call to the number, it answers and a person on the other ends states, 'you will not win, we have eyes and ears everywhere,' and proceeds to laugh, putting the phone down. James rings the number again, the line is now dead, 'the bastards James shouts,' the sweet Bennett gave him it must have been poison, a hitman it is starting again, James calls Leyland to update him and his suspicion of poison being in the sweet, given to Meads. Leyland thanks him; he will update Guy about the situation. After the call, James decides to look at the police security videos watching Bennett or whoever he is leaving, and he can see him turn left and head towards the rail station.

Further enquiries on the rail station cameras, seeing him board the train to London via Darlington and York. More investigation from the other station cameras, he has not disembarked, unknown to the police, Bennett had changed his persona before the train got to Darlington. Locking the door on the first-class booth he was in, opening the briefcase, he takes out a grey suit, removes his beard and glasses, all items put into the briefcase and placed in the top locker. Grey suit on, he gets off at Darlington and gets into his car, throwing the disabled sign away, another successful hit.

Chapter 32

Jimmy has left messages to all his crew, not to be disturbed; he will contact them when he is ready; he has things to sort out. Unusually a drug lord rings a private detective to see if he can find his wife; with his network of dealers. They do not have the where for all to do that type of work. Normally a man like Jimmy can cope with things like this, but the rapid succession of things he cannot comprehend, who could be behind it all. A call to Mo Sam, he is on his way for a chat he will be there in ninety minutes, 'we will meet at your office, I need answers.' Panic sets in straight away with Mo. He has not done anything but with recent events, anything could happen. Mo arrives at his office; he asks three of his enforcers to come to the office immediately if a problem arises. Mo's hands sweaty with stress, hears Jimmy pull up; in his wife's old SUV, Mo walks directly past the enforcers giving them a knowing nod; the door closes behind him. Jimmy starts to speak, and this is not the confident man he is used to talking to. Jimmy explains what has happened in the past few weeks. The number of men they have lost and, worst of all, the disruption to their cash flow. The impact is starting to cripple them, and the suppliers are screaming for their cash. His wife and son leave him a hitman kills his eldest son; Mo can see a weakness in Jimmy he has never seen before; the man is on the edge of a breakdown. Mo tries to give him moral support, 'do you want me to take over the reins for a short while, till you feel much better.'

Jimmy, confused, is now thinking this is what Mo wanted; Mo can see he is about to get angry and has just realised the connotations of his statement, and takes what he said back, 'sorry it came out wrong Jimmy, I only want to help you get back to where we were.' Mo carries on. 'Look, take a few days off, gather your thoughts, then we can move forward,' Jimmy nods his head in approval.

Mo tells him, 'That one of his guys will drive him back, Jake will follow in another car to bring back Steve, leaving the car at your house,' he agrees he sleeps all the way home, thankful to get back in his bed.
The next day Jimmy calls Paul, his enforcer of many years, to inform him about his car being stolen and keep an eye out for it. If you find it detain the idiot who stole it and bring him to the warehouse so he can smell his last rose. Paul has told all their dealers to look out for Jimmy's car, the word passes quickly through their fraternity, and within four hours, the vehicle is seen in the town centre. Paul and a colleague are dispatched to retrieve it; what type of fool would still drive around in a stolen vehicle? Paul only needs to wait for fifteen minutes when a skinny lad looking sixteen unlocks Jimmy's car. With a tap on the shoulder, he turns around to see a broad man with a muscular build; the lad starts to stutter his apologies, 'it was so easy to steal, I am sorry, please take it back and let me go.'
Paul tells him, 'It is not my car, but the man who owns it would like to talk to you,' the lad, now realising the error of his mistake, starts to shake. Paul pushes him into the car, with the help of his colleague, 'try to get out, and your legs will be broken,' the lad stays quiet, not a word spoken during the ten-minute ride, to the warehouse. The vehicle drives into Petals warehouse, and the lad is informed to stand in the middle of the warehouse; Paul leaves him standing, next to a plastic sheet. With the sun beating down on him through the clear plastic corrugated sheeting on the roof, the smell of different flowers drifting in the air, even though he does know a flower from a weed. With the scent of the

flowers, his concentration lost on the smell, his mind was oblivious to the deafening silence, he did not hear Jimmy approach from behind. The silence was broken by the sound of his right leg breaking under the first blow of the baseball bat. After that, Paul could hear the screams, only lasting a couple of minutes. Then a high pitched whistle from Jimmy, for him to collect the body wrapped in the plastic sheet, a routine from their old days in London.

Next, at the rear of the warehouse, a freshly dug hole and next to it a cement mixer Paul puts the body in the hole, and Jimmy says, 'I think a 2 to 1 mix of sand and cement should be ok to fill that hole,' tapping Paul on the shoulder. Paul forever faithful agrees and proceeds with Jimmy's demands, just another day at work for Paul.
After Jimmy's workout and getting rid of his tension, he feels better, 'right, Paul, can you organise three vans? We are going county lines for a few days.' Paul looking perplexed, Jimmy tells him, 'we must move our products around, so we do not lose it all, like Glasgow and Newcastle, without it we have no funds.' Jimmy's business brain kicking in for survival must gain control and respect back from his dealers and kickstart things again.

Chapter 33

Urgent text to Mark, Harry and David from Guy's burner phone, informing them to buy new phones. And meet in a layby near Coventry, the next day at midday. The coordinates are given; they must stop everything and tell no one. Harry and David are used to this type of thing, but this is new to Mark. He is starting to like this espionage stuff, and it is intriguing him. Lydia is quizzing him about his journey, playfully asking in a childish voice, 'can I come? Please let me come.' Mark explains that there are times when patience is the better virtue, 'if I can tell you something, I will unless I am sworn to secrecy.' Lydia accepts this and waves him goodbye, and Mark is using her car, just a feeling, he has learnt to live by them, he did not tell Lydia. As mark drives down the motorway, the sun is at the height where it catches you out on the brow of a hill, blinding a driver who narrowly missed him as the sun caught his eyes. Mark slows down; this is one meeting he does not want to miss. Leaving an hour earlier than he usually would, just in case something happened. Mark pulls into a lane, five hundred metres further on a large layby, big enough for trucks, looking around nobody else here yet. Two saloon cars pull up behind him within twenty minutes, and the people stay in their vehicles. Mark is just about to get out of his car when a large Volvo pulls in front of him; he recognises Guy and gets out of his vehicle; at the same time, the other two car doors open. Guy waves for everyone to come into his car, introductions made, basic pleasantries exchanged. Guy starts to explain what he had learnt when he left Harry and David a few days ago, and Guy proceeds to tell them he has had a secret meeting with the Prime Minister and the head of MI6, Mark, stunned at this revelation. Guy informs Mark he must sign some paperwork, part of the official secrets act; Harry and

David did this several years ago. Mark duly obliges; he loves this cloak and dagger stuff.

So guy carries on, 'after discussions with the PM and head of MI6, neither party knows of our clandestine work.
It begs me to think we are being set up for something, the reason why is evading me at the moment.' Mark mentions that in his last little venture at Jane Steel's, she said that the Ramina cartel is importing knives from Hoffman Brothers in Holland to protect their assets. Harry and David using their expertise, have unearthed messages from the Ramina cartel to Hoffman Brothers, and they are a front to launder money. Unfortunately, their job was to rid the UK of drugs, which has now gone worldwide through no fault of their own. One of the main problems is that even though they can see the messages, the encryption is so good they cannot see where they originated.
Further discussions and Guy informs Mark they are closing in on the person who is drip-feeding Jimmy. Unbelievably a security guard was walking the corridors of power and picking up information to sell on, having taken a while because he was so low-level he was left alone. Guy, 'While we are talking, this individual is about to be transferred to our safe location. A little talk to enlighten him to the error of his ways.'
Guy, 'right then back to the Hoffman Brothers, I will ask Interpol to investigate this matter; hopefully, we will be able to break the cycle of knives coming into the country.'
'Regarding Ravenhurst Holdings, I am one hundred per cent sure this is a major money-laundering set up to clean the cartel's money, and having just bought up the area in Newcastle, which Mark paid a visit to, it is far too coincidental.' Guy, having passed his new

number on to Leyland, was surprised when the phone rang. It was emergencies only; something must be wrong. 'Hello, sir, we have an issue at Middlesbrough.'
'What is wrong, Leyland.'
'DS Meads was killed in our custody last night.'
'Looks like a hitman, poisoned sweet, slow-acting took twelve hours.'
'Good grief, that was the same as the two prison guards in Manchester.'
Harry, 'What has happened, Guy.'
'The only possible lead to the Ramina cartel was killed, in police custody, apparently poisoned.'
Mark, 'The infiltration is deep, to get to him so quickly.'
The rest agree, and Guy decides to break up the meeting; he bids farewell to Harry and David, asking Mark if he can give him a moment of his time. Guy asks him to step out of his car, putting his finger on his lips; Mark obliges, already knowing something is worrying him. They walk twenty metres up the layby before Guy stops him, writing on a piece of paper asking him to give him his phone; Guy takes it and smashes both to pieces, Mark looking at Guy with his arms in the air.
'What the hell, Guy, why did you do that? It was brand new.'
'That call from Middlesbrough has just confirmed I have a traitor within my mists; the only two people who knew about the transfer were in that vehicle with us today.'
'What about the people at the other end of the line.'
'Only the superintendent, the prisoner had a spit hood on to hide his identity, the drivers etc., from a neighbouring police force, who have no connection to him, no name given.'
'Why did you smash the phones then.'
'Both can clone the phones, and they are technically gifted.'

'Buy another phone and ring this number; when it answers, put this code in 91315, this will go to my secure phone and leave your new number.' Mark is not worried he enjoys everything about this subterfuge game; he agrees to Guy's request; Mark shakes Guy's hand and leaves. A despondent Guy, annoyed that a close colleague, could betray his trust, it can only be money, he will not be kind to this person, he already knows who it is. Achieving the hit on DS Meads can only mean they are closer than he thinks. The timescale of five hours to arrange it is powerful indeed

Chapter 34

With his business head in gear, Jimmy has decided to trade in some of his assets to pay for the next delivery. In the two years he has been in the Northeast, the excess money he had accrued from his drug empire. Jimmy started to buy up terraced housing, and his portfolio now expanded to over fifty properties. He will need to offload at least thirty to get the money he requires for his next shipment, currently being held back, till he comes up with some cash. Having already driven the price down on the houses when he bought them, well below market price, Jimmy's aggressive style never failed him. Sellers too frightened to fight for more, the ones that did ask were told to visit him at Petals Flower Distributors. There are three more graves next to the individual who stole Jimmy's car, concrete so solid now. He heard through various contacts a company specialising in bulk purchase of properties. He rings the number of Baxter Holdings, explaining he has a business proposition of mutual benefit to both parties. He needs a minimum of eighty thousand pounds per house, and the current average is around one hundred and ten thousand pounds. Two days later, in Baxter Holdings main office, Mr Baxter walks in with his construction manager and solicitor. Jimmy puts forward his proposal, and he does not like the idea he is not in control. Mr Baxter asks Jimmy to leave the office and can he wait while they discuss his proposal. It was only fifteen minutes, but to Jimmy, who is staring at the collapse of his empire, an eternity.

Jimmy called back into the office; he is not used to dealing with ethical people; after losing his wife to suicide and daughter in prison, Mr Baxter has become a born again Christian. He explains to Jimmy that it is a one time offer. Jimmy used to do, 'It is a fair offer, and I assume we will need to do some upgrades in the current climate. However, we can offer you ninety thousand per house if you agree my solicitor will get on with the paperwork immediately.' Jimmy shakes hands on the deal and leaves all the relevant details with them.

His empire will have that cash injection of 2.7million pounds it so sorely needs at the moment.
While jimmy is organising and rebuilding his empire, the local news channel and paper have issued an appeal for a missing youth, last seen two days ago. The police would like to speak to the two individuals he was last seen with, ushered into a large black SUV, in the town centre car park. Unfortunately, the police could not confirm the registration number as the registration plates were obscured with mud. Still, any witnesses can come forward in the strictest confidence to help solve his disappearance. Paul approaches Jimmy to see if their contact in the police force can deal with the situation. Jimmy nods, 'already done, Paul, no need to worry, just carry on as normal.' Jimmy has not told Paul he cannot reach DS Philpott, assuming he is on holiday, but Paul should have told him before he left for his holidays. The next day at a news conference, the boy's mother begged him to come home, stating he was a bit wayward but not a bad lad; all Jimmy had done was inadvertently stopped, a future criminal from stepping on the town's streets.

Chapter 35

After the meeting with Guy and his colleagues, Mark is driving back to Manchester, surprised that Guy was so open in his assessment of the situation. Seeing in his eyes the disappointment that a long term friend and colleague could betray them. Mark knows all too well how money can change your sense of reasoning. To Mark, it was like buying a car you cannot afford, but your mind sees it differently, making excuses you can afford it, and before long, you spiral into debt. Then out of nowhere, someone offers a lifeline, more money you are now trapped until they say do this one thing for us, and you are debt-free, you are caught one thing turns to another, you can never get away now, do our bidding or the police will find out if you tell someone you are dead, caught forever. Ringing ahead to tell Lydia he was on his way home, would she like a pizza brought in to save time? She asks. 'what do you mean.' Mark responds, 'it will give us an extra fifteen minutes in the bedroom,' Lydia squeals with laughter, 'I better take my underwear off to save ten seconds then,' both laughing. Lydia is waving from the lounge window; he smiles, knocking on the door. Lydia opens the door scantily dressed, Mark says, 'pizza delivery, but I think we will need to reheat it,' placing the pizza on the kitchen table, Mark runs upstairs to catch up to Lydia. The next day Mark leaves his contact Number on the secure line, adding he used to be on the dark web himself, and he will make some enquiries out of hours and update him. The revelations from the day before have hit a nerve in his senses regarding things close to home. While his time with Lydia is good, something is wrong, but he cannot put his finger on it. Mark is cleaning the kitchen worktop after breakfast; Lydia has gone shopping; he grabs the plastic bag out of the

waste bin to take out to the refuse bin, placing the bag in the bin. He hears a noise behind him.
Rosie, the neighbour, leaning over the fence, 'good morning Paul,' Mark turns around, telling her he is Paul's twin brother
Mark, explaining Paul has been in prison for three years.
Rosie nods, 'oh, that's right, I remember now, how is Lydia.'
'She is ok; I think she is happy.'
'That's good, so sad Sharon died; she was so fit, she had only been home for a week before it happened.'
'What do you mean, by the way, what is your name? You knew Paul but not me.'
'Oh sorry, my name is Rosie; Sharon was a great neighbour, always happy and helpful but seemed to change when Lydia came home.'
'How do you mean Rosie.'
She became withdrawn, not wanting to talk as though something was on her mind.'
'Was that unusual for Sharon.'
'Oh yes, she was a chatterbox, similar to myself in the nicest way, of course.' Rosie chuckles.
'Why do you think that happened.'
'I don't know when Lydia came; it was instant; I am sorry I should not bad mouth Lydia. I do not know her; it was so strange.'
'That's ok; sometimes it is best to get it out in the open, don't worry, I will not tell her.'
'Thank you, Mark.'
Mark nods and finally puts the lid on the refuse bin, bids Rosie farewell, enters the kitchen and switches the coffee machine on. He has a phone call to make and hopes Guy has the power to do something for him. He rings Lydia, 'just checking how long you will be, just got to nip out,'

'No problem, I will be hours just going for fancy things for your benefit.'
Marks laughs, 'thank goodness I thought you might be wasting money.'
'No way it's all for you.'
'Okay, see you when you get home.'
Marks senses are on high alert something is not right, especially after the conversation with the neighbour; he decides the call to Guy must be made outside.
Walking to the end of the driveway, he auto dials the number for Guy actually, it's the only number in his new burner phone it rings but goes straight to answerphone, leaving the message 'ring me asap'.
Just as he turns to go back up the driveway, his phone rings
'It must be urgent for you to leave that message.'
'Can you do something for me? Unfortunately, it is well away from your remit, but I must find something out quickly.'
'Carry on what is it.'
'Can you get the exhumation of a body done and an urgent autopsy?'
'Good grief, what is going on, Mark.'
'Let me just say, my suspicions have been raised, and if correct, you are getting set up.'
'Whose body is it.'
'My ex-mother-in-law.'
' It is that serious, Mark.'
'Yes, if I am right, there will be signs of poison, the same as DS Meads and the two prison guards.'
'Give me twenty-four hours, and you will have an answer.'
'Thank you, Guy, goodbye.'
Mark goes to the basic car and opens the rear boot lid; two minutes later, he walks to the house, pulls out a frequency scanner from his pocket and moves it over various items in the house. Walking around the house,

he writes in a small notebook. Going in and out of all the rooms and finally the main bedroom. To his surprise, there are a lot more microphones spread around the room. He may have missed some of them, but now he knows he will be careful what he says to Lydia.

Just as he puts the scanner away in the basic car, Lydia turns into the drive, jumps out of the car gathering several bags, with the biggest smile on her face, 'we are going to have the time of our life tonight,' and glides past him.

Mark runs in behind her, grabs her waist swings her around and kisses her; he must carry on as though nothing is wrong. It is going to be long twenty-four hours.

It only shows how good neighbours can sometimes save the day, and he will send Rosie some flowers tomorrow if his suspicions are validated. So the day passes, as usual, the nighttime a little bit different; he has just found out Lydia has a fetish he is not into but has to keep up the pretence till he is sure what is going on.

Mark is expecting the call from Guy; he must think of an excuse to get Lydia out of the house. Mark looks on the internet, finds a health spa, and arranges for her to go, paying a premium to get her into a full spa. Walking into the living room, he asks Lydia if she is free all day; she nods yes, 'good after last nights shenanigans, I have booked you into a health spa for the full works hoping my reward will be just as good.' Gleefully she accepts his offer; it is only two miles down the road; she walks into the spa foyer in thirty minutes. While he is waiting for the call that could change everything, he goes upstairs. Mark has just remembered that Julia had put a family photograph album on top of the wardrobe. His curiosity that he may find something to help him solve his problem, opening the album he can see they looked like twins, even in their childhood they looked the same. The album set out as though it was a story through their years, then on page ten, he noticed something that confirmed his suspicions, only a tiny detail, but it was enough. Next to a photo is an old newspaper article about Lydia losing the tip of her little finger on the left hand in a gate lock at the London zoo; a court case ensued. Still, they lost the case as the zookeeper was unavailable, transferred overseas, they said. Mark puts the album back in place, no sign of disturbance; he goes downstairs and puts some eggs on to boil, places bread in the toaster, and they say men cannot cook, they will be perfect, he tells himself. Toast is ready, just about to get the eggs; the phone rings he must go outside to answer.

'Hello Guy, please tell me I am wrong.'

'Unfortunately, you are correct, same toxins.'

'I would like to kill her, and I think she may have killed the real Lydia as well as Sharon.'

'Step back Mark, what do you mean killed Lydia.'

'Found some old photo's the real Lydia had the tip of her little finger missing in an accident.'

Good grief, this is intense, Mark

'I think it would be best if you send some men to collect her before I do something we will both regret.'

'Any particular time, Mark.

Mark, 'Currently, she is at the local health spa; I will text the address.'

Guy, 'Where do we go from here, Mark.'

'Carry on as good professionals do, Guy.'

'The fallout from our meeting two days ago is not what I wanted.'

'What do you mean, Guy.'

'This Ramina cartel bought my closest ally, Harry; he is too frightened to say anything, they are certainly

powerful, it was him who was holding back information, misdirecting David.'
'As is most people, that is how they control them.'
'This now means we need to meet to formulate a strategy, and I have found out it is better to attack than defend in life.'
'With you there, Guy, call me when you are ready to meet.'
'Before you go, Mark, what made you suspicious.'
'When we took down Jane and Dawn Steel, she was too good, very calculated, not a beginner.
'I would not have noticed that.'
'Everyone to their trades, oh before you go, to get her to look like Lydia, we are looking for a top-notch plastic surgeon, and it must have taken months, a lot of planning has been involved in doing this, be careful who you speak to.'
As he ends the call, the sound of the smoke detector going off, 'bloody hell the eggs,' entering the kitchen, the stench of a burnt pan and the eggs popping, he curses under his breath.
Then his thoughts go to the original Lydia; they must have tortured her pretty severely to get the amount of information they had, she had the mannerisms and the quips that Julia used to say, his revenge will be brutal.
Mark had given Guy the registration number of Lydia's car, two vehicles parked up either side of the car, waiting for her. Twenty minutes later, Lydia walks out of the spa, refreshed for the night not to come. But, as she unlocks the door, unaware that four men are standing around her, cuffs placed on her, and she is arrested, shouting language unbecoming of a lady, the people in the spa are shocked at what has just taken place.
With a media blackout, peoples phones being unable to upload any photos, the situation must be controlled. Although Guy is conscious that the slightest adverse

information about them must not come to light at all costs, he will inform the PM and head of MI6 what they have found out; hopefully, the PM will authorise staffing to help them.

Chapter 36

After realising that Harry may be a mole, Guy pulled Mark to one side when Harry and David left the meeting in the layby near Coventry. Putting his cards on the table with Mark, he found it difficult to digest that his best ally now is a prolific hitman but knows he is a man of honour and loyalty if given the respect he deserves. That phone call Guy received regarding DS Meads in the car was the nail in Harry's coffin. Harry and David were the only ones who knew what was happening, but he dismissed the possibility of David, as he was not on board when the other police guards were killed. As Mark sets off home, Guy calls the local police and Harry is stopped twenty miles further on, with an officer telling him he has been stopped as he has gone through a speed camera too fast. Just a ploy to keep him there till Guy arrived to take over the situation, Guy already hoping Harry had not informed anyone about Ron Walton. Before he contacted the police, Guy called his friend in MI6 to monitor any calls from Harry's phone, knowing he still had his original, using only the burner phone to contact Guy. As Harry was getting out of Guy's car, he dropped it on the floor, Guy pretending not to notice but saw he was embarrassed, face flushed. The police were starting to exasperate Harry by the length of time it was taking, now looking under the bonnet pretending they were doing mechanical checks. He was getting annoyed just as Guy turned up. He introduced himself to the police, and as Harry steps out of the car to talk to Guy, a nod to a policeman who instantly handcuffs him. Harry is looking perplexed and surprised, asking what is happening; Guy informs him that he is being arrested for aiding and abetting in the murder of DS Meads, John and Linda Lane and two police guards. Harry looks at Guy in disbelief what the hell is going on, shouting at Guy, 'you have known me for years, I would not do that to you; this job is making you paranoid.' Harry is placed into the back of a police car, screaming his innocence. He is booked into a cell with twenty-four-hour, surveillance nobody to see him other than Guy.

Harry will be transferred tomorrow Guy will come back with some new colleagues. It is a long twenty-four hours for Harry, constantly looking at the door, hoping a stranger does not knock on the door. He alone knows how deep the Ramina cartel is in the system. A long sleepless night ensues he is in turmoil, should he tell Guy everything, and throw himself at his mercy. At 9 am the next day, the echo of the key in the door lock and the metal cell door opens. He is requested to stand back; two men enter, handcuffs placed on his wrists, then escorted him outside to a waiting vehicle, paperwork signed, and the vehicle leaves. Harry has not seen these men before, and he is hoping they are Guy's colleagues or he will not get out of this vehicle alive. Then he feels the needle in his neck, instantly nothing but blackness. Many hours later, Harry wakes up, his head pounding, wanting to be sick, legs cuffed to a chair that does not move and cuffed to a steel bar on a metal table that also does not move. Looking at the floor, he can see blood spatter (just paint for effect) in his mind the cartel has got him; his chances of survival is now at a minimum. Then the incessant music, so loud it hurts his ears, shouting for them to stop, 'please stop, please,' this a tactic that Guy does not like, but they must break him before anybody else dies. In Harry's mind, his sexuality has brought him into the crosshairs of the cartel. Being Bisexual, he was caught in a compromising situation with a man, his wife unaware of his penchant for men. The offer not to destroy his marriage of twenty-eight years and his son and daughter will not find out if he does as they say.

The photos were sent to him at his workplace as a reminder that it could explode in his face at any time. He is now just another pawn to use and control for the benefit of the cartel. He was a mine of information at his level in Guy's organisation.

With a slight accent in his head, a voice from behind him sounds like a dutchman; mixed emotions is this one of the cartel's men or one of Guy's men he has not met. The first question will undoubtedly indicate who has got him, 'what have you told Guy Long.'

But, then, with a deep intake of breath, in his mind, it is the cartel he screams out, 'nothing I have told them, nothing.'

'That is hard to believe; you have been in custody twenty-four hours, Mr Graham.'

Harry, 'Please, believe me, I was supposed to be questioned today, but you have got to me first.'

Voice, 'Have you set us up, are you tagged.'

'You know I am only tagged by you, and the tracker is still in my neck. You will stop my heart if I talk, and I want to live god damn it.'

At this point, he feels the needle again blackness ensues, Guy listening in another room, 'move him to another location deep down, we do not know how good their technology is. we need to remove it fast.'

David, 'this is bad Guy, what the hell are we up against.'

'An organisation with money to burn, I,m afraid our worst nightmare.'

Just as they are about to leave, security cameras can see two large vans approaching. Only people who are authorised can enter; eight men jump out of the vans, heavily armed. The site was made to look as though it was not there. An underground car park, to hide coming and goings, entering at one end, further down the road. The exit is a quarter of a mile further down the road; an electronic gate opens on exit, passing through the gates. Guy instigates total lockdown, and they lose visual coverage as the cameras go dark. Steel shutters are closing, covering all exits and windows; Guy says to David, 'Harry must-have information for them to send a kill team .' David nods he has never been involved in an altercation, even at school. As with these buildings, there is always a way out, special tunnels in different directions. The men with Guy are special forces; Guy' issues a shoot to kill order if we can take any prisoners. It is the longest ten minutes David has ever known. But, for Guy and the rest of the team, it is just another day at the office. As they move through the tunnels, the emergency power has come on, and lights start to flicker.

The generator has not been used in years, as the sight abandoned years ago. The generator is half a mile away, and the cables are old, dust kicked up as they run through the old tunnel.

David coughing as the dust reaches his throat; not used to this type of thing, they reach an exit, two of Guy's men open the doors. They are one-hundred and fifty metres away from the main building; as they turn around, they can see six men fixing explosives to the steel shutters, another two are going around the back. Guy tries to phone his other colleagues coming out the opposite tunnel, all phone signals gone, 'they are using a phone jammer to stop communications.' David turns around smiling; that's why I brought this old radio comms phone, smiling proudly at Guy. He contacts his colleagues in the opposite direction, informing them of two incoming persons to deal with. As four SAS operatives come out of the tunnel, four shots to the heads of four assailants, they fall instantly the other two surrender immediately. Two more shots were heard in the distance, confirmation of two kills over the radio phone. Suddenly the grey clouds dispersed, the sun shining, casting shadows across the fields. Even the stark concrete building looked friendly, as the last two men were taken back into the building for interrogation; Guy did not want to issue a kill instruction but, it was a situation kill or be killed. As they enter the building, Harry is well aware he is surplus to requirement, for the cartel and his life is on a short leash unless he gives Guy information. Two of Guy's colleagues take Harry into the medical room; Guy requests anybody with first aid or medical experience to come forward. The chances that anyone has the expertise that Guy is looking for are slim, but things sometimes have a way of happening. A hand raises, one of the SAS operatives used to be a medic in another life; Guy is always surprised what life has got to give. The man steps forward; Guy explains, 'the reason we had a visit from that kill squad is our friend on the table has a tracker in his neck, it requires moving do you think you can do it without killing him.' Angus is looking at Harry, who is now in a complete state of panic; in a cold sweat, his hands are clammy, sticking to the steel table. The former medic turns his back on Harry and speaks to Guy, winking Angus says, 'it will be touch and go depending on how deep it is; Harry faints on the table when he comes around, a small plaster on his neck.

The medic could feel it just under the surface; Guy was so glad it was not a nano tracker like the one he had given Mark.

Destroying the tracker, Guy needs to talk to Harry, hoping he has not told them too much, and find out their end game. Receiving a text message, Guy informed that they have another guest, Lydia, still sedated, brought straight into the medical room, a call for Angus to return. He was surprised to see a female on the table; Guy asked him to do the same procedure, Angus was mystified, needing to do this twice within an hour, wondering what was going on, but he is used to taking orders without question. Angus finds and removes the tracker quickly, handing the tracker over to Guy; he nods in appreciation, and Guy destroys that one as well. So aware now Guy is thinking, whoever they are, they must know that we have at least one or two of their operatives; in effect, four people are about to be interrogated.

Chapter 37

Mark has removed all microphones from the house, and they were even in the shed and garage. He has decided to leave one in the living room to see it; this could be useful to draw someone in. Having already been enlightened by Guy about the trackers in Harry and Lydia and the update regarding the elusive Mr Bennett who had killed DS Meads, Mark will do his best to draw him in. First, he must find out who killed Lydia and Sharon; it will end brutally for them when he does. Mark has decided to vent his frustration on his next drug gang and is heading towards Leeds. Having already killed the Robbins brothers years before in Leeds, he was fraught with anxiety over the fact it never ends. As one falls, another starts up; the only way to stop it is to cut the supply source.

Small steps are too small, and this is why he thinks it must be government-led. They have the money and manpower but do not seem to care; someone somewhere is getting their pockets lined. So far, he has gleaned information through his last couple of ventures and has his sights on Mo Sam; he will be in his territory in one hour. Driving through Leeds, again, he can tell the areas of deprivation where drugs are dealt. Rather than stay a few days to test the water, his anger is reaching the point of no return over the issue of an innocent Lydia being killed. While in his basic car, he has parked up on the corner of a street, he can see a deal going down. The dealer can see him coming towards him, unsure whether he is a customer or the police. The dealer is confident in his environment; he offers him a wrap when Mark reaches him. Mark declines and advises him he would like some information; the individual is named Seth. He tells Mark that due to some issues elsewhere, he cannot do so. Mark offers him a choice of life or death. Seth looks at

Mark, not believing what he has said, 'you must be joking, old man.' Mark is starting to get exasperated by these old man jibes. 'Look, I do not normally brag, but those issues you are talking about is me; you have ten seconds, or you will be dead where you stand.'
Seth bursts out laughing; ten seconds later, Seth is dead.
The knife to the heart was swift and clean, with no time to scream; Mark left his body perched against the wall and returned to the car, proceeds to a new destination four streets away. In the same scenario, a dealer is doing his business. Mark pulls up to him, gets out of the car, and a similar situation takes place; and Mark has the information he wants. Unfortunately, the dealer ended up the same way as Seth. The main stash house is in a different area of the town; it was opened up only two weeks ago, due to problems in Glasgow and Newcastle. Mark picks up four canvas bags on the way, and he feels he may need further cash to move forward; if enough is offered, someone will cave in. He parks up around the corner; there is a buzz about the area, people going to and from the stash house. Mark's handy work has reached them, the sky opens up, and the rain falls, in the moonlight casting different shadows a bit of an advantage for a seasoned assassin. He can see the two cameras, one at the front door another higher up, two quick shots, and they are both out of action. It is where a hitman's patience comes to the fore; it takes another thirty minutes before someone ventures, slowly out of the front door, hoping not to be shot. Looking up at the cameras, he shouts to his fellow dealers that they are broken, not realising they have been shot out. Two more dealers come out, three quiet thuds they lay dead on the floor, in seconds, Mark moves forward in the shadows, waiting to see if any more come out. He waits ten minutes no more people come out. It is now or never;

he moves to the rear of the house. A small explosive device was thrown into the yard as a distraction. Two minutes later, a loud bang, he runs into the house past the three dead dealers, one man in the front room, a shot to the head. Mark listens for anymore, and he can hear footsteps on the next level, using a silencer the other people do not know he is in the house. Mark shouts upstairs, 'what the hell is happening here,' a ploy for them, two heads look over the stair bannister, two more shots to the head, they slump over the stair railing. He carries on up the stairs, checking all the rooms.

Nobody else is in the house; as he enters the room where the money is, he fills four bags full, throwing them out the rear window. Mark drives the car to the rear, fills up the basic car with the bags of money, then goes back into the house dragging the three bodies in and sets the house ablaze. Mo Sam had been told about the attack on the stash house, as Mark was attacking it, now grateful he was not there, a call to Jimmy Lees who is getting irate that someone would dare attack them again, who is it. Yet again, his money has gone; this will cause untold misery for him as Jimmy cannot pay his suppliers now, more furniture broken in his house, wishing the house deal would come through quickly. Mo Sam is confident the assailant does not know where he lives but has told his family to pack some bags rapidly. They are leaving for a few days due to an emergency. Mo Sam tells his wife he will get a few things from the supermarket, and he will be thirty minutes., on arrival home, he can see the empty bags, losing his temper, and shouting for his wife and kids. Suddenly the lights come on, lighting up the pool. As he looks, his wife, son and daughter are tied up sitting on a bench near the pool edge. A pain in his chest the realisation someone is in his house, he runs outside, Mark tells him to, 'stop,' Mo Sam stops immediately. Mark continues, 'before we go any further, did your family know about your drug empire.' The arrogance of his twenty-one-year-old son, 'are you stupid? Do you know who we are, ' again, Mark asks, 'did they know their lifestyle was built on addiction and misery.' Once again, the son pipes up, 'of course we did you, idiot,' every time Mo Sam tries to keep him quiet,

Mark, 'well, that seals your fate then.'

Mo Sam, 'look, we have plenty of money; surely we can come to an arrangement.'

'Another time, another place that might have been possible.'

'Look, everyone has a price; come on, we can come to a deal.'

'Not today, I have seen the suffering that you people cause, for easy money and greed,' at that moment, Mark shoots the son, who topples into the pool.

Mo Sam's wife and daughter are screaming; two seconds later, two thuds and the place is quiet, his wife and daughter are also dead in the pool, blood spreading in the water.

Tears now flowing down Mo Sam's face, he falls to his knees another thud, and Mark is leaving the house, business concluded.

A quick text to Guy, 'Leeds business completed, on my way home to catch a hitman, keep me posted.'

Chapter 38

Jimmy is acutely aware someone is trying to destroy all that he has worked towards; it has got to be from an outside source, his contact, high up in government, has gone silent. He was an old school friend, who became his runner for information always 100% correct, so he had no hesitation trusting what he had to say. When Jimmy came out of prison, one of his first contacts was Phil Melton is old runner, who informed Jimmy that he was high up in government, more in jest than truth, but he could not retract it once he had made the statement. Jimmy thought he had gone up in the world while he was in prison. And friends help friends; Phil, now trapped in his lies, Jimmy asking for inside information and the extra remuneration he would receive, to him substantial, only being a security guard would help him out. After two years, Phil invented the story of the government trying to close drug gangs down, hoping this would keep him busy until he emigrated to Australia in three months. Unfortunately, it coincided with the mysterious request to Sir Guy Long to head up a similar project. Now that Phil is unreachable, he does not know how many people are involved in his capture, adding more fuel to his anger. Jimmy is unaware that Mo Sam has met his maker, leaving several messages to contact him, but to no avail. After several hours reality strikes home; his network is slowly being eroded, still not knowing that a single hitman is causing havoc on his network. With only Manchester and his Middlesbrough branches still viable, he must push Baxter Holdings to complete the sale he requires to be solvent. A frantic call, he is willing to give an extra 5% discount if they can complete in two days, it will be in your bank in two days and a sigh of relief from Jimmy Lees, rare indeed more used to take than give. He called his suppliers to release some more products, and funds were available; the answer he got was not what he wanted to hear. Using their network, they already know the problems he is having and does not want to waste their valuable goods, or assets as they call it.

They have cut him loose to source from elsewhere. If he can find anyone to risk supplying him, unknown to Jimmy, he is the sacrificial lamb for the cartel, as there are no friends in this business; money is king. Jimmy has finally realised there are few friends in the cutthroat world of drugs, his quandary now who will take his money and with a reputation that is now well tarnished, they will try to charge him a premium price. His financial status has dropped more than 80% with Mark's intervention. Jimmy must get himself together, start thinking straight; the county lines vans are doing their work, and a little trickle of money is finally coming through. It could be best to step back until his finances start to improve. Sometimes, it is best to wait. Just then, his phone rings, 'hello, this is your friendly fixer. Have you got any information so I can solve your problem?'
Jimmy, taken aback, is flustered, 'no, but whoever the bastards are, they have just closed my Leeds branch.'
Music to Mark's ears, 'Is there something you need me to do.'
'No, I will be in touch shortly.'
Mark puts the phone down with an air of superiority, thinking 'I,m getting under his skin.'
Jimmy is putting his phone down, suddenly suspicious of that call at that moment; good grief, I am getting paranoid; I must get my head in gear. Jimmy decides to contact his Manchester branch, newly promoted Vince Smalls answers the phone. A small sigh from Jimmy, at least all is ok there. Jimmy asks Vince if he has heard anything regarding Mo Sam, 'only that the police are

saying it is a turf war as usual nothing will be done you know that Jimmy.'
'Yes, I suppose so; keep vigilant, do not trust anyone new to you.'
'Ok, Jimmy.'
Secretly Vince has seen the light and is already organising an escape plan. Vince does not want to be another victim in this war. However, he has no control over it; he will take Jimmy's money and run for his life in seven days.

Chapter 39

Mark is home formulating his plan to catch Mr Bennett; he would not usually ask permission to kill someone, but killing DS Meads means he could be closer than everybody thinks. He texts Guy outside; the reply is simple, 'if you get the information you require, do as you please.' Mark is now a happy man. He enters the house and pretends to ring Guy, 'hi Guy been on the dark web and found information on that Mr Bennett, no picture but there is nothing secret on the web, I have downloaded info for your eyes only if you can call in please, tomorrow at 11 am, look forward to it.' Mark senses that the elusive Mr Bennett will call to get this information before the 11 am deadline. He will most certainly want to gain access to see what he has about him. With the false Lydia arrested, Mark has reverted to the takeaway as most single men do, collecting rather than getting it delivered. He was always aware that his prey could be watching, already changing the alarm code if Lydia had given the code to one of her colleagues. As Mark steps out of the door, the garage light operates as it normally does. He installed a mini camera in the gutter just above it to record anybody coming up the drive; he leaves to collect his dinner. Within five minutes, a ping on his smartphone, Mark pulls over and sees a man scouting the house; who removes the lamp from the outside light, the camera has given him the advantage over this man. He collects his meal and drives home, parking in the next street, knocking on the door of the house behind him, requesting police access to catch an intruder trying to break into his house; they agree wholeheartedly. Mark asks them to stay in the house for their safety. He will only be two minutes, and surprise is always the best option, luckily his garden is quite long and surprising himself how sprightly he was to get over the fence. He can see by the moonlight; his prey is by the side gate, the man is not expecting anyone, then the pain in the knee, he drops his gun, pain in the other knee, 'who are you,' was the surprised tone from his victim.

Mark responds, 'more to the point, who are you,' the man starts to shake as the pain increases in his knees, he stays silent. Mark carries on, 'I assume you are just cannon fodder, with Mr Bennett coming later to clean up,' the man nods a yes in the defeat of the situation. Mark, who do you work for.'
'I do not know, we are given an address, and we kill anyone there, money transfer in the bank, immediately on the kill.'
'How do you tell them, if you want to go to the hospital, it would be wise to tell me.'
The assailant is thinking he is going to be ok, 'a coded text.'
'Would you like to inform them I am dead if you want to go to the hospital, I am only after Mr Bennett?'
The man takes his phone out and duly texts his employer; Mark makes a mental note of the number, a shot to the head all is quiet, five minutes later, he knocks on the rear neighbour's door to tell them all is ok. He drives back to his house, the meal in the microwave, a deep sigh, he is back in his old ways again. After Mark finishes his meal, he places the body in the garage, going in by the side door; Mark will call Guy after Mr Bennett calls tomorrow. Then, off to bed to reflect on the past few days, hoping he can get some answers tomorrow; maybe they can find out why all this is happening. Mark gets up early, having a stable breakfast; he has a long day ahead of him; Mark positions himself at a slight angle in the single chair, his right hand out of view of the front door, a tranquillizer gun in his hand. Leaving the door slightly ajar, giving the impression a visitor had already been,

the clock ticks by, and time seems to go into slow motion, 10 am, and the door starts to open further, a tall man impeccably dressed enters the house. Mark had put blood on his shirt to look like he had been shot; as the man looks in an instant, he feels the dart just above his heart, he reels back, starting to lose conciseness, falls backwards onto the laminated flooring. Mark searches his victim for clues, only a mobile phone and a wallet. With a small amount of money and a helpful bank card, for a good hitman.

Mark gathers his newfound friend putting his arm around his shoulder, and drags him into the garage. On awakening, Mr Bennett finds himself tied up and hanging from the garage rafters. Knowing his fate might be sealed, he attempts to barter his position with Mark, telling him he will give him information for his life.

Mark's first question is the obvious one, 'who has put the hit on him.'

Bennett, 'that goes back three years.'

'What the hell happened three years ago.'

'Holland three high ranking people in the Ramina cartel.'

'How did they find out.'

'Even if you kill me, you will not win; we have eyes and ears everywhere.'

'All these deaths for that.'

'That hit cost the cartel over a billion pounds in lost revenue across the world.'

'I can see why they are angry,' Mark sarcastically replies

'Where is my apprentice? He was supposed to visit you last night.'

'Oh him, he is behind you. Do you all have trackers?'

'I think I have said enough; I assume the end is coming; if so, make it quick.'

'Who is my lady friend.'
'What do you mean.'
'Well, she is getting interrogated as we speak.'
'No, it can't be she was too well versed in her role to fail; how did you find out.'
'Our first hit she was too cool, you could tell she had done it all before, and the real Lydia had the tip of her little finger missing.'
'No, that can't be; we spent thousands perfecting her persona.'
'You did not have the photo on top of the wardrobe; your team
miscalculated, I am afraid; what is her real name.'
'Ask her.'
'What about the real Lydia. where is she.'
'Again, ask her.'

'I will, and it's time to say goodbye now, nothing personnel.'
Mark takes his Glock out of his waistband, Bennett closes his eyes, it is over in a second, he unloosens the rope and lets him fall on top of his apprentice. Then he rings Guy, about to tell him about the reason they are after him.
Guy stops him, 'oh, by the way, fingerprints of your girlfriend confirm she is Susan Bennett, part of a man and wife hit team.'
'Well, Mr Bennett kept that one going to the grave, slightly embarrassed now; I think she was having a better time in the bedroom with me rather than him.
Then he asks Guy, 'can he get someone to collect the bodies later in the evening?'
Even Guy was surprised when he found out about another body; he would ring Leyland and tell him to stop looking for Bennett; he has come to an untimely end.

'Will you update me after your interrogation? We are getting close to finding out who our antagonists are at last.

Chapter 40

The four detainees are in separate rooms, spaced two rooms apart, the empty hallway echos when someone walks past. All the detainees are free inside their rooms to eat, drink and sleep, all wearing red coveralls; toilets are in the room for their use, a small dimly lit lamp in a special housing so no one can break into them. Cameras in each corner watch their every move; there is no privacy in these rooms. There is a flap on the steel door so that food can be served. They are fed sandwiches only to avoid utensils being used. Plastic cups for drinking water only; no tea or coffee will be given. Finally, after two days, the sound of a struggle, one of the hitmen is being dragged from his room a steel door slams shut, a shout, ' take him downstairs to the chamber,' a brisk response, 'yes sir will he be coming back,' all is quiet.

The other detainees are now wondering what their fate is; after one hour, the sound of a single gunshot, looking at the monitor, Guy is looking to see the response from the other detainees, only Harry shows fear. A call down the hallway, 'clean the room he will not be coming back,' a deep intake of breath from Harry; he is the weak link but does he know enough to help them? Guy suspects not. Another long four hours, again the sound of a scuffle with some expletives. Shouting, 'I know nothing, I cannot tell you what I do not know,' ninety minutes later the sound of a gunshot, Harry is agitated, yet another, 'clean the room, he will not be coming back,' Lydia oh so calm. It will be another twenty-four hours, and Harry will not sleep. He is on the verge of a breakdown, Guy did not want to do this to an old friend, but he must get to the bottom of the situation before too many more people die. Harry can hear the footsteps, who is next then the key in the door of his cell, too frightened to shout, too weak to resist he was not made to be a spy. By the time he reaches his next destination, he is willing to sell his soul, looking at the floor more signs of even more blood spatter. Not knowing they would have had him in the room earlier.

They needed to wait for the red paint to dry, everything for effect. Harry sits down on the steel chair, the usual handcuffs placed around his wrists and ankles, the lights become brighter, and that voice from earlier in the week speaks. He cannot see the person speaking, 'Hello Harry, how are you today,'
'If you must know, I am shitting myself,' his voice shaking, the person already knowing he is near breaking point.
'Why don't you start at the beginning? How long have you been with the cartel.'
'Three months before this whole thing started.'
'They found out I was bisexual and took photos to trap me.'
'As all good cartels do, sorry about that, Harry, but the department knew, they could not use that against you.'
'What the hell, how long have you known.'
'In our game, there are very few secrets, Harry.'
'My wife and kids did not know, and they used that against me.'
'Do you know what their end game is?'
'No, for some reason, they are after Guy; I do not know why.'
'What information have you given them while you have been in their employment,' Harry's head drops.
'Again, what information have you given them,'
No response again, his head has not moved; on entering the room, Guy can see he is already dead, the voice shouts for Angus. Within two minutes, the sound of Angus running down the hall, he checks Harry's pulse. His lips are blue, confirming what they already

knew. Exasperation from Guy, how can this have happened? He orders an immediate autopsy. The body is taken to a local police station under a banner of need to know. He rings Dr Mitchell, an old colleague, to meet him there. It will be two long hours at the station before Guy gets an answer he did not want to hear. Somehow the same poison toxin was in his system, as in the previous killings. How did it get into his system? Dr Mitchell enters the room with the remains of a small plastic tube and the smallest electronics he has ever seen.
'This was installed just under his shoulder blade, difficult to spot.'

'What are we up against? I have not seen anything like this before. Have you done a tox screen on it?'
Dr Mitchell, 'that's where the poison came from, Guy.'
'Right, give me that, I will give that to a specialist to check,' foolishly Guy had crushed the trackers. He must get them back to check them finitely. Rushing back things going through his head, a realisation that Lydia will reach the same fate shortly, a call to the base to get her to the hospital quickly before he left the police station, he had asked Dr Mitchell if there is an antidote for the toxin. Dr Mitchell will investigate and come back as soon a possible. It is now a race against time to see if Lydia has the same thing in the same place. It is explained to Lydia what is happening, she did not know about this added feature to her body, and for the first time, a glimmer of fear Guy had not seen before. The hospital has an area purely for jobs such as these. Rushing her through the x-ray, a location of the pellet found. Lydia did not know about this added failsafe from the cartel, a frustrated Guy hoping she would give up more information if they save her life. All cartel members have the same thing in them, all installed under the pretence of the tracker being installed, not

knowing about their added cargo. It will be a stressful two hours for Guy, not known to show any emotions, hence one of the reasons for his meteoric rise up the ladder with a perfect poker face. Dr Mitchell is doing the operation, and he is a calm man under pressure. He locates the tiny pellet and places it in a small glass vial. Within seconds the pellet cracks and the poison leaks out. This particular pellet was faulty, as they are all supposed to activate within seventy-two hours of the tracker being removed, each item talking to each other electronically, all possible lines of information to be erased. Having a complete pellet to investigate has given Guy a sense of hope out of this mess. A call to the head of MI6 is required. Given two simple stitches, the beauty of modern medicine, Lydia is transferred back to Guy's complex and will be interrogated the following day.

When Guy arrives back at the complex, he is told that the other two prisoners died suddenly one hour ago. He nods his acknowledgement this killing system of theirs goes to all levels, it seems.
The gunshots the prisoners heard earlier were just a smokescreen to worry the others. So when Guy gets into his office, he is trying to look back at his past. Why is a major cartel after him? It does not make sense, and he has never been involved with anything in the drug trade. Now hoping Lydia might be able to shed some light on whats is going on, another long twenty-four hours before he can speak to her, he has noticed her demeanour is softening. Lydia is requested rather than forced to the interrogation room, and only one hand is cuffed to the metal rail on the steel table.
Voice, 'hello Lydia, do you know why you are here.'
'Not really.'
'What is your connection with, Mr Bennett.'
She raises her head, 'why.'

'Just answer the question.'
'If you must know he is my ex-husband, is that a problem.'
'Well, I am sorry to tell you, he has passed on.'
No emotion on her face, 'That's sad, we parted on bad terms.'
'What do you mean.'
'It was him who forced me into this situation.'
'Carry on Lydia/'
'By now, I assume you know my real name is Susan.'
'We do.'
'I wanted to retire, he said one last job, next thing I know I wake up a different woman and told I must go into deep cover.'
'Then what happened.'
'It was against my will, forced into a position for his benefit and not mine.'
'How long ago.'
'Two years, I have been playing this part, we parted company six months ago, you can check the divorce papers at the Manchester courts.'

'Who are you working for.'
'I am only telling you this because you saved my life; the only name that kept coming up was the Ramina cartel.'
'Do you know where they are based, head of operations?'
'No, everything is kept secret; only certain levels are party to classified intelligence.'
While Guy is listening, he picks up on the words classified intelligence. A small clue about what and who is behind all of this.
He is hoping it is not what he is thinking, but Ron Walton should be back in a couple of days, and he might bring something to light.

Voice carries on, 'Do you know why they are after your boyfriend.'

'Who would that be.'

'You have been living with him for a few weeks, Susan.'

'What you have known all the time.'

'Again, why are they after him.'

'I did not know until my ex let it slip a couple of weeks ago.'

'What is it about then, Susan.'

'Around three years ago, he took out three high ranking bosses of the cartel, costing them a phenomenal amount of money; they have been after him since.'

'Do you know how they found out?'

'Only rumours and hearsay, you do not know who to believe in this profession.'

'Point taken, the rumours what did they say.'

'They have eyes and ears everywhere, a police file about a hitman who was sentenced to life in prison, someone called Paul Reed, they joined the dots.'

'How did they know of his release.'

'Two security guards, as usual, everyone can be bought.'

'Well, they never got to spend it; they poisoned them the next day, with the same one they nearly killed you with.'

'Did you kill the original Lydia and the mother-in-law Sharon?'

'No, they killed Lydia the day I moved in, by my ex-husband's apprentice he liked to call him.'

'Do you know where Lydia's body is?'

'No, the apprentice took her, and I had to pretend Sharon had a heart attack; I did not know how she died one week later.'

'Would you believe, poison?'

'A recurring theme, it seems.'

'You did not ask how your husband died.'

'I have seen Mark or Paul whoever he is at work, he is the best I have seen, so I assume he did it.'
'Yes, his apprentice as well.'
'Can I ask you a question?'
'You can; I am not sure you will get the answer you want.'
'How did you find out about me.'
'Your boyfriend.'
The disappointment on her face was a picture to be seen, not wanting to believe any of it; they were so good together she would never have killed him she would have helped him she was so happy the way things were with the relationship.
'How did he know he never met Lydia.'
'You will need to ask him if you see him again.'
'I suppose so,' the sadness in her face it looked like she loved him, Mark completely unaware.
'We will suspend our talks for now. Can you take Susan back to her room?'
In the next room, Guy is pondering his next move. It is like a chess game, and he wants to be the one who checkmates in this game of survival.

Chapter 41

Unknown to Guy, his problem started nine years ago when two people went missing in Afghanistan, John Rains and Carl Naim undercover intelligence gatherers following a money trail to the Taliban. Both were involved in an explosion in a remote part of the country and had not informed head office where they were and spent months being moved around by kind Afghans to avoid capture. In that time of healing, both became bitter that no one had come to help them, losing sight of the fact that their inability to keep to their protocol caused their predicament. When they went missing, Guy spent two years looking for them, and they assumed they must be dead as all leads led to nowhere they had become ghosts. Unfortunately, Guy and his team decided they had spent too much time and resources looking as they gave up as time passed. John and Carl had seen the vast amount of money being used to support the Taliban, but they could filter cash to another account using an algorithm they had created. In their minds, they were helping to fight the Taliban and line their pockets simultaneously. And this would pay their way out of the country. However, the best-laid plans can change, and a chance encounter with an Opium grower and the seed is sown to create the drug cartel. What can they call this cartel? After several suggestions, the obvious one was to join their surnames, so Rains and Niam became Ramina. They liked it because it sounded Mexican to them; this might make authorities search in different directions, any misdirect always helpful. Over the next two to three years, their anger knowing no boundaries, their business strategy was to create the most feared cartel in the world, to control by fear and be willing to kill anybody without rhyme or reason not to get caught. As the business gradually grew, so did the tentacles spreading across countries rich and poor nobody will be missed. They even had a fuel farm built, and this was connected to a floating fuel buoy half a kilometre from the shoreline offshore.

It was one of their many business successes; this would fuel up a floating fuel ship. And this would travel further out to sea to fuel another large cargo tanker. This tanker was purpose-built in Korea, fast-tracked like a modular building system. It was completed under twelve months; cash payment every fortnight certainly motivates the supplier. Such was the cash flow of the business, never-ending their product constantly wanted by the idiots of the world, the rich and famous bragging all helps to sell it. While these idiots buy their products, there is no reason to stop; they get profoundly rich while their products addict and kill the end user. Healthcare is under pressure looking after what remains, crime is rife, families destroyed for that next fix, no food in the cupboard, but they rob someone for that fix. The rich have the funds to rehabilitate in private hospitals; the poor join the constant spiral of despair, never seeming to care for the souls destroyed by man's greed. Any other business would be closed immediately, strange how the money wheel perpetuates these things, all pockets lined someone else's problem to solve, but nobody does. So significant is the money they dared to name the fuel ship KoKane and the supply ship Aeroin, a play on words that few people seem to look for, throwing more dirt in the face of the public and police. At the centre of the ship, Aeroin is a moon pool, an open area to the sea, so small submarines could pick up a limited amount of heroin, not too many kilos, to cause problems undoubtedly proficient for the supply of small quantities to townships along the coastline. As you move around the ship, the bare product is loaded into the rear storage areas, then stripped, ready for the process. There are three different areas, all different in use. In the process, it is clinically clean well ventilated. Everyone who works in these areas is fully suited with pressurised suits with hoods over their faces. Once through the process, it is vacuum packed and barcoded with a full delivery address; the system's efficiency is unbelievable, finely tuned over the years with minimum contact with anyone.

The product is placed on an automated conveyor system, covering three levels; the barcode knows which cage to deliver.
Then hydraulic rods push the product into a cage until a delivery request, and once a request is in place, rods from the opposite side push the product back onto the conveyor. The system then takes it to a lift, rods push it into the lift, and the lift takes it up or down, depending on whether it is a submarine or a helicopter delivery. This system alone has increased their efficiency by 30%, recuperating their break-even costs in just four months, currently having another tanker being built again in Korea. This tanker will then feed death and addiction to another part of the world.

Chapter 42

Mark is reflecting on his past, no real regrets, you are what you are in his mind and the old excuse that somebody has to do it; if not him, there would be someone else. The bodies were removed from the garage within one hour of his call to Guy. And a blacked-out van drove right up to the garage. A large board is placed across the gap from the van to the garage, so a prying neighbour could not see, the bodies swiftly removed and the van gone all in five minutes. He is contemplating if he should take out his local drug den, then the final chapter, he will let Jimmy die slowly in his misery, a vengeful end after ordering the demise of his friend Ethan Holton.

After talking to Guy, he finds out that Lydia(Susan) was separated from Mr Bennett. He does not know if she would have attempted to kill him as their relationship seemed to be heading towards better things. He had fallen into that male trap, where sex overtakes your commonsense and reasoning. Julia had used it so many times he should have seen the signs, and this was a masterstroke from the cartel, the long term planning to achieve the end goal; he was in awe of their resourcefulness. Being caught is possibly why he is still alive today. Safe in prison, unaware that a large cartel was chasing him. Thankful for small mercies, maybe he should thank Leyland and his colleague James. Not that he will see them; again.? Mark finishes his cup of tea, steps outside in the glorious sunshine. The temperature is around 29 degrees, a slight cooling breeze, nice day to do some work. He starts the old faithful basic car and heads to an area well known for drugs in Manchester. As he arrives, still amazed that there is no police presence in an area renowned for drug use, it seems that no one cares; he has already spotted a potential informant. Driving up to him, having already changed the number plates. Just in case someone sees him getting out of the car with money in his hand. And looking as though he was about to buy some of his wares for sale.

A quick talk and he has found out that the boss had done a runner with Jimmy Lees money that morning. Finally, he thought it was starting to get through to some people, not realising it was just a frightened man trying to protect his family. His work-life balance had finally reached an imbalance he could not ignore. Vince Smalls and his family were just boarding a flight for Canada, lucky that a relative lived there and for the right amount of money, they could stay in their log cabin indefinitely. The young man speaking to Mark told him where the house was with the drugs, maybe the threat that he would be dead in a few minutes if not offering the information he required. The young man had heard the rumours about the people killed in other parts of the UK and did not want to be a statistic like them. He was gleeful in giving Mark all that he required, and it must have been the sunshine and the pleasantness of the day that Mark allowed him to walk away. Getting back into the basic car, Mark wonders if he has made a mistake, he has never let anyone go before, is it old age, or is he starting to mellow. Looking in his rearview mirror, Mark can see the young man's pace is getting faster; Mark turns the car around the young man is running now. Mark brings the car up beside the individual and shouts; the man turns a single shot to the head, he falls to the floor, no need to stop and check if he is alive, Marks victims are never alive, he drives to the house where the drugs are. The occupants will not expect a daytime visit; all the others have been in darkness, they will be in disarray with their boss Vince doing a runner. Pulling up outside the street house, just a small terrace of six houses, it

seems like they may have taken over on first impressions. His senses are generally correct; he has had to live by them for so long. On entering, he asks to speak to Vince; the men assume it is business, not querying why a man would come in on a day like this with an overcoat on. They are sweating and are in short sleeve shirts.
One turns to tell him he has left the business, leaving them to answer to Jimmy.

Mark asks if anyone else is available, a simple 'no' was the answer, three quick shots all is quiet, he carries on looking in all the rooms, picking up dropped cash, finding the drugs and once again a roaring fire ensues, Mark drives away contented.
Yet again, there are more troubled families. Who has lost their husband or boyfriend for being in the wrong place at the wrong time? Due to the evils of supplying drugs. These are not the only families, the users who can't get their drugs; with the climbdown coming off the drug, it affects all around them, but the suppliers don't care. Where there is demand, their profit increases, the user will not try and barter the price, they need the drugs, and they will pay what is required for those few hours of contented oblivion. While Mark is driving home, Jimmy is constantly ringing Vince Smalls mobile number, frustrated that there is no answer. It has been left on the table at Vince's house, no one to hear it ring. Vince had given the house to his sister, mortgage-free. She will move in as soon as her house is sold. For the first time in her life, she will be cash-rich; she will never see her brother again.
Jimmy storms out of his office and bellows to Paul, 'can you get Ricky to Manchester? Vince is not answering his phone; something is wrong.' It is a long two-hour drive to the designated street where Vince should be. As Ricky approaches, traffic is building up, and he can

hear the sound of sirens not far away. Ricky decides it would be better to park up and walk to Harford Street, a small terrace of six houses. The crowd is quite large as he is getting nearer. He stops to talk to an old gentleman asking, 'What is happening, why the crowd,' to be told,

'That one side of Harford Street is fully ablaze.' Ricky then asks, 'this is a silly question; I have a friend who lives there. Is it odd or even number houses.'

The gentlemen looking at Ricky dumbfounded by the question, 'I do not know, but it is the left-hand side looking from here.'

It is not what he wanted to hear; he turns around to go to his vehicle, glad he is calling Paul and not Jimmy, the phone only rings once, and Paul answers, a few expletives later, he puts the phone down.

Jimmy storms out of his office; he has just checked his account no transfer had taken place the evening before, and overhearing Pauls conversation, he is coming to the point of no return, with his mental state. He can only assume that Vince is dead, not knowing the truth; it's probably the best.

Chapter 43

After recent events at Guy's hideaway, he makes a call to Leyland, knowing that Harry Graham lived in his neck of the woods, noticing the TS postcode on his home address for contact purposes. Requesting if he could call to his house with a search warrant, having to explain that one of his closest allies had been caught up on the wrong side of the line. Telling Leyland he had told his wife he died in the line of duty so as not to inflame the situation, ongoing enquiries deem a visit from the police to clarify a few things. Harry lived in Ingleby Barwick, one of the largest independent building sites in Great Britain; it had grown into a township, with several building companies erecting housing. Harry bought a plot of land and built his own six-bedroom house, and the neighbours enjoyed his company at local barbecues. He was talkative and had many stories to tell, without any indication of working for the government. Claire, his wife, was a party girl enjoying life to the full, no questions asked when he went away to work for weeks on end. Leyland calls James, 'do you want to come on a search and seek, for information tomorrow.'
James, 'what time in the morning, your car or mine.'
'Yours, you get fuel paid for now is 9.30 am ok.'
James is laughing, 'below the belt, sir.'
'Stop calling me, sir,' I have left, remember.
'Ok, boss.'
Leyland was amused at James's respect; it is only fifteen minutes from Leyland's house. A sizeable brick-built house, the front entrance has a large convex glass shape, with the double-width doors set within, in a high gloss finish. White tiles on the foyer floor, the staircase started in the centre and spread to left and right on the first landing, wood and glass balustrading either side of the stairs. They ring the doorbell; on

opening the door, Claire, still showing signs of tears being shed, both offer their condolences and ask to come in. As they step into the foyer, Claire requests they remove their shoes.

Both oblige instantly, feeling the heat from the heated floor on their feet. James shows his badge to Claire, then expertly passes the conversation to Leyland, who takes it up as though they are a team, both look at each other knowingly. Then Claire's eldest daughter Alison walks in with coffee and biscuits. Claire informs them that no one in the household drinks tea, so they must apologise if they do not like coffee. So that over with, 'how can I help you? I assume it was something Harry was working on.'
Leyland nods, 'yes, unfortunately, it was sensitive, and I am sorry we can not tell you more.'
'What do you need from me? I assume that is a search warrant in your hand, DC James.'
'Yes, Mrs Graham,' always respectful.
'Where do you need to be.'
'Did he have a home office at all?'
'Yes, just down the hallway to the left, that was his room; no one was allowed in.'
James, 'Just before we look, Mrs Graham, did Harry ever give you anything, just in case of emergencies just like this, I am sorry to be blunt, but time is of the essence.'
Leyland, 'it was Sir Guy Long who has asked, to come here, do you need to verify with him.' Claire sensing their sincerity, opens up, telling them I hid a small book in the garage, come with me please.' After an eternity of searching, Claire offers the book to Leyland. Looking through it, he can see certain coded pages, on others various names. While they were in the garage, two high-performance motorbikes had pulled up outside, two people came up to Leyland and James,

with guns pointing at them, offering to relieve them of the book, Claire faints it is all too much. One man demanding the book, the other, 'just kill the bastards, will you.' Then two thuds, both men shot in the knees, their guns scrape along the drive as they clench their knee, then a voice from the past, 'Hi Leyland, James, our boss sent me, it is okay to close your mouths now.' Leyland, at this stage, is shouting for Alison to comfort her mother.

James is placing cuffs on the two assailants, a call to the station ten minutes later, the sirens heading through Ingleby Barwick, normally a quiet little town. An irate Leyland is on the phone to Guy, in disbelief of the current situation, not wanting to believe that Paul Reed, alias Mark Andrews is free again. Whilst he is thankful Mark saved their lives, he cannot comprehend why he is standing in front of them and not in prison. However, whilst the heated argument rages on, James, who has never been faced with the possibility of being killed before, is now forever grateful for Mark's intervention.

Leyland has just come off the phone, and everything explained he has calmed down; he thanks Mark and tells him to go before the van comes for their new guests; the fewer people who know, the better. Mark agrees and casually walks away; around the corner, the basic car is waiting; Mark's sense of humour thinking if only it had a tail, maybe he might get a dog. Just as he gets into the car, two police vans pass, followed by a forensics team; the two men are taken to different hospitals,

tapes are placed across the driveway. During the conversation with Guy, he was told about the tracker and must also check for the other item. Remove that first before the tracker and do so within six hours. Leyland, even with all his years of experience, is astounded by the ingenuity of this cartel. Guy explaining that they will get to them while the trackers are in place, like DS Meads. He now realises their mantra of 'dead people do not talk' is all too effective. They must break this cycle and soon. Leyland and James again knock on the front door; Alison invites them in and takes them to see Claire. Both offer apologies for what has happened, stating they did not realise until now how critical Harry's role was in their investigation.

Claire is now shaking, crying, asking, 'will they be back.'

Leyland being honest, said, 'I do not know is there anywhere you can go to stay,'

'We have a cottage, and Harry only bought it about a year ago.'

'Is it far away.'

'It is between Leeds and Manchester.'

'From now on, Claire, we are your only contact in the police for security reasons and your safety.'

'Is it that bad?'

Leyland, 'I'm afraid so, or Harry died in vain.'

Alison enters the room with yet more tissue's;

suddenly, James jumps up, saying, 'sorry if I am wrong,' then tackling Alison to the floor. Leyland is shocked at what James has done, Claire screaming, 'thank you, oh thank you,' Leyland looks to Claire, 'she is not my daughter, she is tied up in her bedroom.'

Leyland, 'how did you know.'

Since DS Meads death, I have been paranoid about necks, and I noticed that small telltale scar on her neck.'

'Well done, I trained a good detective then,' James, with a wry smile, looks at Leyland and nods. Clarie runs upstairs to free her daughter; when they come down, both shaking, Alison puts her arms around James and thanks to him, she is safe now due to James quick thinking. Claire continues to tell Leyland that the

woman on the floor came yesterday evening asking for the book you have, 'I told her I never knew what Harry was involved in, he never talked about work, it was too secretive, which he never did,'
Leyland, 'how did you manage to convince her to keep you alive.'
'I did not; she gave me twenty-four hours to find out where it was.'
'Lucky you, then we arrive, and all hell breaks loose.'
'I think she was waiting for you to leave, and we would have been killed.'
James, 'the neighbours will be talking, so when the van takes our new inmate away, we will leave you in peace.' Just as he finishes his statement, the van arrives. The woman is now creating a fuss until Leyland has a word in her ear, then complete silence, as she is handcuffed and led away to the waiting van. Once outside and the van has left, James turns to Leyland, 'what did you say to shut her up,' only that she will die if we do not remove the tracker.
As her colleagues have installed a failsafe device, at least four of her colleagues have been killed that way recently. Leyland informs James that he will need to bring his computer to his house, as all avenues of trust are now limited to them both. Leyland has never seen such control from a criminal organisation like this. Somehow the leak must have been from Guy's team. He must speak to him, up close and personal, a coded message via text to Guy, to indicate his concerns, they arrange to meet at the same layby near Coventry, and he must be by himself. The meeting is set for 11 am the next day, coordinates are given, Leyland has told Guy he will bring DC James with him, and for once in his life, he will carry a gun he and James are both firearms trained both concerned about the situation. The next day, both cars reach the layby simultaneously, Leyland waving for Guy to come to their car; even Guy

was surprised by the cloak and dagger aspect of Leyland's behaviour. Leyland hands over a note to Guy, he reads it, 'have you swept yourself and the car for trackers and microphones,' Guy with eyebrows raised, confirms, 'no.' He goes to the car and gets out a handheld sensor, and sweeps over his body and around the car. His level of concern has now reached a new high, under his coat collar a small microphone, a new generation one Guy has not seen one so small, under the rear bumper a tracker, now realising Guy has given their position away. He leaves his coat in the car and returns to Leyland and James, requesting they move to another location to talk, silence till they park up in nearby motorway services.
Leyland proceeds to bring Guy up to speed on what has happened locally and what James had seen. Leyland told him to focus on anyone near, and someone close is still passing information on. The only person near Guy now is David; you could see the devastation in Guy's eyes, clenching his fist, 'I will deal with him when I get back. He is the only one who could have put that microphone under my collar.' Leyland grabs his wrists, explaining, 'they do not know, we have found it, can you use it to our advantage.' Guy accepts Leylands argument, and they formulate a plan. Then Guy brings up the tracker problem, James, 'what is your insurance like Guy,'
'It is fully insured if that is what you mean,'
'Looks like a little accident is in order; I hope you do not mind.'
'What have you got in mind.'
'We bring the car back here to the motor services, find an unoffending bollard and reverse into it.'
Within thirty minutes, they return one damaged bollard and one badly damaged bumper that requires replacing. Report the incident to the motor services management, and Guy's insurance will pay for it, all

recorded on CCTV. Leyland and James are still in the layby, waiting for Guy's return. They go their separate ways to confirm their options, each having a coded warning system to help each other.

On the way back, they must pick up the female assassin and bring her to Guy's retreat till things get better. Although technically they can not charge her with a serious crime, she only tied up Claire's daughter. A good solicitor will have her walking free in twenty-four hours, so her transfer must happen quickly. Leyland is trapped between the blurred lines of his old police job and something they are not used to. Although he has always played by the rules, hence his reputation as a good solid copper, he does not want James being dragged into this mess.

Chapter 44

As Mark is driving away from the scene before he reaches the motorway, already knowing he is in Jimmy Lees area, Mark has decided it is now or never that he finally meets him. So he pulls over and makes a call to Jimmy, 'whoever it is, it had better be worth my time.'
'Hello Jimmy, it is the bearer of good news.'
'Who the hell are you, and what good news.'
'It was you who contacted me, Jimmy.'
'A lot has happened recently; who are you.'
'Your friendly remover of problems.'
'Unless it is excellent news, this conversation is over.'
'I have found out who killed your son.'
A short silence, 'give me his name; I will take over and beat him to death.'
'I thought you wanted me to do that.'
'Look the way the past few weeks have gone; I deserve to do it myself, give me the damn name.'
'How will I be reimbursed? I am in your area and could be with you in an hour or so. Have you got any cash?'
'Look, come to my house; I will text the postcode, and you will be paid.'
Unknown to Jimmy, twelve hours earlier, Mark had called to his warehouse of Petal Flowers and placed various explosive charges around the building. Always planning ahead, you must know your prey before killing them. Mark did not know that Jimmy was finally getting a delivery of his precious goods; this would be a bonus, seeing them destroyed. Now struggling with his mental health, Jimmy would usually have taken several precautions before inviting a stranger to his house. But knowing who he was and the voice was familiar, Jimmy was home alone. Unusually, part of his brutality was that someone had to witness his act of violence, deciding to stay to discuss matters with Mark. Normally he would have been with Paul and Ricky

organising the unloading of his valuable cargo, but recent events have made him cautious.
Never in his adult life has Jimmy ever been afraid, this is new to him, and for once, he knows how the people must have felt, not that he cared. Both Paul and Ricky had been with Jimmy for years and knew what to do, everything loaded into particular areas, to minimise anyone seeing them, out of sight, just like their boss told them, they were helped by six of their dealers to speed things up. When the final package was delivered, the small cruiser cast off and started to move up the river; it was two hundred metres away when the warehouse exploded. All eight people inside were engulfed in flames. The local press will report it as a tragic accident, but the police will only find minimum evidence of a possible drug warehouse; this information will not be given to the public domain. A few minutes before the explosion, Mark turns into Jimmy's driveway. As he looks to his right, he can see the raised mound in the centre of the immaculate lawn, not knowing it was the grave of Jimmy's son he had killed. Pulling up in front of Jimmy, his eyes are transfixed on the grave, and Mark introduces himself; Jimmy is still unaware he is there as if he is in a trance; Mark raises his voice, suddenly a reaction.
'Who are you, why are you here.'
'We spoke about one hour ago.'
Jimmy's mind is befuddled; so much as happened he is lost in his thoughts, all concentration is gone. Mark re-iterates that they spoke one hour ago, reality comes to the fore, 'oh yeh, come in.' Mark is disappointed how easy this kill is going to be after all have gone before him. Jimmy turns to go into the house, and for once in his life, he says, 'sorry' to Mark,
'I was lost in my thoughts staring at my sons grave,'
'Sorry to hear that,' then Jimmy feels the needle in his neck, only enough sedative for a few minutes, so Mark

can tie him to the dining table, which looks out to Ian's grave. Spreadeagled across the table, both arms and legs tied to each leg of the table, he wakes to scream at Mark all the obscenities he can think of; Mark sat on a chair opposite his head. Then, turning his head to see Mark, 'who the hell are you.'

'I am the man you set your son on, that did not work out too well, did it,' Jimmy rages at Mark, struggling to get out of the ropes that are tying him down. Mark calms him down, 'it is pointless struggling; you will not get free, an old special forces knot, tricks of the trade, my friend.'

'But why me, why my business.'

'I think the government have got sick of people like you ruining peoples lives with drugs and said enough is enough.'

'There are other people, why me.'

'You know in your chosen profession; you have enemies everywhere.'

'Surely, there must have been someone else.'

'Not really; you ordered the killing of my best friend.'

'Is that really what this is all about? Who the hell has caused my misery.

'Ethan Holton.'

'That was at least three years ago, and he turned me in years ago, the bastard.'

Well, in a strange way, he has got you again; if you had left him, I would not be here.'

'Get it over with; what are you going to do.'

'Keep quiet for just one minute; I have a call to make,' as the phone starts to ring, '1.2.3. that explosion you have just heard is your warehouse being destroyed.'

Jimmy wants the misery to stop, 'get it over with for crying out loud, get it over with.'

'Well, you will die a lot slower than the others,' Mark gets his knife and cuts Jimmy's wrists, Just enough for the blood to start to drip on the floor slowly. Mark slightly releases the ropes from the table's legs, just enough so he can put two cushions behind his back, then sits Jimmy up to look out the door at his son's grave, walking past him leaving the door open. The rate the blood is dripping, it will take hours for him to die; Mark knows not to let vengeance take over you. It is a job he must be professional, gets into his basic car and makes his way to an empty home, Mark along with Guy having a much more challenging task ahead of them.

Chapter 45

As Guy drives back home, he considers his options, and this cartel has got into every aspect of his life, controlling people he respected. They are clinically ruthless in everything they do. He is in dire need of an independent IT forensics person, as it looks like Harry and David have hidden some truths, which he must unearth and soon. Before leaving Leyland and James, they gave him a name of a person they used on occasions and found him to be the best at solving every issue they gave him. When Guy got home, he waved to Mary, then put his hand over her mouth. Mary's eyes widened, then he opened up the collar of his coat and showed her the microphone as he hung it up in the closet, then guided her to the panic room. Mary knew instantly to keep quiet till they reached the panic room; even inside the room, she whispered so quietly,

'What the hell, Guy, what is happening.' For the first time in their married life, he had to explain the seriousness of the situation. And she was astonished at the severity of it all. He further spelt out that she must stay at home and get her sister and husband to stay for her safety till everything is sorted out. Acutely aware that things must come to a head shortly, and hopefully, they can carry on back to everyday living. Mary makes a good old cup of tea. Guy calls the number Leyland gave him, 'hello, is that Clive Williams.' A friendly 'yes' came back the reply, and Guy proceeds to tell him certain parts of his investigation and could he help as an independent advisor, but would understand his reservations. To Guy's great surprise, he agreed that Clive was drinking coffee in Guy's panic room, with two computers by his side within twenty-four hours. Before Clive's arrival, Guy had called David to tell him to take two to three days off one hour earlier. So we all have some breathing space and gather our thoughts for the coming week. David accepted, not knowing he would soon be arrested. While Guy spoke to David, he suddenly remembered Harry's book in his coat in the closet.

Walking back to the panic room, looking through the book, he could see names from his past, and things started dropping into place. It takes only two hours for Clive to find malware checking Guy's computer, and this was only installed six weeks ago. He removes the virus unknown to him or Guy. Doing so will automatically set the failsafe timer off in David, and he will be dead in seventy-two hours. Clive is surprised at the level of sophistication, already realising a lot of money is involved in achieving it. He has given Guy more information in four hours than either Harry or David for what is now obvious reasons. A call to Mark is required, the phone rings twice, 'just a couple of minutes of your time, I can confirm that the three people you killed in Holland were part of this Ramina cartel,'
Mark. 'stop you there, Guy, I only killed two.'
'Who the hell killed number three.'
'Sorry to say, Guy, the obvious answer is the person who hired me.'
'Suppose so, not thinking straight, at the moment.'
'Anything else, my bolognese is starting to burn,' Mark says, laughing.
'Just one more thing.'
'Yes, that would be.'
'Do the names, 'Luca Rosso, Mia Rosso and police chief Brambilla, ring any bells.'
'Mia hired me to kill her husband.'
'Why are they all dead then.'
'We killed him; Mia refused to pay the full contract price.'

'Carry on.'
'She threatened to get more hitmen after us, so I took her and her lover out.'
'Well, you will be pleased to know that they were all high up in this Ramina cartel, no wonder they want you.'
'What can I say, Guy, just a man in demand.'
'Well, I still have not found out why they are after me as well.
'Where do we go from here, Guy.'

'I am hoping we can revert our two new female colleagues to help a new cause, seeing that their old employers were willing to kill them without their knowledge. Would you be ok with that?'
'No issue for me, Guy. life is a big incentive.'
'Okay, let us hope they are willing to help us.'
'Oh, by the way, my original task is complete. So are we ok to part company?'
I was hoping you could stay till the current situation is resolved.'
'Thought you would never ask, I am in till we get these bastards dead or alive if that is ok with you.'
'Would have liked them alive, to face their day in court, but with the amount of money they have, I do not believe it would happen, anyone trying to catch them will be taken a big risk, so the smaller the group, the better.'
'I think you could well be right; the smaller the information pool, the better.'
'I will contact you in a few days.'
'Okay, Guy, hoping you have some success.'
Putting the phone down, Guy is conscious that he has never dealt with a situation like this before, and he must take his military hat of and seek specialist help. But the more that knows, the worse it will get for

everyone. Another phone call and Leyland and James will be at his house in twenty-four hours, and this is now the main nucleus of his team.

Chapter 46

The next day Leyland has rung Guy and asked if they could postpone their visit till the following day. They have been requested to attend the suspicious death of Jimmy Lees, a known drug kingpin. Before they arrive deep down, they have an idea who may have killed him, as with all of Mark's previous killings, there will be no evidence, splitting hairs as to the rights and wrongs will test their moral code to the limit. It is far too coincidental that an explosion at his warehouse, all within twenty-four hours. Whilst the officers are processing through the house, they find a computer, James hoping that Jimmy did not have a fancy signing password. After three attempts, he is in with a simple JimLees password. It opens up on a page showing a large transaction, with the reference RC; he calls Leyland to look. Both look at each other. Could this be a possible real lead to the cartel, as the transaction is for two million pounds? Surely it must be; they will take it for Clive to look at when they get to Guy's house tomorrow. Before Mark arrived, Jimmy had just paid the cartel for the goods that had just been delivered the day before. Feeling happy that things were getting better, he went outside to get some fresh air, never to turn it off again. James tags the computer for evidence, telling forensics they require it urgently for a couple of days. Then his phone rings, a request to attend the site where the explosion happened. It takes thirty minutes to get to the site, and the typical journey would take about ten minutes, a backlog of traffic due to roads being closed off. On their arrival, they can see DI Short and DS Philpott; now aware of Philpott's affiliation to Jimmy, they must tread carefully about what they say and do. DI Short is oblivious to the situation regarding Philpott and will be for some time to come, and both are surprised to see Leyland with the obvious question as to why he is there. James interjects having to tell lies to avoid complications, saying he was consulting on another matter.

A half-truth rather than a complete lie seemed the better option to him. So James moves on with the conversation, 'do you believe this was Jimmy Lees drugs warehouse.'
Philpott is now relieved that Jimmy does not have a hold over him. Even though it was self-inflicted, he will destroy the backup file he had on Jimmy as there will be no need for them now. The biggest problem for him now is that Pillpott has got used to the financial inducement he was receiving from Jimmy on the twenty-eight day of each month. The lifestyle of his wife and himself has now come to an abrupt stop; what can he do now, strange the money you get, you uplift your lifestyle and never put it away for that rainy day, thinking it will never come.
DI Short jumps into the conversation, 'yes, but we found something else,' he proceeds to take them to the rear of the non-existent warehouse, to an area twenty metres away towards the riverside. Then he shows them the recent concrete works in the ground, some more discoloured than the others, with them being older.
Philpott held back and let Short carry on, 'looks like we could have four graves; one is as recent as a week or two.'
James, 'we had heard he was a nasty piece of work. Have you had any scans done yet?'
'As we speak, they have just arrived; we should know within the hour.'
While they are discussing things, Leyland excuses himself just got to make a call. He is ringing the Chief Superintendent to confirm that Philpott is still under

surveillance and someone is with him at all times at work; he confirms this and calls over James. As they are talking, a commotion, the people checking the newest assumed concrete grave have confirmed a body. They will check the rest, and all will be dug up, and another three bodies will be located. It will be several days before the identities come to light, one being the young man who stole Jimmy's car, and the other three were people who would not sell their houses to him,

Which have now been sold to Baxter Holdings; when Mr Baxter finds out about this, he donates the houses back to the original families as a goodwill gesture. James informs his colleagues that they have been called away to the job that Leyland is the consultant on and will be uncontactable for a few days. This statement, for some reason, makes Philpott's annoyed, 'that bloody James. always was the gaffers favourite.' Short, 'don,t take it; personally, it's just the way the job is, we never know what's going on.'
'I suppose so,' Philpott calms down, not knowing he is part of their investigation. Then, as Leyland walks away, James says to him, 'I will only be a minute,' giving a stupid excuse to Philpott, 'is that a cartridge next to your foot,' he turns, 'oh sorry, my mistake and returns to Leyland.
'I am getting paranoid; I just wanted to look at Philpott's neck, to see if there was a scar,' luckily, Philpott will not die soon. They both agree he was just the local contact for Jimmy, in-house to minimise suspicion on him and not involved with the bigger picture.

Chapter 47

Back at Guy's place, Mary has got to used to the northerner in Guy's special room. Bemused by that fact, he only eats fig biscuits and no other, and he dunks them in his tea. It must be a tradition up there, she thinks. She catches her foot under the loose rug as she brings in the umpteenth packet of fig biscuits. Falling forward, Guy catches her and she puts her hand on the corner of the coffee table for support. As she straightens her clothes, she asks Guy to help her with some urgent post. Looking at her, he knows something is wrong and follows her into the hallway.
'What's up, Mary? Are you feeling ill?'
'No, when I fell, I felt something under the table. Could Clive have put it there?'
'No, he has been fully vetted by Leyland; they have used him on many occasions.'
'I am worried Guy, what shall we do.'
'Did you call Daisy and Dominic to come?'
'No, I forgot too.'
'Right, ring them now, pack your bag and go to them directly.
'But guy, I cannot leave you here.'
'I,m a big boy Mary, no need to worry about me; I have some reinforcements coming tomorrow.'
He could see the worry in her eyes, but he pushed her upstairs, 'go quickly,' she rushes upstairs, her mind all over the place, she rings Daisy, 'I must come to you immediately, I will explain when I get to your place.'
Daisy 'what wine shall I get in? It must be urgent to be coming straight away.'
Mary is walking downstairs; Guy standing at the bottom, tells her he has ordered a taxi, 'we cannot use our cars just in case they have trackers on them,' she nods in acceptance, wondering how Guy can cope with all this. Mary gets into the taxi, and Guy talks to the

driver, requesting he take the long route and be aware if someone is following him, this is exciting to the driver, a bit of deception and extra money.

Before the taxi leaves, Guy kisses Mary goodbye and tells the driver to make a note of any car and registration. The driver informs him, 'I have cameras front and rear; I can come back if you want me to,'
'I would appreciate that, and a cash benefit will help to cover your time.'

The ecstatic driver drives away with a nervous-looking Mary who starts to tear up; the driver passes her a tissue, used to having some emotional women and the odd male in the back of his taxi. Walking back into his special room, Guy asks Clive, 'fancy a bit of fresh air,' Clive nods and follows him. Once outside, he explains what Mary thinks she may have felt. Clive explains that he should be able to backtrace it; it will only be short-range. It is bliss to Guy's ears; at last, they are making silly mistakes or could it be a trap, he may need the help of one Mark Andrews. A quick text to Mark via the new burner phone, they have had quite a few recently, but it is a small price to pay if this can keep their adversary away. The response was instant. He would be there in the morning. He will call into one of Guy's safe houses to pick up some essential tools that they may need. While he was texting Mark, he was trying to understand what could have turned David in the back of his mind. Harry could understand that being bisexual in this type of work was always prone to being used. With David, he thought was clean that he knew about, not realising it was pure greed, with an offer of untold wealth that he could dream of, he would have a tracker placed in his neck. Once again, they inadvertently forgot to tell him about the added extra, just under the shoulder blade; in many ways, Harry and David were working against each other as they both did not know they worked for the cartel.

Each hides different aspects of the case, which Clive is unravelling, now with surprising results. The only problem that Guy will have now, as they are not talking openly about the situation, could his listeners become more suspicious. They will need to create a false narrative for them to follow, long enough to resolve this case.

Whilst still outside, Guy checks if Mary has reached Daisy's house, she tells him that she is standing outside, and the driver is coming back to see him. The driver returns to see Guy, giving him the SD card; Guy asks him if he would like some coffee while he waits, accepting his offer with gratitude, 'black only please, we work long hours for our money.' Clive takes the card, and five minutes later, he requests Guy to check if he can see anything unusual, luckily all is well, and Guy knows Mary is safe. The driver is now fifty pounds richer, and he thanks Guy for his kind gesture; if ever you need a taxi again, please ask for Phil; he gets into his taxi and drives away with his tax-free cash. By the time Phil reaches the end of the long pebblestone drive, Phil likes the noisy drive. He can hear people coming and going, driving or walking. Clive calls him into the lounge area he has located where their listeners are, and it is only twenty miles away. The address is familiar to him, but he cannot remember where Guy asks Clive to search for the owners, surprised to find it is Charles Raven, more dots in the puzzle they must solve. Frustration on Guy,s face, Harry and David kept this from him; he must find out Raven's connection to this cartel. Never before has Guy seen such a powerful organisation. But why him? What has he done to warrant the release of such venom? It will be another hour before Guy will have an inkling of the names of the people who are his antagonists.

Chapter 48

After his conversation with Guy, Mark has decided to look on the dark web for possible clues; there are always avenues to find out specific information if you know where to look. Mark has used this system for his needs, which was another part of his life now long gone. Always amazed that this wonderful invention has become the byword for hate and criminality. To be used to ruin peoples lives by the stroke of a key. It will be another two hours before he gets into a website that deals in drugs, with a speciality designer drug called B16; this offers the end-user bliss for two to three days. Alleviating to tell them that it is more addictive and will destroy their bodies within twelve months, most salesmen never tell the truth, as long as the sale is completed. If they do not ask, they are innocent of deception, everyone wins, and the cartel gets richer and richer. The cartel's arrogance has grown, and for some reason, they have shown an area of land, stating our product is homegrown in our backyard, showing acres of land. On closer inspection of the photo, Mark can see something. Still, it is not clear to see, 'where is that bloody magnifying glass,' it takes another fifteen minutes and upturned drawers along with a lot of mess on the worktops finding the object of his desire. Hoping it was worth the effort, moving the computer screen to a better angle, he looks through the glass, 'eureka' even he was surprised he came out with that statement. He takes another long hard look; in the background, he could see the loading jetty and pipework, a possible landmark that Guy's man may be able to find, but it also indicates fueling for a boat. There is something else further out to sea a stronger magnifying glass is required, a quick run out to the DIY shop. Rushing back, he is on a high, and he may be getting somewhere to help Guy. Placing the glass over the screen, a smile starts to form at last yet another clue, and he can see the floating mooring buoy they are using a ship. In the morning, Mark gathers clothes and essentials for a week just in case. Setting the alarm, Mark has installed more cameras in the event somebody tries to get in, linked to his phone.

Chapter 49

On the way to his hideaway to talk to his prisoners, Guy wonders how he can stop Mark and Leyland from coming to blows, their past does not bode well, and he hopes this does not interfere with things. They, along with James, must bury the hatchet for the good of the investigation and work together. He knows deep down that Leyland will try to get him back behind bars, but a promise is a promise in Guy's eyes. It is 6.30 am when Guy drives up to his hideaway. Both women have been prepped for the interview, and he decides to talk to the unknown assailant first. He enters the room, she has not given her name, informing her his name is Guy, at this, she indicates that she has heard of him and replies, 'Trish' then Guy places the two vials on the table, and he shows her the one with poison in it.
'Your employers regarded you as expendable; did you know about it.'
'No,' with an air of surprise
'Well, as soon as this tracker is removed, the other vial would have killed you in seventy-two hours; we can show you several bodies down the hall to give you proof if required.'
Trish stays silent, not wanting to believe they were willing to kill her to keep her quiet, 'no, they would not; I have been loyal for three years.'
'Say that to the bodies downstairs, Trish.'
Guy grabs her by the arm, dragging her to see Harry and the two assailants, gasping other than Harry she knew them they had joined the cartel simultaneously. Before the cartel changed their policy, nobody could give anybody up if they did not know them. So all had anonymity nobody knew who they were and the guarantee of the poison; it was a win-win for them. He takes her back to the room; sitting her down, he explains that he will guarantee free passage anywhere

and a new identity if she offers enough information. Silence as she stares into space then looks at Guy, 'but they are everywhere, you cannot stop them.'
'They have indoctrinated you to think that way.'
'I am confused; I don,t know what to do.'
'Bluntly Trish, help us or die, your choice.'
He could see the torment in her eyes, but if you chose this line of work, your consequence is a life or death situation. Walking out of the room, he tells her, 'you have thirty minutes to choose, or you go to the nearest police station, let us see how long you will live then.'
Leaving her to ponder her future, Guy goes into the next room to a waiting Lydia (Susan), showing her the vials that could have ended her life. He has not told them they were injected with the same nano tracker as Mark; if they both decide to help, Guy will know where they are.
'Well, Lydia, you have had some time think I am going to give you a one time offer, help us, and we help you start a new life anywhere, and you will be free.'
'How do you want me to help.'
'Help us finish this cartel, and your problems will be gone.'
'You make a compelling case.'
'It is a win-win for you.'
'On one condition.'
'That would be.'
'I must talk to Mark.'
'Will tomorrow be okay.'
'Thank you.'
He returns next door to speak to Trish, 'decision time, what have you decided.'
'Prison, I will be safer; no one can get me there.'
'You were warned, last chance to change your mind.'
'Prison damn it.'
'As you know, they have eyes and ears everywhere; I cannot and will not guarantee your safety.'

'I will take my chances.'

'Okay, I will organise your transfer.'

Within one hour, Trish was transferred to the local police station and charged with attempted murder, placed in a secure jail, she asked for a solicitor. Another restless night and Trish is on her way to the nearest high-security prison.

Whilst on the way to the prison, they will need to pass through a small industrial park, this route designated by the chief superintendent. Along the longest road, four vehicles surround the van shooting the tyres and a well-placed shot into the windscreen. An officer falls forward, loud shouting to release the prisoner. The back doors open, the prisoner is thrown to the floor, and an officer is instantly shot. One of the men shouts for Trish to come to one of the cars. Trish gets into the back of one car, and it speeds away into the distance; as it turns the corner, everyone is shaking hands, and the two officers come back to life; job well done.

Chapter 50

As soon as Guy left the room the day before, he organised the abduction of Trish to open her up to her imaginary cartel captors, hoping to get another clue to move forward. On the way back home, he is wondering how long this will go on for. Suddenly, he hears the sound of pebbles under the car; he had driven home in a trance, not realising how he got home. This simple event will drive him on to solve this vendetta against him. That one word has opened up yet another thought in his head. Just as he is about to enter the house, that noisy sound of pebbles under wheels again, it is Leyland and James. They shake hands and go through to the lounge, that smell of fresh coffee in the air. Clive enters the room with the obligatory fig biscuits smiling, ' Hi Leyland, James, long time no see,' they shake hands, both also grabbing the fig biscuits. 'Must be a bit of a delicacy way up north,' with a slight note of sarcasm Leyland and James looking at each, thinking we have touched a nerve here, not realising Clive has had six packets in the past two days along with an entire jar of coffee, no wonder he cannot sleep. Leyland remarks on Guy's home, saying how beautiful it was and big, so big he felt he could get lost in it, also pointing out the memorabilia from around the world on his past- adventures he assumed. James handed over Jimmy Lees computer for him to look through; he decides to peruse it while they wait for someone else, he tells Leyland.'

'Yes, we are waiting for your saviour Leyland, I know you do not approve, but he might be one of the few men who can end this nightmare we are in.'

Leyland looks at James, 'I am sorry to say I think he is right,' James agrees wholeheartedly. While Mark is just about to enter the driveway, his ears start to burn, 'someone must be talking about me; I hope it is good,' he thinks. Impressed by the magnificent Edwardian house set in its surrounding grounds, immaculately manicured lawns, trees trimmed to perfection, expecting to see an old horse and carriage on the driveway.

It was picture perfect, and thinking he would have loved the more sedate life of that period. Even the bell push was a bell pull, and when he pulled it, the gentle sound of a time lost in history he loved it; the door opens, and Guy welcomes him in. He introduces him to Clive and knowing looks towards Leyland and James, 'they have met before,' Guy explains to Clive, who is curious but has learnt in life, they will tell you when you need to know. They move into the dining room, Mark once again drifting to a time gone by, the polished wood panelling up to the full door height, the high ceilings this one was in a vaulted shape, solid oak floors and seating for at least thirty people, the elegance of it all he thought. Guy breaks his concentration, who tells them of the microphone in his special room, and they must talk quietly. He explains the situation about his two female prisoners, and he hopes to speak with David the next day. Also, one of his old contacts should be home in two days, who might have some answers. James proceeds to update them regarding the demise of Jimmy Lees, and police are looking at all avenues. Both James and Leyland look at Mark, who puts his hands up in the form of denial, indicating the possibility of a copycat killer. James carries on regarding Jimmy's computer, and they feel sure that a payment was made recently to the cartel. Clive chips in, 'I think you are correct, looking back there were regular payments for years, then recently hiccups missed payments, some of the e-mails become aggressive between both parties.' Mark pretends to whistle and looks towards Guy, both fully aware of why this has happened. James pipes up, 'did the name Philpott come up? Possible payment as well,' he turns to Leyland for approval, still learning it seems. Clive punches some keys, and if by magic, every payment made to Philpott in the past three years, James looks to Leyland, seeing the disappointment in his face. Leyland did not know that Philpott volunteered his services freely; this would have been harder to take. All four men turn to Mark, looking for his input, then pulling the rabbit out bag. He tells them about the website, giving Clive more ammunition to hunt this cartel down.

Carrying on, he notifies them how they are blatantly advertising their new drug B16. Leyland and James had previous experience with this, knowing how violent it turned Ethan Holton while coming off the drug. Leyland is not prone to violent retribution, but the world is getting worse, which could make it ten times worse. 'We must do something; they are destroying our society as we know it, for blood money,' James nods his approval, Guy agrees and Mark smiles some more work to do. Mark carries on, 'they have shown their plantation on the front screen, I am sure with the consent, of course, that Clive could tap into an eye in the sky and find it. Clive looks to Mark, appreciative that he has already noticed how good he is. He then tells them you can see a pipeline in the distance, going to a jetty, 'I think this could be a fuel line.' Clive has brought up the image and connected it to the TV for all to see. With the bigger version, everything becomes clearer; he has various tools on his computer and expands the image using pixelisation software to enhance what they can see. They can now see the mooring buoy in the distance and the front end of a ship being loaded and a name just visible, that name being Kokane, Guy speaks first, 'the arrogant bastards, they have just changed the spelling of cocaine, they are laughing in our faces.' Leyland is surprised that his old boss is swearing but can see why '. Right then, we must stop this and soon. 'Leyland looks to Clive, 'it looks like your services are uppermost now; is there any way you can find out about that ship and if they have any others.' Clive buries his head into his computer; within a couple of minutes, he writes down information into his notebook. The rest of them put their heads together about tackling the situation when Guy mentions the microphone again and that Clive has pinpointed it to a particular house twenty miles away. Informing them all that this name came up at the beginning along with his business partner. Both being high-level politicians and businessmen, 'it looks like my former colleagues hid them under the carpet, so to speak,' the frustration in his voice could be heard.

Then Guy points out, 'we must get into his house hoping he does not destroy any information on his computer.' Clive asks for their names again, forgetting he already made a note of Charles Raven. Turning to him, he repeats, 'Charles Raven and John Hurst, they are also are current directors in Ravenhurst Holdings.' A few strokes of Clive's computer keypad and he turns to all telling them, 'they have a swiss bank account each and bank accounts in the UK, salary's paid into the UK only and looking at their financials, normal spending no indication where their swiss money is coming from.' Clive carries on he is on a roll as they say in proper circles, 'the ship we saw was built in Korea another was built at the same time, you will not like the name of the other one either Guy. It is Aeroin, both ships built to a different specification.' Leyland interjects, 'can you find out what type of ships they are? It could help us, I hope.'

'Ahead of you, Leyland, one was built to supply fuel, and the other was called a processing ship, never heard of that before.'

Mark, 'If it were me, where would you process your drugs, so no one could see, but look normal,' the others looking slightly perplexed he carries on, a drug processing ship constantly on the move, getting refuelled by another bringing the raw product to you to process.' The look on their faces was priceless to Mark, always being the villain and now the hero something new to him, he liked it. While Mark is wallowing in his small victory, Clive butts in with a decerning tone, 'eh guys, they are getting another built; it will be ready in about four to six weeks.'

At this, you could see Guy's anger rising; Leyland jumps in, 'fresh coffee anyone, Clive can you show me the kitchen please.' Bringing the situation back to normal, Guy shouts to Leyland a simple, 'thank you,' all is calm now they carry on talking, and Guy gets his head into gear 'let us get back to things at hand. We have the battle to win, plans and strategy to make,' his old brigadier hat back on. Clive is having a great day on his computer. He has looked at the family tree of Raven and Hurst, and they have a connection with two names that Guy had given him earlier in the day; this is an essential clue that will bring things to light for Guy. With this connection, it finally dawns on Guy, which starts to bring things into perspective and the realisation that something catastrophic must have happened nine years ago for these two men to create such an evil organisation.

As Guy's face looks ashen, the other men realise he is now aware of who is behind it all; Guy slowly sits down, 'can someone open the bottle of whiskey on the dining table, please.' One quick swig, James thinking that could not have touched the sides, 'another one please,' again knocked back like a true army man.

After what seemed an eternity to the rest of Guy's small team, he begins to tell them who he thinks their adversaries are.

'Around nine years ago, I headed an international team of intelligence gatherers; we were extremely successful and managed to stop many things, such as bomb threats home and abroad. But, as part of that, it was also to find out where the money trail was coming and going to in Afghanistan, the two men I think are involved disappeared, we searched for them for two years and finally gave up, nobody had heard or seen them. Leyland asks him why he thinks it could be them, and Guy replies, 'the information Clive has just given me. It indicates a family connection to Raven and Hurst; they are cousins, and the meteoric rise up the ladder can only be done with some extreme money, such as a drug cartel.'

It is too coincidental, and there are too many factors pointing their way. Leyland concurs the old police adage there is no such thing as coincidence; in the criminality scene

Clive breaks into the conversation, 'while you are talking about them, Revenhurst Holdings have just bought a lot of properties in Newcastle three days ago,'

Guy, 'good grief, what is their strategy.'

Leyland, 'got to be large scale money laundering, by the look of it, hard to imagine how much money this cartel has.'

Guy stuns them all, even more, when he tells him about an additional purchase of an area in Glasgow, looking slyly sidewards towards Mark. It is another area in which Mark intervened to clean up the place.

At this point Guy, turns to Clive, 'Can you just check if they have put any offers in for properties in Manchester and Leeds.' Then, two minutes later, the

others wondered what was going through his mind and a surprised Clive, 'how did you know Guy.'
'From what I can see, they will try to purchase properties in Middlesbrough next; they are all areas that Jimmy Lees drug empire was involved in.'
Leyland, 'it does not make any sense, destroying the buyer of your drugs and stopping the money flow, it is crazy.' Mark, listening calmly, says, 'can I put a suggestion forward for you all to consider.' All turn to him regarding him as the labourer to the engineers, a slight snigger from Clive; Mark making a note for future reference.
Guy, 'any suggestions as to what this might be about would be appreciated.'
He carries on, 'I think the drug gangs have been unfortunate sacrificial lambs in the bigger picture.'
Leyland was surprised by this statement, 'but to what end, it does not add up to me.'
'So they can buy the areas up and start to control within. They will be buying the properties so cheap, they then move their people in and begin to take over the town, flooding them with drugs, then society goes to hell.'
James, 'what type of people are they? Life means nothing to them.'
Guy interjects, 'if this is their strategy, it is long term, so they must be passing on the baton, good grief this could be catastrophic, we must stop this.'
Leyland, 'is there anyone you know that can help.'
'I will make a few calls, and I will not be here tomorrow if Mark's scenario is correct; we have got to act fast, we need information quickly any suggestions.'
Clive, 'what are we going to do about our eavesdropper.
Guy, 'I have an idea, leave that to me, if it works, we will have some information in two days.' The rest of them look at each other.

Clive, 'anyone for a fig biscuit.'

Chapter 51

The following day, Guy is up and out before breakfast; rather than making breakfast for four men, he has arranged an urgent meeting with the head of MI6 and the PM. Also, requesting the appointment is behind locked doors. He left early to avoid the constant traffic jams trying to get to the centre of London, and he regarded this worst than any assignments he has been on in his many years of service for his country.

At 11 am Guy is shown into a room he has never been to, with two guards outside, a sign of how important Guy had emphasised this meeting. As the door opens, both men are seated, formal shaking of the hands and Guy gets straight down to business. He explains the severity of the situation, and the cartel has many people in high positions worldwide. Guy decides not to tell them about the trackers in their necks; it is the only way at this moment in time that they can tell who works for them. He dare not contact Interpol now because of the possibility of yet more undercover cartel people apologising for his paranoia; that is how bad it is.

MI6 involvement will certainly help; if only they could keep it secret long enough to tackle the cartel. It means Guy could then minimise contacts with local police forces; this in its self will open a can of worms. However, he and his team are now aware of the extent that the cartel has infiltrated most areas of the police network. He now realises they are mainly a standalone team against this cartel; this could be an advantage in so many ways.

Just as he reaches his vehicle, a text comes through on his phone, 'do we need to meet, regards Ron Walton,' a sigh of relief, hoping that Ron might be able to help. He suggests a meeting in one hour at your house Ron, telling him he will come by taxi, his paranoia coming to the fore. He walks around for ten minutes, stops a taxi, travels towards Ron's; Guy stops the taxi twenty minutes into the journey. He gets out and walks for another ten minutes and does the same until he comes to the village where Ron lives.

Looking around to see if anything suspiciously stands out, then he starts to walk to Ron's house; Guy has never had this feeling of dread before; a call to Mary might help. Finishing his conversation with Mary has brought him back down to earth; she always was levelheaded. Knocking on the door, Ron opens the door with the biggest smile; they have not seen each other in some years, Ron under the impression he had retired. As soon as Guy gets through the door, he asks Ron if he can look at his neck; Ron is perplexed, he agrees; he has never seen this man worried in all the time he has known him.

Ron, 'what is going on Guy, I have never seen you like this before.'

Guy whispering, 'Can we talk outside.'

Stunned by this request, Ron abides by his wishes, 'what's up, Guy.'

'Please, it is important.'

'What the f---k is going on.'

'Please, I need to do this; all will become clear shortly.'

'Okay, Guy, can you carry on?'

'How long have you been away.'

'Four weeks, Guy, why.'

'Can I ask you a question first before we proceed'

'Of course, no secrets between us, Guy.'

'Do you remember the names John Rains and Carl Niam?'

'Strange, we spent two years looking for them with no success and a request from on high to carry on looking for them three months ago; that is a bit spooky, Guy.'

'Who instigated the search, Ron.'

'It is top secret, Guy, even I cannot tell you.'

'Let me guess; you were requested to attend a meeting behind closed doors by two politicians and only to report to them.'
'Good grief, Guy, how do you know.'
'I am hoping you have not reported your findings yet.'
'I only got back late last night, and I am going to speak with them tomorrow.'
'Where is your phone, Ron.'
'In the dining room, why.'
Guy asks him to speak quietly, get your phone, but please do not talk anymore for one minute.'
Ron brings his phone back, giving it to Guy, who removes the back and shows him the listening device; Ron's face goes white, not wanting to believe what he has just seen. He takes it to his garage and puts it on his workbench for future attention. Coming back, he asks Guy, 'what is going on.'
'Manipulation Ron, manipulation I am sorry to tell you.'
An angry and frustrated Ron decides to make a calming pot of tea; Guy is now sitting at the patio table outside along with the tray of cakes and tea. Ron was shaking with anger as he poured out the tea.'
'I suspect your home may have been bugged while you have been away, is there anywhere you can stay? It is for your safety as well.'
'What the f—k is going on, Guy.'
'Do you know who you met when you were given these instructions?'
'Yes, I do.'
'Carry on.' Guy hoping it is the names he is thinking of and if it is, a rare mistake indeed.'
'Charles Raven and John Hurst,'
'I knew it, and now it is starting to add up.'
'My next question could be vital to our survival.'
'Go on, then hit me with it.'
'Did you find Rains and Niam?'
'Well, for two dead people, they are very much alive.'

'I knew it; where are they.'

'They move every three months; they have several houses all over the place, where they have got their money from baffles me.'

'With that information, your life is definitely in danger.'

'What do you mean, Guy.'

'Well, I believe they are the main bosses of the most ruthless cartel I have ever known.'

'No, not, John and Carl.'

'It is starting to look that way, Ron.'

'We are being used for their ends, Ron.'

'What do you suggest, then.'

'We are lucky that you texted me, so hopefully, they do not know we have made contact.'

'If you can go to that meeting and tell them you are at a loss and think that they must have died nine years ago, you can find no trace of them. I believe they have used you because they know you are the best at your skillset; if you cannot find them, nobody can.'

'Okay, Guy, can you give me some background as to what you think it is about, please.'

After several cups of tea and digestive's no fig biscuits in this house, Guy runs through everything that has happened in the last few weeks. Ron is grateful for the update; he is savvy enough to carry this ruse through to convince Raven and Hurst that it is a lost cause. As they are talking, Guy reminds him to scrub any information on his computer; Ron suggests to Guy that it might be best to take it with him, just in case something happens. Telling him, 'you know we are always on a knife-edge in our chosen profession, always looking over our shoulder. He goes into the house, bringing out the computer giving Guy the password just in case. They shake hands, both wishing each other well and Guy leaves, taking the same precautions on his way back to his car, arriving home later that day. Ron arrived in London for his scheduled appointment the following day; he was shown into the usual meeting room. The meeting only lasted thirty minutes; both men seemed happy that he had not found anything that would indicate that Rains and Niam were alive. Ron leaves the building, glad he has given them false information, hoping Guy can finish his task. Crossing the road to get to his car, another vehicle speeds up; having been watching him, Ron sees him and tries to jump out of the way. Unfortunately, Ron is hit, and the driver speeds away, not waiting to see if he is alive; three to four people rush to assist him, hoping he is not dead. He staggers as he gets up, thanking them for their concerns, gets into his car and texts Guy for his address; he needs help immediately.

Ron is guided to a layby four miles from his house; he parks up; two minutes later, Guy arrives with a colleague; they get out of the car and walk over to Ron.

Mark walks around the car with an electronic sensor and finds the obligatory tracker under the rear bumper, and Guy puts his finger to his lips, indicating for Ron to stay silent, opens the door and takes his coat. Then he shows Ron the hidden microphone under the collar of his jacket; Ron's jaw drops, still wanting to scream with the pain in his legs. Ron can hardly move now, now so glad that he had an automatic car rather than a manual, so Mark and Guy assist him to their vehicle, asking him to lay down in the boot, get his breathe back and tell them what happened. While he is talking, Guy contacts the medical staff at the local hospital, and he has used their much-needed facilities before recently. He informs Ron medical staff are in place to look after him. While they were talking, Mark had got out of the car and taken a petrol can from the vehicle, and he was now dousing Ron's car with petrol. Mark explains the need to set it alight; they need to think

Ron is dead, they agree. Mark returns to the car, and within seconds the car is engulfed, flames in the air, as they leave the layby and go to the hospital.

Four hours later, Ron is now resting in a hospital bed, and he is fortunate indeed to only have a broken left arm due to his lousy landing and severe bruising down his torso. Although there are guards outside his room in another three days, he will assist the rest of the team, and local newspapers will report the sad passing of Ron Walton, who passed away the victim of a hit and run; he was a pillar of the community.

Chapter 52

While Ron recuperates, the rest of the team have decided that Guy must talk to Trish. But, unfortunately, she has declined their offer of help, having been rescued by the cartel.? So, for two days, Trish was located in a windowless room, echos of feet walking past, nobody speaking, constant loud music, banging on the metal door, no food or water. Screaming for someone to come, 'I am one of you Carl will kill you when he finds out what you have done to me.' Then a voice over a speaker, how do you know Carl,'
'He is my boyfriend, you bastard, and he will kill you, I can assure you.'
'Can you prove it?'
'Only if you ring, the coded number.'
'Cannot do that.'
'Why the hell not.'
'Our remit came from our local contact, and we do not have a number.'
'He should have it.'
'Who do you think we are? We are low, low level on the pay scale, we will need to pass on to our supervisor, until then you will need to wait.'
'For goodness sake, 18942 on the encrypted phone, my reference, Loose Canon.'
'And this will tell him what.'
'That I am okay, are you an idiot, or all hell will break loose.'
Trish could he mumblings in the distance, then loud shouting further away, everything inaudible, after one hour the voice returns.
'Our supervisor has spoken to Carl, and he has given us specific instructions. That you and we must adhere to is that understood, Trish.'
'Of course, Carl must be obeyed, or there are consequences.'

'Firstly, a new passport is required, your choice of name.'
'Lisa Canon sounds good to me.'
'When you leave, no contact whatsoever till you are with him.'
'Don't tell him I told you, as I think he is getting paranoid.'
A slight snigger from Trish, 'that is why we are such a successful organisation idiot.'
'Point taken, he emphasised no phone, no electronic mail complete silence when you leave here, till you are with him.'
'Yes, can I have some food now, arsehole?'
'We will need a photo for your passport,'
'But I am a mess, no photo while I am like this.'
'Do not worry, we have female colleagues here, so we should be able to supply your needs.'
Half an hour later, a meal is brought in with makeup and a hairbrush; the meal finishes with a different looking Trish, as her photo is taken.
'Give us four hours to do the passport, and you will be on your way.
'Thank you, moron.'
A long four hours pass, then the door opens to Trish's room; a man in a mask enters, telling her anonymity is how we survive; he hands her the passport, she snatches it from him. A spit mask is put over her head, and she is guided outside and taken to a van; she can feel the chill of the early morning air.
'Now, where are you taking me.'
'You tell us, we can drop you off anywhere; we need to carry on with Carl's wishes.'
An irate Trish gives them an address in Ingleby Barwick, where she had left her car. Dropped off at her destination, the van is in the distance when she gets the hood off. Around the corner, her car is waiting, and before Trish gets into it, she strolls to the next road to

see the police tapes and two officers outside, the house she visited. Trish is unaware she has a nano tracker in her body, and the passport has a third-generation microphone under her photo in her passport.

Chapter 53

Once Trish had left the building, Guy went to see Lydia further down the hallway; she had agreed to help in any way she could now ever grateful they had saved her life. Finally, after two hours, Lydia has decided to do something; Guy did not want to ask, but she accepted willingly as long as he did not tell Mark, as the end justified the means. He then explains that she will have a hood over her head for secrecy until they arrive at her destination. When she leaves, Guy heads back to the team to catch up with the ongoing situation. As he enters his house, the smell of the usual coffee and a tray of different biscuits, not believing they have spent their own money to help out. Even with a bowl to put cash in for food, it looks like the local takeaways will be busy until this mess is sorted out. Their first question was to ask how Ron was, hoping his injuries would soon heal. Gulping his first cup of coffee for several hours, Guy explains Ron had found out that Rains and Niam are very much alive; the team gasp in astonishment. He also explains that Ron had a meeting with Raven and Hurst the morning he was run over, and he believes they were getting rid of loose ends. But, he continues to say, 'it looks like the latter are as ruthless as their cousins.' At this point, he turns to Mark; opening his briefcase, he takes out a plane ticket and gives it to Mark along with a passport. 'Time to do what you do best, Trish has bought a plane ticket to Italy; can you follow, please? Feedback is essential.'

Leyland looked at James, knowing someone would die; they were not happy being in this situation. But, they will look in the mirror when it is all finished, hoping they can justify it.

Leyland, 'could we not do that Guy, it will free up Mark with the Raven situation.'

'While I have been away, the Raven issue is being dealt with as we speak. Secondly, Trish has already seen your faces at the house in your neck of the woods.'
'Bollocks five stars to you, Guy.'
'I do have a task if that is okay, Leyland, James.'
'Fire away Guy, what would you like us to do.'
'I have got a key to Ron's house. Could you give it a look over, please?'
Leyland, 'any particular reason.'
'They attempted to kill Ron; I am assuming rightly or wrongly they will go to his house to find anything that might incriminate them.'
'That's our remit, time to do some police work, James.'
'Oh, by the way, I think his house will be bugged; Ron's phone was so again, I am assuming.'
'Give us the address, and we will be on our way.'
As Guy passes over the keys to Ron's house, the front door closes, and Mark throws a travelling bag into his basic car and heads to the airport.
Ten minutes later, Leyland and James head in the opposite direction towards Ron's house, both concerned the way this unusual case is going. They arrived ninety minutes later, both aware they must not speak, opening the door to a scene of devastation; the house had been completely ransacked. They step back away from the house, and a quick call to Guy, all decide that they should walk away; the least the local police know, the better for now. Leyland wipes his fingerprints off the door handle while James looks around, cursing himself; he should have seen if he could get some fingerprints off the handle, thinking that's what retirement does to you. Finally, they get into their car and go back to Guy's house. On the way, they discuss what they have inadvertently got involved in, and both men hated the drug scene for what it did to people.

By the time they get back, Mark is already on a plane to Milan, a route he has travelled several times with Julia; he's seated two rows back, watching her every move. Inside, a wave of growing anger that this man Carl Rains was one of the instigators of Lydia and Sharon's death in an attempt to get him. They go through customs to collect their baggage on landing, and Mark casually bumps into her talking Italian. She stares at him, 'I do not speak Italian,'

Mark replies, 'Sorry, I am from Manchester, you are so beautiful. I thought you have got to be Italian.' Her stance softens. 'oh, oh, thank you, I am a bit embarrassed now.'

'No need to be; my name is Mark.'

'I am Trish.'

'Please to meet you, Trish.'

'Have you come on holiday.'

'No, just a couple of days, business to attend to.'

'Similar to myself, is your business in Milan.'

'No Lake Como.'

'Very nice I used to live there in a past life.'

'Look, it is the day of modern women, can I invite you for a meal? I have a reservation in a hotel in the centre of Milan.'

'It is the day of modern man, how could I refuse such an offer and I will pay, is that okay.'

'Of course, how could I refuse.'

The taxi arrives at the hotel in twenty minutes; on entering, Trish gathers her keys from reception; Mark steps back so she can go to her room, turning around, 'bring your bag with you.'

'Certainly, Trish,' he follows her up to her room, entering she says, 'we have just got time for a shower; it will be quicker if we shower together,' a smile from Mark.

Both are looking flushed, just getting to the restaurant for final meal orders, meal over with; they decide they need another shower, both surprised by their stamina. Trish cannot believe that she has had sex three times with this stranger, but he managed to release pent up feelings, and her orgasms have never lasted so long before. Trish opens up to him that she is going to see her boyfriend mainly to settle an old score; he left her high and dry, in a situation she thought she would not get out of. He is very controlling and a billionaire, but she realised that money does not make you happy after the last few hours, always wanting more. Carl did something without her consent, which must be redressed, so it does not happen to anyone else.

Mark made a call when he arrived at the hotel, and he had organised for a Glock and silencer to be delivered at the hotel reception for pickup; he still has friends in Italy.

Mark, now realising that she will kill Carl, this is a revenge mission for her; it must be about the poison they put in her back, which Guy had removed. But, unfortunately, this is a loose canon literately, in the sense of the word, which might stop them from getting the information they require.

He asks if she wants to share a taxi to Lake Como, he is going to visit an old neighbour, and he can drop her off if that is okay.

Trish readily agrees, and they talk about how beautiful Lake Como is again that calm blue water, no ripples like a mirror reflecting all around it, then the taxi stops. Astounded at where they have stopped, as Trish gets out, he says, 'I use to know the people who lived here; they died tragically just over three years ago. The taxi driver concurs, stating Mrs Rosso and the police chief found on the patio both shot. Trish, surprised, gets out and walks to the villa; Mark tells the taxi driver to stop around the corner; he cannot believe the irony as he was the one who killed them. Thanking the driver, he gets out of the taxi and immediately rings Guy to update him, asking, 'do you want me to save him.' Guy, 'Normally, I would rather have him alive, but his computer is his most valuable asset to us right now. So you need to make a judgement call on our behalf; whatever you do, I will stand by you.' In Guy's mind, if they keep him alive, there will undoubtedly be an onslaught of killings to free him, 'can you make it look like she killed him.' Mark points out that Clive gave him a USB he can access to download at your end.

Mark thanks him; he has now walked down the side of the villa and can hear raised voices on the verandah, and can see Trish is pointing a gun at Carl.

Trish, 'you bastards, you put poison in our bodies to keep you safe.'

Carl, 'look, Trish, all our operatives have it, a safeguard for everyone, its just business.'

'I am your girlfriend, you bastard. Do you have one in your body?'

'I am one of the bosses; why do I need one, you stupid woman.'

'They wanted me to join them, but I refused.'

'Who wanted you to join them.'

'I don't know; if you had not sent a team to get me out, I would be in prison now; your tracker worked, they found me.'

Then Trish suddenly stops, putting her hands up, 'oh no, I did not have the tracker in; how did you find me.'

'We thought you were dead, and I never sent anyone.'

'Carl, what have I done.'

At this point, a quiet thud like compressed air, she lay on the floor; Carl looks up to see Mark indicating for him to sit down.

Carl, 'who the f---k are you.'

Mark, 'currently your worst nightmare.'

'Look, I have money to burn, walk away, and you will be wealthy beyond your dreams.'

As Mark shoots him in the ankle, the screams and blasphemy from his mouth are unbecoming of a drug lord; then, Mark ties him to the dining room chair. As Mark is tying him to the chair, he notices the burn marks on his hand and arms, 'I assume this is the reason you became an arsehole.'
'You don't know what I went through.'
'Oh, the explosion in Afghanistan, blah, blah.'
'How the hell do you know, we were left to fend for ourselves; nobody came.'
'My information is they spent two years looking for you.'
'No, that can't be.'
'Well, the short time I have known Guy Long, he is an honourable man, and I would rather believe him than you.'
'What are you going to do to me.'
'When I leave, it will be like Mrs Rosso and the police chief; only they were swift, yours, on the other hand, will be a bit slower.' Mark places the USB in the computer and rings Clive, 'Can you do your work, Clive.' Fifteen minutes later, Clive confirms they have everything they need.
'It was you who killed them.'
'Yes, that was my honour; she refused to pay the final 25% of our contract for killing her husband, saying she felt he was not worth the money.'
'It was nothing to do with drugs.'
'No, I did not know she was involved with them.'
'What about Holland, my three friends.'
'The same someone offered a ridiculous amount of money to kill them; I never even saw their faces.'
'We started a war for nothing, and we thought you were getting too close to us.
'Paranoia is not good; why did you kill my mother-in-law and sister-in-law.'
'Purely revenge.'

'Is that why you are after Guy.'
'Yes.'
'Well, just to let you know before you die, your ship Aerowin will be at the bottom of the ocean in a few days.'
'How do you know about that.'
'Your arrogance, there is always a trail if the right people are involved.'
'No, you can't do that.'
'If you poke the donkey enough, it will retaliate.'
'My colleague will get you all.'
'Yep, we will see about that, daft question, why no security.'
'Needed to be low profile; you would not have found me if my girlfriend had not been so stupid.'
'Correct, and goodbye,' deciding to get it over with quick, one shot to the head, Mark unties him, throwing the body to the floor.'

Mark starts to look around the house; even these people have backup books, if only for birthday cards; walking into the main living room, he notices a painting slightly lifted off the wall. The closer he gets, Mark can see the painting is hinged on the righthand side, pulling it from the wall a safe slightly ajar; not believing his luck, Trish must have disturbed him, and he forgot to close it. On opening a substantial amount of cash and various pieces of paperwork.

It must be essential to put them there in the first place in Marks mind. Grabbing its contents, he places it all in a holdall that Trish had brought with her. Taking her passport out and removing the microphone, no loose ends. Then he looks for any security camera hard drive; this is found; he removes it and goes to the end of the verandah. Throwing it and the gun into the lake, mesmerised by the ripple on the calm water, time to leave. Knowing they will question the amount of money at the airport, he goes to his old bank in the town, who remembered his past dealings. The money is put into an old account for future accessibility; it has become his emergency fund if needed. Paperwork is placed neatly in the holdall, and he makes his way to the airport, a call to Guy telling him he will be with them by the evening. Complaining he never got time to get the suntan oil out.

Chapter 54

While Mark travels home, Guy suddenly remembered Harry's book the cartel was after, going to the cupboard under the stairs, the rest of the team asking if he had any magicians or goblins in there. Then, with a wry smile, more of a snigger, he comes back with the book. Surprised by its contents and disappointed that so many people could be bought for cash in their pockets.

There were seventeen police personnel across the country, and this struck at the heart of Leyland and James, their moral compass severely tarnished by these revelations. Of course, they knew about Raven and Hurst, but for Guy, when he saw two names, he threw the book away, screaming in the air running over to the dining table and gulping from the bottle of whiskey, for the first time they had seen genuine anger from Guy. He starts shouting, 'No, it can't be them .' he gathers his thoughts and tells Clive to stoke up the coffee and get those bloody fig biscuits out; we have a lot of work to do. While they have their coffee and biscuits, Guy informs them of the two people he was shocked at; one was a close friend in the military, and the other was the head of MI6. He had given up sensitive information in his last meeting with the PM, with him in the room, cursing himself that he did not look at his neck, glad he kept this from the conversation. Clive, can you use your skills to find out about him? If we need more people, even hackers, we must sort this out. Why would he crossover? It is a dangerous game to play. While you are at it, can you check on his family? They could have a hold on him, but what.

'The byword is extreme caution from now on, and we can not trust anyone till this is over.'

Leyland, 'If we start to take the police personnel of the streets, it will set warning bells off, and we will be in the firing line.'

James, 'can I make a suggestion, Guy.'

'The table is yours, James.'

'We have seventeen individuals; can we not invite them to your special facilities, under the guise of a special assignment, they have been selected to attend to assist in this endeavour.'

Leyland, 'my goodness, where did that come from? It's brilliant.'

Guy, 'I concur we can hold them till this is over, hopefully.'

James turns to Leyland, 'if we invite Philpott, he will not overthink into it; he knows we are on special assignment anyway.'

Guy, 'can you organise please.'

Leyland, 'it will need to be a request to each division superintendent, and times staggered to avoid suspicion.'

Leyland contacted his old superintendent, who already knew about Philpott and agreed with their proposal; he will draft the request to his counterparts suggestion the people for the task force. Leyland had given him times for each individual to be at a pickup point; punctuality is essential to be a part of this task force. It will take two days to gather them all together in Guy's special place, and they are picked up in a blacked-out van for security purposes. To the individuals, this added a sense of mystery and a heightened sense of excitement, all hooded as they approached their destination; some argued others accepted it for what it was. On entry, they were all checked for their trackers, and there was only one without a tracker DS Phillpot; James will need to do some further investigations, not realising Philpott only worked for Jimmy Lees. The rest all received the obligatory sedation needle and tracker, and poison removed. Having got hold of a heavy lead-lined box, Guy had all the trackers placed inside, in separate boxes with labels of their new captors, hoping the box would block trackers. At the same time, Lydia was playing her part in trying to end this nightmare.

Chapter 55

Like any good assassin, Lydia stalked her prey; knowing his daily routine to the office, she would like to kill him, but her remit is purely information gathering. She has already purchased an older vehicle for the sole purpose of a fender bender; already discussed with Guy, even she needed permission to buy on Guy's expense sheet. Charles Raven lived in the affluent area of Amersham, just off the M25. To get to his home, you must travel down a private tree-lined road before you can see Raven Manor. Many neighbours class it as a modern horror in architecture built in sandstone, with an abundance of tiny windows and the main doors made of grey steel more a fortress than a home, the neighbours would say. So Lydia waited in a side road till she could see the shiny black Bentley coming her way; they are half a mile from Raven's house; as he passes, she pulls out behind him. A couple of minutes later, he indicates to turn left to go up the tree-lined road, and then he feels the collision. He jumps out, arms in the air shouting obscenities, then realising it was a woman, instantly calmed down.

'Are you okay,' Lydia's window slightly open tries to explain that a wasp got in the car, and she panicked and pressed the accelerator by mistake. Opening the door, she swings around and to Raven in what looks like slow motion; her long legs touch the floor, the black high heels crunch in the pebbles. Her black pencil pleat skirt had ridden up, showing a stocking top, the white blouse with just enough gap to gaze at her breasts. Lydia was in her element; she knew he was hooked before she got out of the car, by the slight bulge in his trousers just opposite her line of sight. Lydia, 'I'm so sorry; I can give you my insurance details to sort things out.'

Raven, 'that's okay as long as you are okay.'
Then the crocodile tears, 'Oh, I'm so sorry, I don't know what to say, this is my first accident.'
'Look, do not worry, we can sort it out over dinner tonight.'
Lydia showed her sense of humour, 'if I knew that having an accident would get me a date, I will need to do it a lot more.'
Raven laughing, 'a pleasure to meet you, my name is Charles Raven'
'Thank you! mine is Susan Hanson.'
'Do you live local?'
'Just in the next village, my first day here, I am in a small cottage for one week, trying to get over a breakup.'
'What? Someone broke up with you; they must be mad.'
'I am starting to get embarrassed now, looking coyly.'
'Oh, you don't have to be; you are stunning.'
Lydia pretends to courtesy, 'why thank you, kind sir.'
'Give me your address, and I will send a car tonight, for 8 pm.'
'But what about this, the cars, the mess.'
'Leave that to me; no need to call the insurance company.'
'Are you sure? Do you think it will be ready by Friday?'
'Certain of it, money talks around here.'
'Oh, that's wonderful, even more, it sounds as though I have hit a rich man, my goodness, you must be married.'
'No far too busy for that.'
'Am I a distraction then.'
'A pleasant one, believe me.'
'One of my colleagues is just coming down the drive, and he will take you home, oh and he will be the person to pick you up tonight at 7.45; there's my card if you need to contact me.'

'Thank you so much, and I am so grateful for your kind help.'

Another shiny black Bentley is making its way up the long driveway, and the registration numbers are sequential; it quietly pulls up near them. Susan thanks Raven, and she makes her way to the vehicle; a man comes out and escorts her to the car, her high heels struggling in the pebbles. Raven smiling as her long legs swing into the spacious rear seat, again that slight sight of a stocking top, Susan knows precisely what she is doing as any good seductress will tell you.

He waves goodbye just as a trailer truck arrives to pick up both vehicles.

Raven is chatting to the driver, with plenty of nodding and shaking of heads. Both cars will be repaired by Friday, for a bonus, money talks again. Susan attempts to talk to the driver asking the obvious questions, has he worked for Mr Raven long, is he a good boss etc. The driver is called Simon, telling her he has been with him for seven years, and as a boss, he is probably one of the best, pays very well for his services. Susan slides forward in the sumptuous leather of the car's interior, towards the front seat. To look at the immense dashboard, she can see the butt of a gun to his left-hand side.

'Will you be there tonight.'

'Yes, do not worry, we will be in another part of the house.'

'We, how many are there? I am now getting worried, a single woman in a house of men.'

'No need, the chef and two others, like myself, so you will be safe.' He laughs as they pull up to the address Susan has given him. Then, getting out, she bends forward to say goodbye, once again enough sight of her breasts to make him think, the boss could be lucky tonight. As Susan enters the cottage, she finds a wine bottle and has a quick drink, not realising there would be a protection team of three men, one she did expect. They had to barter with the current owners to have a two week holiday, on the pretence they needed the cottage for a drama they are filming in the village. She starts to run various scenarios through her head, the usual pros and cons and has come up with a visit to the hospital after the crash. A call to Guy can he arrange for her to stay overnight at the nearest hospital. If Raven checks on her, all part of the ruse, a man like him must be cautious. Thirty minutes pass, and Guy return's her call giving her the contact information; all calls are to be monitored from that room. Once settled in, she rings Raven telling him how sorry she cannot make it; feeling ill after the crash; she went to the hospital. They are monitoring her for two days, and she should be back at the cottage by Wednesday, and can we re-arrange for Thursday.

As suspected, a phone call to the hospital to check she was there, so Raven is suspicious, she will need to be careful.

Raven rings the hospital to speak to Susan on Tuesday evening to verify her car will be ready on Friday and find out if she is still there. Before moving in, two of Guy's team had installed security cameras so small you needed to know where they were to locate them for Susan's safety. This footage went straight to Clive's and Susan's phones

But while Susan was in the hospital, she had two visitors, one of which was her designated Bentley driver Simon Lock. They also installed two cameras and a microphone. Now she can see how his paranoia is working; this will be difficult to access his computer in the short term. However, this could be the excuse Susan needs not to see Raven. Over the next hour or so, Susan is mulling things through her head. And then she realises, if she can get Leyland and James here, they could arrest the driver, who broke into the cottage. After contacting Guy, her plan is put into place. Returning to the cottage, knowing the cameras are downstairs, she stays upstairs out of sight to get ready, coming down five minutes before the scheduled pickup. The driver has already left, and Raven is looking at his computer and can see how captivatingly beautiful Susan is, his mind going wild at what he thinks the night will bring, how wrong could he be. Raven can see the driver when the door opens; he shouts to his chef to get things ready as the door closes. At this point, Leyland and James appear and, with raised voices, tell him, 'armed police, down on your knees and hands behind your back.' As part of the sham, Susan says, 'what is going on? He is only Mr Ravens driver.'

The driver interjects, 'good grief; I am MI6, you can check on it.'

James, 'we will check on that at the moment; you are under arrest.'

'What for, 'we will tell you down at the station,'

'I will need to ring my boss.'

'Not while you are under arrest.'

'Crying out loud, you will be in a lot of trouble for this; my boss is powerful in politics.'

Leyland, 'you will need to come with us as well, miss.'

Before their visit, Susan had packed her case and taken it to the rear into the cottage's backyard. James was already placing this bag in their car. James suddenly realises how beautiful Susan is. Standing the driver up, Susan injects him with enough sedation for at least two hours; Leyland and James place him in their vehicle for his journey to Guy's special place. James looks at the back of his neck, sure enough, the now-familiar raised tracker. Also, before they left, Susan left a shoe on the path and a piece of torn fabric on the small gate lock, implying a struggle had taken place. This type of thing is not second nature to Leyland and James, wondering if they could survive in the world of intrigue. On the way to Guy's unique hideaway, they call into the local corner shop to get some aluminium foil and masking tape. Half a mile down the road, just before the M25, they pull into a layby and proceed to put a thick layer of foil on Simon's neck, held down with the masking tape. This, they hoped, would act as a deterrent on the tracker signal. Twenty minutes had passed, and there was no sign of Simon and Susan; an annoyed Raven contacts his other two protectors to see if they can find them, Simon is not answering his phone, and his tracker is offline. Finally, the two men arrive to find the Bentley still with its key in the ignition. On the path is Susan's shoe, and they see the torn material in the gate lock. A call to Raven with the update, surprisingly he tells them to come back, he has just realised, he is now vulnerable with no protection at all. He is more important than Simon or Susan,

his cousin Carl Niam said, 'you above all are more important than the rest.' Raven told his men it had gone higher up the chain and had sent an e-mail to Carl, waiting for a response, which will never come. Having also sent a text to a burner phone. Which is located in the glove box of a car, which belongs to the head of MI6. The text was straightforward: 'Simon missing, do you know anything .' it will be twenty-four hours before this text is seen. Leyland. James and Susan arrive at Guy's unique hiding place, not realising that they have a full day before MI6 will start to look for Simon Lock.

Fifteen minutes before they arrived at Guy's hiding place, they placed a hood over Susan's head until complete trust is gained; they must protect themselves. Susan accepts this, realising she is on a fine line; Susan wants to get back with Mark and will do anything to help.

Simon wakes up, disorientated and confused, still not sure why this kidnap has taken place, but still a gentleman, he asks if Susan is okay, 'have you harmed her.' Oblivious to her role in his abduction, if only he knew.

Then the realisation that his neck has aluminium taped to it, 'What the f—k is going on.'

For the first time, Guy comes forward to speak to him, always wanting to be in the background, but it is now at the point of no return.

'Firstly, did you know about the tracker in your neck?'

'Yes, I was told at my interview, look what is going on here.'

'Did you know you also have another different type under your shoulder blade?'

'No, what do you mean.'

'We will get back to that shortly.'

'You must be joking.'

'Who do you work for.'

'I have told your colleagues, MI6.'

'That would be John Graves.'

'How in the hell did you know that.'

'That will become clear shortly.'

'What, what do you mean.'

'Can I come back to the tracker? Why was that put in your neck.'

'Purely security, if we ever left, it would be taken out.'

'And has anyone left recently?'

'Yes, one only. in fact, I replaced him.'

'Look, is this necessary.'

'Well, your life is hanging on your answer.'

'Okay, Stuart Rogers.'

'How long ago.'

'One year ago, around May.'

'Where is he now.'

'Strangely, he passed away about three days after leaving.'

'Why did you break into Miss Hanson cottage.'
'What the hell, how did you know.'
'We have cameras as well. Simon.'
'But why.'
'Why did you do it? Was it of your own volition?'
'No, Charles asked us too.'
'Any particular reason.'
'He is always suspicious of everything and everyone; that is why all who work for him are fully vetted for employment.'
'What does Charles Raven do.'
'All I know, he is a politician and also a property developer.'
'Have you heard of a company called Ramina?'
'Not, at all.'
'Have you heard of Carl Naim and John Rains?'
'Yes, Charles was proud of Carl; he is some fancy billionaire, I think he is related.'
'What is your job for Raven.'
'Purely a protection team; there are three of us.'
'Who put the team together.'
'You seem to know. It was John graves.'
'I am going to leave the room and will be back in thirty minutes.'
'Okay.'

Leyland and James have been watching going into the next room, and all men concur they all think he is telling the truth. Then, returning to speak to Simon, Guy releases him from his cuffs and apologises for his inconvenience. But can we point out the reasons, and for him to make up his mind. Simon nods, and all the men sit down to talk. They point out that his previous colleague Stuart Rogers died due to the other vial in his back; this triggered three days after the tracker was removed. Working for MI6, he knew he would have to face situations, sometimes life and death but being so close as to have poison in his back made him physically sick.

Asking for a bucket to be sick, three seconds late, all three men turn away, not wanting to see Simon convulse into the bucket too. What hurt Simon more was his boss John Graves was involved, like Guy and Leyland, both people with high moral standards, that trust is now broken. They cannot tell him everything but take him to see Angus, the SAS medic, and remove the vial from his back; this done successfully, Simon is now a happy man. It now looks like Guy's team is gathering momentum; it seems to be getting bigger daily.

Chapter 56

Two hours earlier, Guy received a call from Mark requesting that he go rogue; the least he knew about it, the better. Only to say that their antagonist's money generator will be stopped. When Mark arrived at Malpensa Airport, he changed his ticket to go to Amsterdam; instead, he has decided to level the knife factory on the city's outskirts. Having looked at the yearly turnover of the business, it is far too much for the factory size, and money laundering came straight to Marks mind; it will need to be stopped. Within forty-eight hours, Mark has the tools of his trade, picking a prime position; he has monitored the factory and noted only four people are working there. Again more questions to be asked, large trailers arriving daily. Boxes are unloaded, and then two containers arrive and are taken into the unit. Twenty-four hours later, the same containers are removed, with different markings, loaded onto trailers, and then they leave. Minimum security possibly trying to avoid close scrutiny will benefit Mark; of course, he will complete his task tonight. Mark noticed a blind spot when they took the containers in, and he now knows the final delivery of a container is half an hour before they finish work for the day. As the sun sets, darkness falls, Mark has already made his way towards the unit; outside the unit, old decaying containers doors hanging on one last rusty hinge, ideal for hiding. They are part of the environment; being there for years, nobody looks at them anymore, the trailer truck slowly ambling through the main gates, reversing into position just opposite Mark four metres away. The first container rises as the forklift lifts it one hundred millimetres and reverses back, turning simultaneously. As the forklift went into the unit, Mark has jumped on the trailer behind the last container, the forklift returns. The last container rises, and has the container is lowered one metre, nearer floor level; at this point, Mark can get onto the container roof and lay flat on the top. Luck is on his side as the container is left inside the unit doors, away from prying eyes.

Mark waits patiently until the security lights are the only ones left on; he remains static for ten minutes. Mark is curious about the containers why such speed to turn them around; as he opens one, it is full of money, time to hurt the cartel. But, knowing that the alarm system will pick him up, a few vital minutes is all he needs to lay explosive charges down the centre of the building. Also, one in each of the money containers, reaching the back door, Mark cannot hear the sirens, then Mark realises the cartel would not want the police there. He need not have rushed the job; shrugging his shoulders, Mark kicks the back door open, halfway up the embankment, the first explosion, music to his ears, then the second, third, fourth it was like a musical crescendo. Loving every minute, if only Mark had a conductors baton, he could have waved his arms in unison. It only took seconds but so lovely to watch; he turned and got into his hire car, making his way to the hotel, fire appliances passing in the opposite direction. Fire tenders hold back as they run hoses out to try and contain the fire; in a short time, molten metal forms. Finally, the fire services decided the fire would not spread to other buildings. And reduce their manpower, enough people just to cool the building down. Unknown to Mark, the cartel is engineering 150mm circular stainless steel tubes four meters long with an internal cap 600mm from each end tag welded in place. First, one cap is lightly welded in place, the tube is filled with drugs, and the second cap is also slightly welded in position so it can be removed easily later. There were several tubes in the building, with drugs installed, with a street value of over ten million pounds. In the containers, the money was a total of twenty million pounds, and the Ramina had just lost over thirty million pounds of revenue. Within two hours, urgent calls were made, firstly to Carl Naim, who was untouchable, the second to John Rains. Finally, a furious John shouts venomous anger down the phone at his Dutch dealer, 'leave it to me; I will sort it out.' Twenty-four hours later, four men who worked at the building were executed and left to remind that the cartel does not accept failure.

John now worried that he could not contact Carl, a phone call to his Italian contact to go to his house. John has turned into an obsessive control freak, with the power he has over life and death, with the snap of a finger, someone dies, he loves it.

He is now fully aware they are under attack. But, from who, John Hurst, his cousin, has already informed him that Guy is chasing his tail, unaware Guy is gathering enough intel to decimate his organisation.

Mark has been on the phone with Clive for some information, which has warranted him to change his flight plans. Mark thanks him, and, 'could he tell Guy, he will be away for a week at least,'

Chapter 57

Simon gives Guy and the team all the information on Charles Raven that he knows; they all agree that he is now compromised with Simon missing.
Leyland asks him, 'do you think the other two men are part of his organisation.'
Simon, 'they have been with him seven years, I have not noticed anything.;
'Do they seem close, or just work colleagues.'
'I wish I could give you an honest answer on that; I do not know.'
'John Graves was not the head of MI6 when they were employed.'
'Well, John was second in command when Stuart Hinds was off ill for a year; this is when they started.'
'It is undoubtedly deep-rooted; we need to be careful; how can we get hold of Raven.'
'He goes to Parliament every Tuesday and Thursday's around ten o clock.'
A shout at the window, 'Lydia, we will need your skillset to help Simon.'
A surprised Simon turns round to see the woman he knows as Susan walk into the room, placing his head in his hands, 'what the.' Lydia puts her finger on his lips, 'all will become clear shortly,' shaking his head, he looks around, the rest of the team smiling.
'Any suggestions, what to do next,' came from Guy, after two hours throwing ideas around, till they come up with what is too simple for words. The following day, they arrive at the same stretch of road that Susan had her accident; Raven's car is driving towards London; as it approaches, Simon struggles to get to his feet, the Bentley slows down. One of the protection crew is driving the Bentley, and the other sat next to Raven, the vehicle stopped, and the driver got out; as Simon starts to speak, he shoots Simon in the chest, at

the same time a searing pain in his leg as the sedation dart hit home.

Just as the other man gets out of the rear, he feels the same pain as his colleague in his leg, noticing Susan coming towards him. Falling to the floor at the same time, Raven struggles to get his phone from his pocket. And the look on his face when Simon knocks on the window. Inviting him to come out of the car, still in a state of shock, thinking three people have just been killed in front of him. Simon was forever grateful that Guy suggested the bulletproof vest; he had never worn one before, not thinking one of his old colleagues would attempt to kill him, this as verified who they work for. A black van arrives, and Guy's special forces men drag the two men into the back of it. Simon now feels the bullet's impact, the adrenalin now ceasing, the bruise will be a constant reminder for the next few days of what could have been. He is driving the Bentley back to Guy's hiding place, Susan putting a hood over Raven's head in the rear, while Simon follows the black van to the deep underground car park. All the men were placed in various parts of the building, one particular room with a furious man shouting, 'do you know who I am.'

The two men confirmed to have the extra vial in their backs, and Guy offers them a way out if they assist. However, they do not believe and ask for a solicitor to talk to and John Graves to be present; Guy responds, 'well, as he is involved with the same cartel as you, I don't think we can do that.' Both vehemently deny they are not involved, and Guy tells them both that Raven does not care about you; cannon fodder is all you are to him.

Looking at them both, 'right we are going to take those trackers out and see what happens, ' then James enters and places a body bag next to them,
'Look, we are in the UK; you cannot kill us.;

'We are not, and in three days, those vials will.'
'What do you mean.'
'As I said, you are nothing to this cartel; as soon as we remove the tracker, the other, for some reason, does not see it, and in seventy-two hours, you will not be of this earth.'
'You are trying to scare us.'
'Would you like to see the bodies we have in deep freeze further down the hallway? It is not pleasant?'
'Both men decline, looking at each other as they are separated, to go to individual rooms.'
Angus is called to do his standard procedure to remove the tracker, and Guy informs him to leave the other vials in place.
Each asks Angus if what Guy had said was true, both thinking he is telling lies, what was the point of the question if you will not believe the answer. They are both placed in one room; in one corner high up is a digital clock counting down seventy-two hours; Guy has had enough of trying to save people; too many people have died needlessly to prove a point. Both men look at each other; Guy informs them, 'you both will die in three days; your choice is a prison sentence for the attempted murder of your colleague Simon Lock and aiding and abetting a drug cartel.'
'You cannot do that,' a raised tone from both men
'We will see in three days; I am going to see your boss now, and I can guarantee he will not have a tracker or vial of poison in his back.' Then, as Guy turns round to leave, one man succumbs to his demand.,
'Take it out. I will talk, only if you prove it is there.'
'Not an issue.' Guy calls for Angus, who removes the vial in front of the other man, his face ashen.
'Can I have a bucket? I think I am going to be sick.'
'Bucket, please, someone.' James throws a bucket in the room, then thinking seems familiar with these MI6 people. At this point, Guy asks Leyland and James to

interview them formally, all recorded and statements taken. The sound of Guy's Steel tipped shoes echo down the hallway, heading towards Raven's room, the key in the lock a loud click, and the door slowly opens. Raven starts straight away, demanding his lawyer be present; Guy lets him rant away; he could tell the man's anger is rising; Guy bangs the table. Then the deafening silence and Guy speaks calmly.

'Charles Raven, you are being arrested for the attempted murder of Simon Lock, along with the other two MI6 agents.' Raven starts to shout, 'do you know who I am? You cannot do anything to me.'
Guy carries on, though not an officer of the law, he will ask James to do it legally. 'also aiding and abetting a drug cartel known as Ramina, in the supply of drugs into the UK, and money laundering through your Ravenhurst Holdings.'
Raven starts to laugh; such is his arrogance, I am untouchable, I know people so high up in society, your feet will not touch the floor.'
Guy stops him, 'and also for your involvement in the attempted murder of Ron Walton,'
'Don't be so ridiculous.'
'Have you been in touch with Carl Naim? Bet he has not answered your call yet.'
'What do you mean.'
'Well, last I heard, he had a bullet in his head, his girlfriend also dead.'
'No, it can't be.'
'If you send hitmen to kill a hitman, he will retaliate.'
'You are lying.'
'Your lifestyle has just stopped.'
'Look, we have so much money, we can buy anyone; it will not go anywhere.'
'Only if you are alive.'
'You would not dare kill me.'

'I never said I would do it; a certain hitman would have no hesitation.'
'Look, if you let me go, I will guarantee this will all end.'
'I wish I could be sure, but people like you do not care about society, only money, too many deaths, for your greed.'
At this point, a knock on the door, and in walks Ron Walton, still with a plaster cast on his left arm, the look on Raven's face, 'but, but you are supposed to be dead,' came from a surprised Raven. Ron walks over to him and throws the most brutal punch he could muster, breaking Raven's jaw.
Ron looks to Guy, 'the talking is through; let's destroy the bastards.' Ron was always straight to the point. Then, Ron looks to Raven, 'well, look on the bright side Raven, you will lose some weight before you go to prison; you will only get liquid food now.'
'Right then, we need to get Mr Graves; how can we tempt him away from his lair,' a call to Clive, who is still at Guy's house. A muffled sound at the end of the phone, 'are you still eating fig biscuits,' a little chuckle from the other end, 'hello, Guy.'
'Can you get any financials on John Graves? We need to visit him; also, we are going to Raven's house; we will give you access to his computer.'
Still spitting out crumbs, Clive responds, 'no problem, Guy, is everything okay at your end.'
'Yes, thank you.'
Walking towards Raven, who winces, expecting another punch, Guy, gets Raven's house keys; once again, obscenities rain forth on them both as they leave the room. Another call to Clive, can he check if the MET commissioner's name is in Harry's truth book (as he called it)? If not, they can trust him. An urgent call to the commissioner, Guy, partly explains their situation and the need for urgency for a court order for Raven's

house. Even the commissioner is worried about which judge to call now, but Guy's sixth sense comes into play; he sends Leyland and James with two other colleagues to Raven's house to get the computer. The men speed to Raven's home, turning left into the tree-lined drive, rain beating down, the trees bending in the wind; from a distance, they can see the front door open, the lights casting light across the front paving. Their vehicle headlights switched off as they coasted to a stop; Leyland and James held back while their professional friends checked the house. On entering, the men can see two others rummaging through drawers in the dining room, a request to turn round with their hands up, shots ring out, and both are dead on the floor. They call Leyland and James in; one man had the computer in his hand; they look at each other. James 'how did they know.' Leyland shrugs his shoulders; baffled by how organised they are, his phone rings.

'Hi Guy, we are in, but two men tried to steal the computer.'

'Good job, we did not wait; by the way, did the judge assign a warrant to enter.'

'Thank goodness was there a problem.'

'Took longer than expected, Leyland.'

'You don't think the judge is complicit, do you.'

'Further investigation required; maybe the computer will give us the answer.'

'Okay, see you at your house then.'

'Before you go to the house, can you bring back those two bodies?'

'Will do, Guy.'

Leyland and the rest of the men take the bodies back to Guy's hiding place, then Leyland and James head towards Guy's house. Unfortunately, by the time Guy had given Angus instructions to fix Raven's jaw, with the aid of his friend Dr Mitchell's phone instructions, he arrived two hours late at his house. Clive was surprised that Raven had not closed down his computer, ever confident that no one would dare attempt to attack them.

The information gleaned would be the straw that breaks the cartels back, and as Guy suspected, the judge who gave them the delayed warrant was on their list. They now know all the people involved; there will be a difficult few weeks ahead of them.

Chapter 58

Mark landed in Turkey after his discussion with Clive; they have located the ship Aerowin two miles off the coast of Turkey. Before leaving Italy, he made three more calls to some old former special forces friends, explaining the situation and willing to accept the challenge. Again, Mark enjoyed using cartel money to destroy them. But, again, his use of the dark web and certain explosives obtained will severely dent their operation. On day two of his arrival in Turkey, he has arranged a meal to discuss the seriousness of what they are about to do in forty-eight hours. All agree with Mark that these drugs are a scourge on society. And anything that will hit them in the pocket, the better. The men run through their tasks, Mark indicating he will be the primary risk-taker, the weather forecast for that evening is a north-easterly ten-knot wind with a light swell. Unusually the ship has limited nighttime watches, yet more arrogance unaware that someone knows about their operation. John Rains is making frantic calls trying to find his business partner, and now Carl's cousin Charles Raven has disappeared; what can be going on. John received the call he did not want to hear from a contact in Italy; Carl's decomposing body laid by his girlfriend, he slumps back in his chair, not wanting to believe what he has just heard. Nobody knows about Ramina; we have made sure, always covering our backs. Any issues swiftly dealt with, no leaks people too frightened of the consequences, death a big motivator.

Even though Guy and the team are getting results, finding Carl's and Trish's bodies means John will go deeper underground and become harder to find. But as long as Ron Walton's information is correct, Rain's hiding could be shorter than he thought. Mark and his friends have gathered in the shadows of the rocks; it is

11 pm; luckily, no moon shining on the sea surface; loading up the dinghy, they push it into the water, struggling against the tide, the outboard motor starts up, surprisingly quiet. The men jump into the dinghy and take up their positions, and head towards the Aerowin.

Half a mile from the ship, they turn the outboard motor off, using the current to guide them towards the target; twenty metres from the ship, they glide into the water. All the men know precisely their jobs; two go either side of the vessel, placing explosives every four metres. Mark had already seen the ship's blueprints and learned about the moonpool; one man was controlling the dinghy. As Mark reaches the moonpool, he swims around under it, in a circle to see if he can see any people present. Unknown to Mark, they had timed their entry exactly on shift changeover; the area was empty. He raises himself onto the flooring, looking around; all is clear. To his right, he can see the lift that brings their product down to load the mini-subs. Placing an explosive into the lift, he sets in motion pressing for level three, turning round; he puts another explosive behind some machinery, then slowly slips back through the moonpool. Making his way back to the dinghy, within two minutes, the roar of the dinghy motor at full throttle, the only sound that someone had been near the ship. As they make their way towards the beach, loud noises from the main deck, some people can see the wake of the dinghy, putting two and two together start to jump overboard.

Unfortunately, the explosions begin sequentially from front to rear, and the people caught in the explosions before they hit the water are already dead.

The lift stops on level three, explodes and, along with the vapours, create an even bigger explosion; the ship and personnel disappear under the waves in minutes. Some people on the beach can see an orange light and muffled sound in the distance, and the ship disappears from the skyline. Even Mark and his friends are surprised by how quickly the ship went down; they shake hands on the beach. All leave in different directions, one taking the dinghy with him, the minimum amount of evidence as possible, only several footprints in the sand. Mark had booked a ticket home on the 7 am flight to Manchester; the cartel has now had the biggest hit on their supply network, along with the Holland hit.

They are now at least a billion pounds in lost revenue, with the cost of a new ship to pay for as well.

John Rains has not received any information as yet regarding these hits on his cartel. As Mark walks through customs more animated than usual, the team is unaware of what he has done off the coast of Turkey. Several charred bodies reached the shoreline two days after the explosion, instigating a sea search for several days; nothing was ever found.

Chapter 59

The team are putting together all the information they have from Raven's computer, and it transpires that Raven and Hurst are the money men, moving it to and froe, minimising any contact with it. If they can find Hurst, they can stop the money movement, which will hit the cartel again; time is not on their side; he has gone missing.

A knock on Guy's door, all jump this is not how their lives should be, Clive shuffles to the door; those fig biscuits are taking their toll, a shout from Leyland, 'my what a big arse you have Clive.' A muffled reply as he opens the door and Mark's head pops through it, a sigh of relief from the rest, a warm smile from Lydia, Leyland looks to Guy, 'we need to resolve this quickly, Guy or none of us will have a normal life, ever again.' Mark sits down and is introduced to Ron and tells them of his little adventure. Some are happy, others not so happy as the repercussions could be life or death.

James stands up, 'currently, we have the upper hand, but in a couple of days, I suspect we will have an onslaught upon us.'

With yet another fig biscuit in hand, Clive, 'can I put a suggestion forward,' carry on from Guy.

'We all should make a video, telling everybody what is going on, mainly in case anything happens.'

James, 'that's a bit desperate, isn't it.'

Guy corrects James, 'I think Clive is right; we have seen how ruthless this cartel is and how far they have got into our judicial system.' Clive tells them all that the video will have metadata to confirm the time and date, and if they all have a copy, there is more chance to get it out on the internet as a last resort.

'You have got to remember; they have at least one judge on their side, there might be more than one also

MI6 individuals, possible police backup, we need to start reducing their impact on us, sooner rather than later.'
'Are we 100% sure who is involved, replied Guy?
'Yes,100% sure.' from Clive.
They sit down and individually tell their stories, all with compelling proof of the cartel's involvement in trying to kill them. All have different USB's, and one will post to a friend, with a note only to open if something happens to them. James and Leyland will send theirs to the chief superintendent, Guy to the PM, Mark unusually to Lydia, as he feels her survival rate is more significant than his. Lydia does the reverse, Clive, putting his on the internet cloud, and Ron to a fellow intelligence officer; he trusts with his life. There is a mood change within the room, a lightening of the load. As if they were letting their frustrations out in the open as they renewed their zest to finish the job at hand. They all shake hands; this one action between them has bonded them for life; Clive breaks the silence, 'tea, coffee, fig biscuits,' a resounding yes from all. A softer tone ensues as they discuss their next step; this is soon stopped when Mark receives a warning tone on his phone. After his latest adventure, Mark forever cautious had put a camera at the front door, realising things could escalate quickly; he did not expect such a quick retaliation. Looking at his phone, he can see six people heading towards the front door, fully armed with balaclavas on, two SUV's with a driver in each waiting for their colleagues return. Shouting to everyone, 'we have visitors. Do you have a safe room for Clive and Ron, Leyland and James?'
Leyland and James try to argue their position to help; Mark tells them, 'these are not your typical criminals, Leyland, it is kill or be killed, we can do this.' Mark tells Lydia to go out the back and come in behind them, and this will be the first time Mark will see her skills.

She rushes through the kitchen, gathering a knife on the way out the back door. Running down the side of the house, that flush in her face the excitement rising, someone will die by her hand today. The people think they have the element of surprise, but little do they know the surprise awaiting them. The front door opens, one individual steps through into the foyer; the sixth man is two metres from the front; Lydia comes around from his blindside, the last man falling to the floor, his throat cut.

The man in front of him turns, hearing the noise as he sees him on the floor. Looking up, he feels the knife pierce under the throat to his brain, immediate silence as Lydia helps him to the floor. The rest of the men enter the house; as the fourth one enters, Guy ramps the music up, the noise is deafening, two hold their ears, two shots ring out, two dead on the floor. The last two feel the pain in their knees; Marks trademark shot to get some information. They hear the SUV's startup, and Mark runs outside, fires a shot at the first vehicle, the tyre pops, the second shot at the driver, he slumps forward towards the steering wheel. The other vehicle crashes into the rear; Guy and Lydia run towards the second vehicle to apprehend the driver. All the men have the telltale sign of the tracker; Guy wondered how many people they have on their payroll. The rest of the team come from the panic room, seeing everything under control through a camera in the room.

Clive's fig biscuits have not left his hand, and they lift their two captors onto the kitchen chairs, the third one just coming through the front door. The third was a woman, the designated driver, she was told, straight in and out, a simple job and easy money, no tracker. Mark and Lydia go and check on the dead driver, the same as the woman, no tracker; on the way back to the house, Mark and Lydia start to talk, both agree to

discuss things later. The woman now moved away from her two colleagues, away from earshot, James attempting but failing to strike up any meaningful discussion. Leyland searches the men's pockets, only one phone between them; hence the man he took it from is the lead assailant, and he is now separated from assailant Number two. Lydia sedates Number two at Guy's request in another room; Leyland and James initiate sounds of the man being beaten up for information, screaming, and punching. Twenty minutes later, they come back into the room and whisper in Guy's ear; he blurts out, 'are you sure he is dead.' Leyland offered his apologies but emphasised that James got over-excited, 'but he will hold back on the other guy if he must, I think he was enjoying it.' Assailant Number one's eyes wide open, waiting in anticipation, sweating the pain throbbing in his knee.
'What do you want to know.'
'Who sent you.'
'It was just a text.'
'How long have you been with the Ramina cartel.'
Shocked to hear the name, he responds, 'Nobody is supposed to know about them.'
'Well, we do, so let us carry on.'
'Look, I do not know; it is just a text.'
'Well, lucky for you, we will not kill you, but your employer will.'
'What, what do you mean.'
'Everyone who works for them has a vial in their back. Sorry for the pun, a backup system.'
'What vial.'
'Poison, if we remove the tracker, you have seventy-two hours.'
'No, it can't be.'
'We have several bodies to prove it, and you are far from the first to visit us.'
'I do not believe you.'

'Simple answer, we remove the tracker and wait for you to die.'

Now sweating more profusely, 'Look, we are just mercenaries, offering our services to the highest bidder.'

'Does not help us; take the tracker out looking at Lydia,' she moves forward, 'no, no, it was Judge Powell.'

'Did you get that, Clive?' as he looks at Clive

'Certainly did.' Clive replied

'Thank you, and we will take out both vials for your safety, but be aware, you will be a target from your former employer now.'

The man nods his acceptance, fate sealed in prison, better than death, even though he dealt in it.

'Oh, by the way, your colleague will be with you.'

'But, you killed him.'

'No, just gave him a sedative.'

'Well played, I take my hat off to you all.'

All the team nods in agreement, and Clive spoils the silence, 'anyone for a fig biscuit,' everyone laughs. Having called his colleagues at his hiding place to collect their prisoners and bodies and the vehicles outside.

'Before you go, how do you tell them you have succeeded? how is the money paid.'

'Coded message by text, just a number.'

'The number, please I will show you how ruthless this cartel is.'

'What do you mean.'

''We have to do this; sorry, Lydia, can you remove the vial? believe me, it is essential, or you will die.'

He takes his shirt off; Lydia slides her hand down his back, locating the vial, surprisingly she removes it with little pain she moves to the room, assailant Number two, still asleep, pulls his vial out. Leyland comes forward with a small glass bowl; the team know more about Guy's house than he does now, puts the bowl down, and Guy places both vials inside it. Then, turning to assailant, Number one, Guy asks him to text his code to the number given. As soon as the text has been sent, the vials break, releasing the poison, the assailant screams obscenities at the bowl, now realising how ruthless they are. Knowing how they get rid of loose ends, their team forever increases, with all the loose ends the cartel leaves behind.

At this point, Guy turns to him, 'do you want to join the good guys and get your sentence reduced? If so, help us, bring them down.'

Explaining 75% of the situation, Guy hoped to get some infighting within the cartel to fight from two sides. Then, knowing they do not tend to tell each other, he will use the two assailants to visit Judge Powell. Clive finds out where Judge Powell resides, and he will have some visitors tonight. Mark and Lydia are instructed to bring the Judge to Guy's hiding place. Both look at each other; Lydia smiles, at last, a time to reconcile and make things better with Mark. Judge Powell.s house is on the outskirts of London, in fact only three miles from Raven's home. Not as big, a reference to the money difference in their lifestyles. The judge had a specific perversion that the cartel swiftly took advantage of; nowhere to turn, he was easy to control.

Along the way, apologies between Mark and Lydia and their reasons for their decisions. Then, all forgiven, they stop half a mile from the house and park up in a lay-by.

Even though it is nearly dark, Mark can see that telltale flush on Lydia's face, her hormones rising, and his thoughts go to, for Queen and country; he must do his duty. Luckily they have taken one of the redundant SUV's, with plenty of room in the rear, nearly fully unclothed before they get to the rear seats; it was spontaneous and wild, both now realising their relationship will go further.

Forty minutes later and fully clothed, they plan their attack, unknown to them while in the throes of passion Judge Powell had passed them and is now in his home. The driveway is only fifty metres long, and the house is fully lit, cameras on two corners, a cautious man indeed. Mark had brought his trusty drone, getting it from the rear of the SUV; he sends it soaring into the air; as it circles, he can see that there is no external security, looks like a front door entry, he tells Lydia. Driving down the driveway, he stops ten metres from the front door, and Mark steps out of the SUV; Mark always kept an old police card as DC Lunn, asking Lydia to stay in the car till the front door opens. A lady answers the door, 'Hello, my name is DC Lunn, here is my card, can I see Judge Powell please.'

'Can you come in, please?'

'I have a police observer with me. Can I bring her in, please?'

'Of course, please both come in; I am sure Peter will be okay with it.'

'Thank you, and I assume you are Mrs Powell.'

'Oh yes, I am so sorry.'

Mark enters the house, closely followed by Lydia, and they are both shown into the living room, Powell sipping on a glass of expensive whiskey. He looks up, surprised by the intrusion,

'Who the hell are you.'

'DC Lunn, Judge Powell.'

Aggressively he raises his tone, 'what do you want.'

'We would like you to look at a short video.'

'You have come to my home to show me a f—king video.'

'Yes sir, just to help in our enquires.'

'Look, this can be done at my office; get out of my house.'

'Cannot do that; look at the video now.' A raised tone from Mark. Powell, taken aback by Mark's aggressive response, once again Powell tells him to get out of his house. Lydia, can you bring Mrs Powell in so she can see the video, please. Powell starts to say he will look at it, 'too late now; your type is always the same.' Mrs Powell comes into the room with Lydia, 'We are sorry to show you this, Mrs Powell, but your husband is too arrogant to listen.'

Lydia plays the video, turning up the volume, and within seconds she could hear the words, 'who sent you to kill us.' And the reply, 'Judge Powell, money sent on completion.' The sorrowful eyes of Mrs Powell and the tears flowed, turning to her husband, 'I knew you were a pratt, but this, what is going on in your head.'

Then the Judge starts to laugh, 'do not worry, they cannot prove anything; dead men cannot talk.'

Mark carries on with the video, which shows the vials in a glass bowl and breaking when he receives the text.

'That can't be the system is foolproof.'

'It seems you are the fool, Powell.'

Slumping back in his chair, Mark informs Mrs Powell, 'I don't think you will be seeing your husband for some time.' Then, she responds, 'what did he do? The video says something about killing, and I was not listening properly.'

Replying, Mark tells her, 'he sent eight people to kill us.'

'Oh my goodness, I must get a whiskey to calm my nerves,' she leaves the room; at this point, Mark has a word in Lydia's ear. She moves to the side of the door, where Mrs Powell will enter; Mark moves behind Judge Powell. As Mrs Powell comes into the room, without looking, she fires a shot from a pistol towards where Mark would have been standing, hitting her husband in

the shoulder. Then, instantly from the side, in one swift stroke, her throat cut by Lydia, Powell now bereft, his wife gasping for air, dying on the floor.
Lydia turns to Mark, 'how did you know.'
'Already two glasses poured out.'
'The old experience counts then.'
Mark tells Powell, 'you have a lot to talk about, come with us now.'
'My wife, what about her.'
'Nothing can be done for her, and if you were not such an arrogant man, she might be alive now.'
Lydia approaches Powell, and he feels the needle in his neck. Instantly asleep, Mark gathers up the computer; this seems to be the one weakness in modern life, everything about yourself on a piece of electronics, along with your faithful mobile. Arriving back at the military hiding place, which now seems to be a second home, their prisoner unloaded, they will leave interrogations to Guy. But, first, the team need to get hold of the head of MI6 and hopefully the final piece of the jigsaw, John Hurst, which he hopes will guide them to the head of the snake, John Rains.

Chapter 60

The evening before, Guy gathered his team together and explained that he hoped they were on the last leg, but he would like to tell everyone to contact their partners and tell them how much they love them. This following week will be a game-changer for them all, and hopefully, we will all survive to tell our tale. The next day, he stepped out into the crisp morning air, early morning dew on the grass, slight breeze from the southeast, the odd tree branch swaying, in the back of his mind thinking what a wonderful life he has had, ever grateful for the wonderful support of his wife and children. It is now approaching 7 am; the rest of the team are stirring; they all know their tasks for the coming week.

Three years ago in Holland, an incident brought John Rains to where he is now seated in the former office of his slain friends, and this office is where the revenge against Mark started. Even though he only killed two out of the three-drug lords, a former dutch special forces man called Luuk killed the other. The office on the tenth floor, in the high rise office block owned by the cartel, is one of many properties in the city of Amsterdam. Under the guise of a shipping company specialising in shipping container movement worldwide, ideal for drug transportation. Gone are the computers showing their drug operation; these gave away their original drug manufacturing operations, and it took two years to bring everything back up to speed. That impact nearly finished them for good, and he and Carl vowed it would not happen again. And through his new network and the dark web, he found out that Paul Reed, aka (Mark Andrews) was in prison; the man who killed his friends formulated a plan, which included destroying Sir Guy Long and Mark. He, along with Carl, was unaware of the efforts that Guy and his men at the time were making for two years to bring them home. As a typical drug lord, the body count did not matter; as long as they get Guy and Mark, everybody else did not matter. John is still frantically trying to contact significant people in his organisation. But his pool of generals is slowly decreasing; what can be happening? Carl came up with the idea of the tracker and poison vial, which was one of the most effective ways of controlling everybody.

Lower-level foot soldiers, controlled with the tracker, unknown to them or anybody else if removed, would die along with their secrets. The next level above could override the protocol and signal the poison vial to break. So on and so on, the general above them could override on anyone at any time, with the power of life and death at their hands. Hence the reason Judge Powell felt so confident, that there would be no witnesses to his crimes. And he is under the impression he is safe and that he only has a tracker in him?

As John stamps up and down in his office, clenched fist, shouting orders to all in his path, everyone cowering, all-knowing by his manner something is wrong. John used to be calm and collected in his formative years until the explosion that changed his moral compass on life. Such was the impact on John and Carl; their view of life changed for the worst, the opium dealer they met and killed then took over his fields of death. Easy money, every day easy money, more and more, they became untouchable, and revenge on those who got in their way, no mercy for any of them. Then, ping in the corner of the office, an e-mail which will send him on a path of no return, informed of his close friend's death alongside his girlfriend. He sends an e-mail to Judge Powell and the head of MI6 John Graves; he is coming to England for an urgent meeting, no more correspondence until he reaches the UK. Clive sends a text to Guy, urgent you must return home immediately, an e-mail of great importance on Powell's computer has arrived. Walking inside his hiding place, he calls his team together. We must get back to my home; I think Clive is eating two fig biscuits at the same time; he needs us now. All rush to various vehicles; as discussed previously in one of their many meetings, they must use different routes, just in case someone knows about them. Leyland and James in the police Mondeo, Mark and Lydia in the acquired SUV, finally Guy and Ron in the Volvo XC90. All arrived within ten minutes of each other, hoping there were no speed cameras on the way. Clive gathered them around and read the e-mail out to all, a muted cheer from Leyland, who could sense the end was finally coming. Leyland puts his old police hat on asks Clive to check if John Rains has a reservation on any flights into London. But Clive was more bothered with answering the e-mail, spraying fig biscuits over the computer, trying to explain in his flustered manner. James looked at the previous e-mails returned to John, noticing how short and straight to the point Powell's replies were. Silence for a few seconds, as they all looked at each other, then Leyland started to laugh, all the rest followed, breaking a sombre moment, Guy comes back with his common sense and says. 'Reply with, see you all at my house Wednesday 8.30 pm prompt, Powell.' It was promptly done and dispatched by Clive, glad Guy took over the initiative.

James noted that John Hurst's name was on the list of recipients, thankful they now have a chance to end it all.

Ron asks Guy, how well do you know John Graves, 'Well, I thought he was a friend, but it looks like money certainly talks in this case,'

Ron responds, 'the same here; they must have stitched him up, well and truly, or it is just plain greed.'

Guy jumps in and turns to Clive, 'any luck with Graves financials, we need a reason to go after him.'

James agrees, 'at the moment it is circumstantial, we need conclusive proof of cohesion with the cartel.'

Mark jumps in.'I assume you will visit them on the day in question of their meeting.' A resounding yes from most of them, except Clive, now choking on ginger biscuits, Guy wants his house back to normal.

'Well, Lydia and I will visit Mr Graves abode to retrieve his private computer. Do we know if he is married or any children in the house?' also, do we know his security at his house.'

Clive informs him he will have the information in twenty-four hours. Guy jumps in and turns to Mark,' can you do two houses in one evening.' Mark smiles, 'a challenge for us, Lydia.'

'The last name on that list of recipients was a friend of mine, former Captain Roger Stains, and I do not know how he is involved.'

Clive shouts over, 'same again, Guy, more financials and security for Mark.' A nod from Guy, 'Clive, have you eaten all the biscuits.' Then, a coy Clive replies, 'one ginger biscuit left, Guy.'

A sudden burst of laughter, the only way to break the intense seriousness of the situation.

The only thing that Guy is worried about is the volume of prisoners, and even if they are locked away, the money behind them, they will soon be out, as they have already found out money talks at all levels. So if they can get the final four people in their inner circle, they all can breathe that little bit easier, but as he has already found out, who do you trust.

Chapter 61

It is a tense couple of days, as the team try to organise their different roles. The only ones showing excitement are Mark and Lydia; the buzz of going into strangers homes and not getting caught is right up their street. In those two days, Raven and Powell are screaming about their legal rights. So in their meals, they were sufficiently sedated and transferred to an offshore facility, where they could shout to their heart's content. Guy has known of this place for five years, having used it for mock assaults on this type of facility. Clive has found sufficient information on Powell's involvement, referencing the video they could take forward for prosecution. They already have Raven for his instructions to kill Simon, one of his own protection team, and several items on his computer. Having already sent a team to clean Powell's house and remove Mrs Powell's body, Guy and Mark could not understand her actions for trying to kill Mark. Powell would not say it could have been instinct, and now they will never know. Finally, Mark and Lydia have all the information they require. And ask Guy if they could leave and stay in a local hotel for the night; everyone overhearing turns and starts to clap; it is the first time both have ever been embarrassed, realising they do have some humanity within them.

John Graves loved power, and with power comes wealth; if you want to climb up the inner circle, you need to know the relevant people to cross palms with to reach the next level. In his tenure as head of MI6, he knew the whereabouts of Rains and Naim eight years ago. Choosing not to tell anyone, this in his eyes, was the perfect chance to reach his financial statement in life; it would be of great mutual benefit to both parties as they got to know each other and also agreed that the cartel's cousins. Charles Raven and John Hurst would gain a meteoric rise in politics and gradually gain political status. Using this, they could use their position to filter funds to all who worked for them and buy up the derelict buildings that drug gangs used to control.

Mark and Lydia left the house like two giddy children, and now it was out in the open, their relationship could flourish. By the time they reached the hotel, they were like newlyweds, so much, so the manager gave them the wedding suite at a discount, a complimentary meal sent up to the room. After the meal, both rushed towards the bed, Mark joking, 'you have left your knife at home,' Lydia giggling, 'I don't need a knife, this is going to be wild, wild sex.' Then, two hours later and slightly exhausted, Mark, 'good grief, I hope we have energy for tomorrow nights job.'

Lydia starts laughing, 'it's after the job you should be worried about.' Mark smiles; he will never forget Julia, but unfortunately, life goes on, and you must take everything good in life while you can. They plan every detail for the evening's work; the addresses are five miles apart, on the southeast side of London, access is easy straight off the M25. They have decided to go to Roger Stains house first, thinking there will be minimum security. As discussed at the team meeting, all entries will be after 8.30 pm if the alarm goes through to their mobile phones. Back at Powell's house, arriving two hours earlier. Guy has prepared for their visitors, at the rear three vehicles to take each individual away to his hiding place. The three drivers act as security at the front of the house to give an air of importance. It will also give them more time to look in places that his search team might have missed. Within the first hour, a false space behind a bookcase offered more valuable information and photographs to help them, along with substantial amounts of cash, vanity will get you every time. There will always be

someone who arrives early; on this occasion, Roger Stains, security, informed Guy, a visitor at the door. The door slowly opens, he enters, and three metres ahead, Guy turns, the look on Roger Stains face the realisation something is wrong, transfixed waiting for Guy to talk.
'You have let the military and me down, Roger.'
'Don't know what you are talking about; I have come for a meal with Judge Powell.'
'Well, that will be in prison.'
'What have you done? They will kill me.'
'Get involved in drugs, prepare for the consequences.'
Roger turns to run; just as he reaches the door, a security man's fist hits him square on the chin; Roger stumble back, and James places cuffs on his wrists, blood starting to run down his face. Shouting non-military profanity at Guy, then being dragged to a waiting vehicle to the rear of the house. All captives will have the obligatory hood placed over their heads. Another car comes up the drive, only two security men outside now; the car stops and out steps John Graves. With an air of arrogance, he looks at the men up and down as though he was on a military parade. Walking forward, he rings the doorbell, then two loud knocks on the door, whiskey in one hand and cigars in the other, he walks into the hallway. He had not been to Powell's house before and was looking at the various rooms he could see, basically comparing lifestyles, ignorant to the fact that four men were staring at him. Then coming out of his self inflicted trance of jealousy, he can sense two men next to him; Leyland and James grab his arms, whisky and cigars fall to the floor as they handcuff him; Guy is trying to avoid bloodshed; far too many people have died. A stunned silence as James tells him his rights and the reason for his arrest. Suddenly it kicks in, 'do you know who the f—k, I am, Guy tell them they have made a ridiculous mistake.'

'We have significant proof of your collusion with a drug cartel, money laundering and the attempted murder of one of your colleagues Simon Lock.' Then, stuttering his innocence, as he is taken towards the second waiting vehicle.

Having landed two hours ago by private jet at a remote airstrip owned by the cartel, initially only wanting to be in the UK for four hours. A large limousine glides by the side of the jet and stops, the jet door opens, and out steps John Rains. Cursing at the cold air, it is several years since he has been in the UK, thinking to himself it will be a short but necessary visit. The driver gets out of the vehicle, tips his brimmed hat and opens the limousine door.

Rains slides into the rear leather seat, drops the chilled fridge door and pours out a glass of wine.
Then he pulls out a gun from a holster underneath his left arm, checking that it is ok, and takes the safety off; he will have order, not failure. In hindsight, Guy has saved the lives of the inner circle of the Ramina cartel, as John was going to kill all to prove a point. At 8.29 pm, the limousine turns into the driveway to Powell's house, then stops; Guy and the team can see the headlights of the vehicle which had stopped, wondering why Rains has stopped. Rain's had requested the driver to stop to screw the silencer on his gun, then a beep on his pager, thirty seconds which seemed a lifetime to Guy and the team, the vehicle moves forward to the house. Pulling across the front of the house, the security guard opens the limousine door, out steps their visitor. Looking around, he asks the driver to stay; I should only be a few minutes and walks forward to the front door, walking straight in expecting to see Powell, Graves and Stains. Instead, the silence was deafening as he looked left and right,

then walking forward, he heard a voice, 'Get down on your knees, or four guns will take your head off.'
'Come out, you bastard, where are you.'
'Get down on the floor.'
'Not till you show your f---king face.'
Guy steps out from an entrance to the right, no gun in his hand; being military, there is no need, hoping he would give in, but desperate men do desperate things. The man instantly grabs inside his jacket and swings around towards Guy; a shot rings out Leyland pushing Guy out of the way; James tackles the man to the floor. A frantic few minutes, and he is subdued and handcuffed, but Leyland is lying motionless on the floor. James frantically runs to him, trying to find his pulse; Guy ringing for an ambulance, which will arrive within minutes, he can hear the limousine speeding down the driveway. Unfortunately, due to the involvement of a gun, the police will also come. Instinctively Guy rings his old friend, the head of MI5, and he is taking a risk; he could not remember if his name was in Harry's book of truth.
So he only skimmed the surface of what had happened, asking him to help as too many questions would hinder their case.
The ambulance arrived, closely followed by a police car, stopping directly behind the ambulance. An officer proceeds to step out of the car, a call from inside the vehicle, and he gets back in. The officers start shouting at each other, arms gesturing, then silence as the radio comms tells them to leave now. The vehicle is screeching down the drive, with two angry police officers inside.
The telephone conversation has given them some breathing space, the worried faces of Guy, James and Ron looking on as the paramedic's fight to save Leyland. Ten minutes later, the emergency doctor arrives, and the sound of a helicopter landing on the

pristine lawn. Leyland's lifeless body, strapped to a stretcher, then carried to the helicopter and airlifted to go to the nearest trauma hospital, all too shocked to speak.

Their prisoner with a hood on is physically dragged to the last car at the rear of the house. Having been sedated before the ambulance arrived. The rest jump in Guy's car and follow the other vehicle back to his hiding place. Minimum conversation on the way back, but all agree James should contact Holly, and along with James, stay at the hospital until they have some answers. They decide to speak to Rains in the morning; Leyland's life is far more important; James has arranged to meet her at the hospital, she is unaware of how critical he is. It will be a sleepless night for all concerned; Holly asks her sister if she could also meet at the hospital; Ivy flies in from Portugal the following day.

Chapter 62

Mark and Lydia are oblivious of the chaos at Powell's house; as they stop outside Stains house, the lights are on; Mark and Lydia are slightly disappointed; there will be no challenge in entering. Nevertheless, Mark gets his faithful police card out and knocks on the door, and an elegant woman answers the door, 'my, who might you be, certainly too good looking to be one of my husband's friends.' Then Lydia comes into view, 'oops, sorry, did not see that coming,' the flirtatious woman then tells them, 'sorry my name is Jane, Jane Stains it is not the best of surnames, but I loved him at the time, come on in, anyone for gin.'

Mark goes into his old routine showing his card as Eric Lunn and telling her that her husband has been arrested.

'Well, finally, he has been caught out; what is it, something daft.'

What do you mean, Mrs Stains,' keeping their pose as police officers, as usual, she did not look at the badge, people can be so trusting. 'He dabbles in things, he will not tell me, but the money comes in regular, more than a Captain's salary, even I can tell that.'

'Please have another gin, Mrs Stains; we will not be much longer.'

'Why, thank you, I will.'

'Carry on Jane, and you were saying the rather large salary,' from Lydia.

The drink overtaking her commonsense, and in a slightly drunk stupor, she opens his computer; giggling, she says, 'he thinks I don't know the password, but when you have sex, things are said, I wrote it down.'

'Could we have that, Mrs Stains? It will help in our enquiries.'

Another swig of a full glass of gin with a bit of tonic, 'no problem, it is 69threeway69,' a slight slurring, 'I could never figure out what it meant.'

Lydia was just about to tell her, and Mark jumped in, 'can we take the computer with us? It would help us a greatly.'

'Oh yes, oh, oh, I think I am going to be sick, so sorry, let yourselves out.'

By the time they reach the front door, the dulcet tones of a woman throwing up are not pleasant to listen to. Nevertheless, outside they both agreed that it was the easiest break-in they had ever done. Mark's phone rings as they get into the car, and Guy informs him of the situation. Not one to show his emotion, only coming to the fore when Julia was injured and later at her death. But strangely, he respected Leyland for his morales of right and wrong, knowing he could not be bought at any cost, and the sense of family had developed in this small team. Lydia grabs his hand, 'come on; we have got to finish this.'

He agrees and punches in the address to the sat nav; five miles further into the country, they turn into a country lane, a farmhouse with the lights on. Mark, ever cautious, goes to the rear of the SUV, opens the tailgate and lifts out his new favourite toy, the drone. This piece of modern technology has paid for it,s self, time and time again; Lydia comes to his side and watches him control it like a toy car, amazed at its agility and the clarity of the cameras. Within minutes, they can see movement to the side of the building; 'he could have a protection team inside the house,' Mark turns to Lydia.

'Time to take a risk,' he tells Lydia.

'Let's go; I'm all excited.'

They get into the car and discuss their options, and the car gently stops outside the house; they wait a few minutes to see if there is any form of movement. Then,

Mark says, 'it's now or never,' he kisses Lydia and steps out of the car, his badge in his hand. Lydia also steps out, in the shadows by the side of the house; she sees a glint of metal in the moonlight, reacting instinctively, and that quiet sound of compressed air, a body falls forward. Mark rings the doorbell as if nothing has happened, no answer; he presses and holds the bell push, the bell constantly ringing. The sound of running footsteps, and a lady comes to the door in her dressing gown, 'who are you at this hour,'

'DC Eric Lunn, this is my card, ma'am.
Once again, the casual look, not really looking at it.
'It is in regards to your husband.'
'Has something happened to him?'
'Yes, ma'am, he has been arrested under various offences.'
Lydia was trying to hold back a fit of laughter in how Mark was talking to the well to do woman.
'He can't be; my god, he is the head of MI6, for goodness sake.'
'Sorry ma'am, but if the Queen had committed a crime, we would arrest her as well.'
An annoyed Mrs Graves, 'sarcasm does not become you, Lunn.'
'I guess not. Can we come in, please? It is a serious matter.'
'I suppose so.'
'Thank you, is there anybody else in the house.'
'No.'
She nods her approval; Mark and Lydia enter, looking around just in case; Mrs Graves leads them into the living room; Mark ever-suspicious looks to Mrs Graves, who has now taken a small pistol out of her dressing gown. Mark casually says, 'It is an offence to point a gun at any police officer.'
'I do not believe you have arrested my husband.'

Lydia comes forward, 'Mrs Graves, do you know Judge Powell and Roger Stains.'
Mrs Graves softens her tone, 'Yes, they are close friends.'
'Well, they have both been arrested, as well.'
Mark sees her relax and grabs the gun, 'there is no need for this, Mrs Graves.'
She flops in the chair, looking distraught, 'what do you want then.'
'If we could take his computer, it would help us.'
'But what has he done? I cannot get it into my head, can I see him.'
'Unfortunately not yet.'
Lydia walks forward and takes the computer; at this point, Mrs Graves turns aggressive.
Lydia pushes her back in the chair; shocked by Lydia's action, she stays silent, not moving.
As they leave, Mrs Graves comes to her senses, shouting, 'I will contact your superiors,' Mark laughing, 'good luck with that.'
At this, Mrs Graves starts shouting expletives, Lydia responds
'By the way, there is some rubbish to move at the side of the house.' She runs to see and finds the body of a man she did not know, 'who the hell is he,' Mark and Lydia turn around, surprised by her reaction, they move to the body, still warm and search his pockets. No wallet, just his mobile using his thumbprint; it opens up on the text page; Mark shows the page to Mrs Graves, instantly she is in tears, 'oh my god, what is my husband involved with.' The page read, (KILL ALL IN THE HOUSE, RAINS), inadvertently they had killed a hitman. Mark rings Guy for yet another cleanup crew; this is getting too regular even for Mark. Mrs Graves tells Mark they can search the house for any evidence they think they can use. While Mark and Lydia search, Mrs Graves is packing her things into two

suitcases; within an hour, she shouts to Lydia, 'slam the door on your way out; I have left a number to contact me.' Two minutes later, her car speeds down the drive, making Lydia's hormones rise, the cheeks flush, 'where are you, Mark.'

Mark tells her that he will check if the wives are in from now on; it is much easier, and fewer people die; he must be getting old, he thinks. But, unfortunately, Mark's thinking is getting somewhat blurred, as Lydia is removing his trousers.

Chapter 63

In the aftermath of Leyland's shooting, Guy has arranged for the MET commissioner and the head of MI5 to be picked up, and brought to his hiding place. They were forewarned about the need for hoods and accepted Guy's reasoning. However, James is meeting Holly and Ivy at the airport, and he has to inform them that Leyland is in an induced coma to keep him alive. It is not a pleasant drive for James, both women tearful, even more so in the hospital. Holly told him that Leyland saved her from depression and alcohol after her marriage to Ethan and his lies. He will need to be a good listener at the hospital; deep down, he would rather be chasing down the people who had caused it. Guy's guest's arrive, and both men are ushered down the corridor and taken into Guy's meeting room; through the one-way mirror, they can see Captain Roger Stains lying on a table. Standing next to him is Angus, who is about to take out the tracker and vial. Both men look at Guy; he asks them to be quiet and watch, both unaware of what will happen next. Then they see the scalpel, shocked when Angus removes both vials, and then they ask what is happening. Guy explains all the incidents that have happened and how Rains and Naim created one of the biggest drug cartels they have known. Then, having placed the vials in a glass bowl, Angus shouts Guy, 'it's breaking Guy,' looking at him, they both run to the next room.

'No, no, it can't be,' Guy's frustration, they have done it again, looking at the lifeless body of John Graves. He explains they can control it remotely, and it is their way of managing their employees. He swings around and runs down the corridor, bursts into the room that John Rains is in, next a loud roar of anger from Guy, 'No, no, no,' he is on his knees staring at another lifeless body. Moving forward, he knew in himself that Rains would

not kill himself; it was the body of the limousine driver that is why they stopped on the driveway.
As Stains was apprehended, he hit an abort signal on his pager. As he sat down in the car, the pager in his back pocket warning Rains to abort his visit?
The same pager Graves and Powell have in their possession. These pagers were only given to people within the inner circle of the Ramina cartel. Rains drove straight to the small airstrip, climbed onboard his private Jetstream plane, a false flight plan given to the authorities and disappeared within hours of Stains arrest.
All the men arrested during Guy and his team's endeavour will stand trial, with the considerable proof that Clive had gleaned from the various computers. However, Stains and Powell will serve the longest due to their involvement with Rains and Naim.
Guy had found out that Stains was using his connections in Afganastan to bring drugs into the UK via army containers; this enabled the authorities to stop entry into the country and cut another supply line off.
Leyland is still in a coma.?
A worldwide chase to capture John Rains and John Hurst, his cousin, now in hiding, they must break this cartel for good.

If you want to find out how it all started, you can purchase the first book. ....**Holidays are Murder**

To find out what happens next, coming in 2022 will be the final instalment. .... **Chasing Rains**

Printed in Great Britain
by Amazon